Madhumita B
She was a writer and editor with *The Telegraph* newspaper in Calcutta for a decade, interrupted by a stint in the non-profit sector. She still writes for *The Telegraph*, recently concluding an interactive serialized story called 'The Husband Hunters', and freelances as well. She lives in Gurgaon with her husband and her puppy. This is her first novel.

THE MASALA MURDER

MADHUMITA BHATTACHARYYA

PAN BOOKS

First published in the Indian subcontinent 2012 by Pan
an imprint of Pan Macmillan, a division of Macmillan Publishers Limited
Pan Macmillan, 20 New Wharf Road, London N1 9RR
Basingstoke and Oxford
Associated companies throughout the world
www.panmacmillan.com

ISBN 978-81-923-9801-3
Copyright © Madhumita Bhattacharyya 2012

The right of Madhumita Bhattacharyya to be identified as the author of this work has been asserted by her in accordance with the Copyright, Designs and Patents Act 1988.

All rights reserved. No part of this publication may be reproduced, stored in or introduced into a retrieval system, or transmitted, in any form, or by any means (electronic, mechanical, photocopying, recording or otherwise) without the prior written permission of the publisher. Any person who does any unauthorized act in relation to this publication may be liable to criminal prosecution and civil claims for damages.

1 3 5 7 9 8 6 4 2

This book is sold subject to the condition that it shall not, by way of trade or otherwise, be lent, re-sold, hired out, or otherwise circulated without the publisher's prior consent in any form of binding or cover other than that in which it is published and without a similar condition including this condition being imposed on the subsequent purchaser.

Typeset in Bulmer MT Std 11/14 by Jojy Philip, New Delhi 110015

Printed and bound in India by
Replika Press Pvt. Ltd.

For Ma and Baba

I wasn't sure how I ended up here. But then again, if anyone tells you they know the truth about the cause and effect of their lives, they are probably lying.

Reema Ray, Private Eye.

Except, I was no longer really that. Now I was Reema Ray, Food Writer.

I didn't think it was who I was meant to be. But seeing as how I didn't believe in destiny, I took what came my way, when it came my way. A girl's gotta eat, and as long as that remains true, she might as well eat as well as she can.

That's not to say that I sold out altogether. I didn't give up on being a detective; I couldn't, hard as I tried. It's just that I no longer expected to be paid for it on a regular basis. My agency was still stumbling along, in name if not in place, and I was part of what you could call a league of volunteer investigators, trying to keep the streets of our city safe on a pro bono basis. And we were doing it all without the help of a steady source of funds, clients or superhero powers.

So who is 'we'?

A little group I had come to think of as the CCC: the Calcutta Crime-Fighters' Club. We had no formal name. This is most likely due to a lack of imagination on the part of my fellow members, though they insist it is because our anonymous status helps us stay under the radar. As far as I could see, however, it would take a fairly powerful tracking device to pick up on our existence, given how we had solved no real crimes together. We talk a good game, though.

You might understand why a girl could get a bit desperate.

So when I found myself in a seemingly irredeemable slump, I baked. When I ran into trouble on a case, I baked. When I felt like nothing made sense, I baked. Baking, in fact, had seen me through a number of tight spots, so much so that I was forced to give away baked goods in order to reduce the strain on my waistline.

And thus I had arrived at the Pastry Principle. It was the only truth that seemed to remain constant in my life. There were numerous components to it, all quixotic enough to produce ready answers to just about any conundrum. They are as follows:

Rule #1: If it tastes *very* good, it will most likely make foie gras out of your liver.

Rule #2: Anything that is worth doing is worth doing yourself, whether or not your arms fall off in the process.

Rule #3: The magic is in the hand that kneads the dough, as all the best recipes are short on ingredients and long on technique.

Rule #4: As a corollary to Rule #3, the only rule I have ever found to have no exceptions – nothing is ever as simple as it seems.

ONE

The meetings of the Calcutta Crime-Fighters' Club had taken on a certain sameness of late. This might have been because the city's criminals were being kept indoors by the August rains that periodically turned the muggy streets into fast-flowing rivers. Or perhaps they were scared of us, the fearless CCC.

I scanned the circle around me, and had to try hard to suppress an eye roll. Villains everywhere would be sure, when confronted by our forces, to tremble, but only because they would be busy laughing so very hard at our fearful symmetry. My companions, clockwise:

Dinesh Dutta Gupta, criminal lawyer: DDG was the founding member of the CCC, which I had chalked up to his unrealized lust for power. He had the matching walrus moustache and belly to bolster this theory. He had influence as it was, but there was only so famous he was going to get as a corporate lawyer in Calcutta. The CCC was the product of his higher hopes and, to be fair, without him, his contacts and his funds, it would have stalled before it started. Yet, unable to see past his petty concerns, DDG was just this side of insufferable.

Terrence D'Costa, fellow PI: he worked with one of Calcutta's larger private investigation agencies. He projected a laidback-man-of-action vibe. My only problem was that he seemed to expect every woman within a three-kilometre radius to want to dive into his bed. With him in it. Me included.

Prashant Ojha, Inspector, Calcutta Police: I wasn't sure what he was doing in our midst. At 5'2" and 83.5 kg, he struck me as barely mobile. Apart from being a useful link to the cops and, more importantly, our all-access pass to the National Crime Database, such as it was, he seemed to contribute little. He hardly even listened except when DDG did the talking.

Santosh Mukherjee, lawyer: spent an awful lot of time defending people who were so guilty they almost locked themselves up. The rest of the time he championed the cause of the friendless, resource-less and hopeless, who repaid his help through eternal gratitude and little else besides. As a result, he had no money at all.

Despite this awe-inducing roll-call, my CCC membership at least was evidence that I wasn't the only one frustrated with the state of law enforcement in town. I was, however, the youngest and the only female, which seldom worked to my advantage. The only one of the gang who liked me, or took me seriously in any way, was Santosh da. Which could explain why he chose to introduce me to the group in the first place.

I had Santosh da to thank for my solitary hour of detective glory, where my work had translated to criminal charges (real charges! with handcuffs!), and he had me to thank for the only paying case he seemed to have won in the past decade.

It was about a year ago that Santosh da had come to me when he had been forced to seek outside intervention from someone with more experience handling tawdry affairs than he had. Lucky for me, at the time, Tawdry Affair was my middle name.

He found me in my little office in a little north Calcutta lane teeming like a beehive with scores of nooks and crannies. I had found it in a pinch. Rent of ₹2500 a month made the price just right, and the security deposit was low. When I started out, it was about all I could afford on my savings. And then there was the little corpus I had built up over the years, gift money mostly from grandparents and the more sensible aunts and uncles on birthdays; my parents too when they were moved to generosity by some academic or extra-curricular success. When other girls went out shopping, I hoarded like a packrat and wore the same clothes for as long as I could. They couldn't understand it then, and they probably wouldn't understand it now if they were to see what my paisa-pinching years had bought me.

But I loved my little cubbyhole. That eight feet by eight feet space held everything I needed: desk, computer and filing cabinet, a couple of chairs for visitors, and my lifeline – a coffee maker. If my visitors wanted milk or sugar, they were out of luck. But one got biscuits if one was lucky. The gorgeous scent of coffee was enough to make me forget the walls that hemmed me in, grey and grainy and cemented over in a recent round of repairs during which no one had bothered with plaster or paint. In my only concession to interior décor, I had taken down the fluorescent tube and put up my own lampshades, and imported my favourite reading light from home. It was a stark look to be sure, but during my optimistic moments, I managed to convince myself it was industrial chic.

When Santosh da came by, I was sifting through photographs taken at the behest of one more in a long line of suspicious husbands. It turned out his wife was making regular post-prandial stops at a hotel in Sudder Street – which I had nicknamed Shudder Street thanks to the number of infidelity cases that led me there. The prints were a bit of drama I participated in with this sort of client. A CD would do, of course, but they wanted the hardest kind of proof, and I would give it to them.

I put the pictures away in my drawer as Santosh da paused by the door and took me in as though he had expected someone – and something – quite different. 'Reema Ray?' he asked.

'Yes, and you must be Santosh Mukherjee.'

'Mrs Aarti Kumar sent me to you,' he said as he took the dusty seat across from me.

'Yes, she called to let me know you might be coming by. How can I help you?' I asked, although I already knew the answer to that question. In one way or the other, everyone who came to me was out to get a cheater.

'It is about a case involving infidelity. Mrs Kumar told me that it is what you specialize in.'

Put that way, I wouldn't let me get within ten feet of a husband – not even my own. 'I do seem to get a lot of those sorts of cases,' I shrugged.

'Well, I don't. I am a lawyer and I have never handled an infidelity case before. I tend to work more with human rights matters: child trafficking, dowry death and so on. I only took this case as a favour to a friend. And I don't know where to begin.'

'Why don't you begin by telling me why you need a detective?'

'My client thinks his wife is cheating.'

He stopped, and I looked at him expectantly as he stared at a spot on the wall somewhere behind my head.

'Yes?' I prompted.

'He feels she has been trying to kill him,' he spat out at last.

And so, right from the get-go, it was a fair bit more interesting than the usual cases I got, most of which went as far as me trailing a cheating spouse with a camera and handing over compromising shots and information to their divorce-seeking 'better' halves. With the door thus opened for intra-marital arm-twisting – let's call it that instead of what it really is (blackmail) – my job was usually done. It always seemed to be the same drill. With the exception of the pre-marital 'character' check, which had even more of an *ad nauseum* nature.

'The wife has been having an affair with one of their mutual friends. Last month, my client ended up sick and is certain that it was some sort of poisoning. The pathological lab couldn't find anything, but he believes his wife has been putting something in the food.'

'Mr Mukherjee, without any evidence ...'

'I know, I know, nothing can be done. That is why I have come to you. Evidence is exactly what I need. My client doesn't just want a divorce – he wants his wife proven to be an attempted murderess.'

Santosh da was squirming in his seat so much that it qualified as a workout, but if he was expecting me to be shocked, he was disappointed. Poor Santosh da had no clue as to how much sleaze I had seen in my young career. And my parents wondered why I was still single.

'There is no proof, only suspicion,' he said with a frown. 'It feels very dirty.'

I had to agree with him there; the one thing you would always find when marriages fell apart was dirt. But business was business. 'How would you like to proceed?' I asked.

'The husband can arrange access to the house for you. Perhaps you can look around for anything suspicious? Any traces of poison?'

'Mr Mukherjee, without any idea of how the poison was administered, I would be going in blind. It would require a huge amount of testing, which might turn up nothing at all.'

'My client understands that and is prepared to pay.'

'Fair enough,' I shrugged.

In the end, I got lucky. I snooped around, taking samples from everything the kitchen had to offer for testing. The cocoa – and a lovely Belgian tub it was too – had been laced with arsenic. Tasty. It wasn't hard to establish that Santosh da's client's wife had indeed been cheating. But that had been her only transgression. It was the lover, sick of her insistence that she couldn't get a divorce, who decided to take action. He had given the cocoa as a gift, knowing all along that the wife was allergic but that the husband loved the stuff. She made him a cup, but it didn't contain enough juice to kill him at one shot, leaving him very sick – and highly suspicious.

The husband duly filed for divorce; the lover was arrested for attempted murder. Santosh da got the only decent pay cheque he had received in what must be years, but was still generous enough to pass on part of the loot to me, which allowed me to hold on to my office for a few more months.

Santosh da told me about the CCC soon after, yet I may not have joined had he not narrated the story of the one major success they had already achieved. About five years ago, the mother of a teenaged daughter disappeared from her Mullick Bazar home, never to be seen again. A few months before I had met Santosh da, the daughter, all grown up, contacted Terrence's agency for professional help in finding her mother. But since she was without financial means, she was turned away. That was when Terrence brought the case before the CCC.

There had never been any evidence of kidnapping nor had there been a note. The daughter, a student of psychology, said that she believed her mother may have been mentally ill though there had never been a diagnosis, and was afraid that she may have simply strayed from home all those years ago.

But it turned out the mother was not really missing at all. Under threat of a new investigation, the father quickly confessed to having his wife committed to an institution of questionable repute. Unable to face his daughter with the truth, he had kept up the lie for years. Santosh da managed to pull some strings and get the lady a spot in a better-run home, and the daughter had taken on an active role in her care.

There is so much of the PI's job that has nothing to do with crime in the eyes of the law. People who need the kind of help that a police officer, doctor or shrink can't provide. I suppose that is what drew me to the CCC – it was my one chance to step out of the sleaze and actually be of some use.

And yet, it turned out that it is not so easy to identify hidden crimes and then find your way into them, and to the bottom of them. The CCC often got sidetracked by cases with no oomph, no human drama – a failing I attributed to DDG's sudden hunger for public recognition. The latest crime under consideration was a string of robberies which, in my view, the police were best placed to solve. But try telling that to my companions.

'Did you read the details that have emerged about the latest dacoity at Picnic Gardens? It is very daring, very daring,' said DDG, appearing even more bobble-headed than usual.

'Yes, if that girl had not sent that secret text to her boyfriend, who knows what would have happened to the family,' chimed in Ojha.

'The police have a good description this time,' I pointed out.

'Has it been linked conclusively to the other crimes?' asked Terrence, ignoring me.

'No, but they are investigating a bandit named Chhote Jimmy, from Bihar, in this connection,' said Ojha.

'Won't the CBI get involved, now that it has crossed state lines?' I asked.

They ignored me once again and I decided to sit back and listen to the four men with dreams of glory glistening in their eyes swap details gleaned from second-hand sources. Finally, Santosh da turned his attention to me. 'Reema, you are very quiet today,' he said. 'What do you think of this case?'

'It makes less and less sense for us to attempt interference. It is too big and, besides, it is so high profile that half the force must be working on it. What additional skills do we bring to the table?'

The silence that followed stretched for a few more seconds than was comfortable. DDG was the one to break it. 'So do you have any other cases that might be of interest?'

'As a matter of fact, there are a couple,' I said. 'One was the corporate matter I had mentioned last week.'

'That SlimCo business?' Terrence asked.

'There are reports that it was they who incited the violence at the Parsons Chemicals factory.'

'That hardly seems big enough to merit an investigation.'

'Five workers were hospitalized following the riot,' I said. 'And then there are allegations of industrial espionage; Parsons has apparently stolen SlimCo's weight-loss product formula.'

'That might be an interesting angle but if I remember correctly, your source in all this was dubious, at best,' said Terrence.

'I wouldn't call him dubious.'

'A journalist for the *Kolkata Chronicle*? Please,' said DDG.

'Okay,' I said, trying not to snap, 'if you aren't interested in that, there was the alleged dowry death of Sunita Sharma, Lake Gardens. Santosh da mentioned it last week.'

'It is a personal matter,' said Terrence.

'What do you mean?'

'Without being brought in by the family, we'd make no headway.'

'Why not?'

'We can't go snooping around in a home without permission. If you can get the victim's family to cooperate, we could at least think of looking into it.'

Despite my best efforts, I felt my shoulders slump. I knew he had a point.

The men turned their attention back to the robbery. Ojha agreed to follow up with the group on any developments in the investigation and Terrence was going to reach out to the latest family that had been hit to see if they were willing to let us in.

'If there is no other business, I need to get going tonight,' said Terrence, rising from the circle and flashing a grin in my direction. 'I have a date.'

So we adjourned, and I walked out of the little para clubhouse Ojha had arranged for this meeting. I waited till the other men, save Santosh da, left.

'How have you been?' I asked.

'I have been very well, Reema, thank you for asking. Very busy with a new case.'

He looked as content as always, dressed in the same white shirt and black pants he always wore. Somewhere there must be a battered black jacket and tie to match to complete the lawyer's uniform. Clean and well ironed, and yet faded and fraying at the collar and cuffs. I imagined he had a cupboard full of identical clothes, some of them older than me.

'How about you, Reema? I have been reading your articles. My daughter enjoys your magazine very much.'

I cringed. In the face of Santosh da's selfless exertions, I felt like a first-rate money grubber. Despite the fact that I was always just one missed pay cheque away from financial crisis.

'I've also been busy, Santosh da, but mainly with writing. Not many cases anymore. I finally had to give up my office.'

'Oh, that's a shame. When?'

'About two months ago.' My menacing landlord, who in all fairness had done nothing worse than ask for the monthly rent, ensured that I had to give up my effort at professionalism and lick my wounded ego in the comfort of a home 'office', otherwise known as the dining table. There sat my laptop. My camera and old case files were stowed in the steel almirah in the bedroom. It was a good thing my clothes didn't take up much space.

'I am sorry to hear that.'

'It's not so bad. At least now I don't have to commute.'

'But is it safe receiving clients at home? You must meet many unsavoury characters.'

'I haven't had a new client for a while,' I admitted. I had one job a while ago for an old customer investigating a potential groom, but that was about it.

'I wish I could help,' he said, staring dejectedly at his battered black shoes that showed their bruises despite the layers of polish.

I could have hugged him, but I had a feeling that Santosh da would not know what to do with that. So instead I gave him a sad smile and said goodbye. Santosh da walked to the nearby bus stop, and I watched him with a sort of envy.

And then I turned on my heel and, just like a princess in a fairy tale, I entered a world where the grit and crime of the everyday were forgotten, replaced by the world of glamour, as glitzy as cheap rhinestones on a knock-off handbag.

The other half of my schizophrenic world was waiting for me at the HQ of *Face* magazine. I didn't have to go in much since I was a freelancer, but I preferred to do my own proofreading. I walked into the production room and looked for Shweta, but my friend found me before I found her and lost no time in handing me a slender stack of prints.

'Here,' she said, already halfway back to the graphics designer she was bearing down on. 'You've got half an hour. We're very late!'

I went through my pieces, handed in my changes and hung about for her to finish so we could discuss the next issue. As I sat in her cubicle, I flipped through the loose prints strewn about her desk.

'Lust lives for happily marrieds!'

'20 tips for a beautiful bathroom!'

'When the time is right for botox!'

Somehow I had become a part of this universe, too. Beauty-magazine writer by day, crime fighter by night. Or was it the other way around?

After my meeting, I decided to walk off the funk I found myself in. I was beginning to think that there was only so long I could pretend that the extremes of my life were working for me. Did I want to be a detective or a journalist? If the answer was detective then I couldn't afford to reject cases, as I had been doing, just because they were distasteful. If I wanted to be a journalist, why wasn't I more committed to it?

With time to kill before I made my next and final stop for the day, I meandered my way through the crowded Chowringhee pavement, dodging hawkers, gropers, walkers and gawkers. Just when I began to regret my choice of route, I broke free of the chaos to a clear stretch. I was in front of a new designer store, right outside the Grand. A mannequin stared out at me from her home in a glittering shop window, boots up to her knees, stockings sheer and shimmering, navy blue dress grazing her thighs, bag upon her shoulder, not a nylon hair out of place. This was a girl with places to go, people to meet. In fact, she seemed to have as much of a sense of direction as I, if not more: at least she had decided that for her, only designer would do.

I looked around at the men and women of the city I called

home – Calcutta. Here I stood, with no real career, no money, not even the glimmer of what might be called a scheme. Here I stood, Reema Ray, and it was time at last to find my dream.

Or perhaps I should have called it my new dream, otherwise known as Plan C (A and B having already run their short-lived course).

Dreaming, however, had never been my problem.

TWO

Being a frequent house-sitter, I had a key to my friend Devika's place. I let myself in and heard a clatter of dishes coming from what was unmistakably the direction of the kitchen. This was unusual.

I headed towards the racket to confirm that it was indeed my friend – the roving fashion editor at the magazine and the woman who had hired me – who was frantically at work in unfamiliar terrain. She hit the button on the blender, remarkably without causing bloodshed. I saw lemons everywhere, ice being crushed and a head-spinning amount of golden spirit going into a cocktail mixer.

Devika finally spotted me. 'Margarita night!' she announced above the clamour. 'You're cooking!'

I breathed a sigh of relief. Refreshments of a liquid nature constituted the one aspect of the culinary arts Devika did display more than considerable skill in. 'What's the occasion?' I asked.

Devika beamed at the universe in general and me in particular, eyes aglow, lips parting to reveal two perfect rows of pearly whites.

Devika's good looks were a victory of nurture over nature, backed by endless reserves of unflappable energy. 'Vivek is going to be home for a couple of weeks.'

'Ah! Does that mean what I think it means?'

'Yup! I need to start my detox as soon as possible if I have any hope of getting my senior-citizen eggs to get their groove on. But I can't do it without one last night of sin!' she yelled above the fresh batch of shattering ice.

The pre-forty baby bug had bitten Devika in earnest. It was now or never, she had concluded with some urgency, though her pilot husband's crazy schedules did nothing to help their chances of speedy and natural conception. I knew Devika didn't want to go through the whole infertility rigmarole – if it didn't happen eventually she had always said she would adopt. And there was only one rather inconvenient problem in the interim: in the absence of an infant, Devika Joshi seemed entirely content exercising her maternal instincts on me. Her latest obsession: matchmaking. She could hardly be kept off the subject.

'So what have you been up to today?' she asked.

'Not much. I dropped into office to proof my latest pieces and before that I had a CCC meeting.'

'Ooh, your superhero squad!' Devika giggled.

I rolled my eyes.

'Any cute men there?' she asked.

'Not one, as I have told you before.'

'Come on! Who'd believe that? No Bruce Wayne types? My Spidey sense tells me otherwise.'

'Then your Spidey sense is malfunctioning thanks to the alcohol fumes in here. And if you call me Batgirl again, you'll get it with the lemon juicer.'

Devika was unfazed by my threats. 'Reema, you need a man in your life!'

I took a deep breath and thought of the collective mojo of the CCC. It's not like I didn't have men in my life. In fact, you might say I had a few too many. They simply weren't the kind a woman of my age would in any way call suitable.

'What did you think of Kevin?' she asked as she carefully lined glasses with salt.

Kevin was an American writer who had come to town to research Bengal handloom. An ever-hopeful Devika had introduced us, and I had given him a gastronomic tour of the city. We had got along famously, but that's not what Devika was fishing for. 'He's gay, Devika.'

'What nonsense! Just because he is a fashion writer doesn't mean he's gay! He's so good-looking!'

'As is his boyfriend, whom I met one evening.'

Devika scowled.

'Anyway, I'm not going to start a real relationship looking like I am.'

'What?'

'I can see every bite from every single food review sticking to my derrière. I need to get back to kickboxing with a vengeance.'

'Rubbish!'

'You wouldn't get it. You are so thin,' I replied, dangerously close to sulking.

'And look how that's working out for me and my fertility. You are so tall! And perfectly proportioned.'

'By which you mean I have child-bearing hips.'

Devika shook her head. 'By which I mean you are attractive to pretty much all men.'

I knew what that was code for, and I tugged self-consciously at my neckline.

'You look great, Reema, you always have,' Devika said in soothing tones. 'When you first came into my office for your interview, I was about to suggest that you forget about writing and become a model.'

'What rot! And anyway, that was a while ago, and before I started to eat for a living. Now I'd have to lose at least—'

Devika waved me into silence with a blinding flash of diamonds. 'I have never been able to understand your lack of confidence in your looks, when you seem so self-assured about everything else. Devika's Style Rule #1: Curves are good. Always.'

I stood in stony silence. At 5'7¾" I could hide a little bit of weight, I knew. But the hot-chocolate skin and the head of uncontrollable curls made me stand out, much to my discomfort, when all I ever wanted was to blend in. The petite, fair prettiness of my mother was the standard against which I had always been measured, and I had never come out on top. Stand on a ramp so a bunch of strangers could stare? Never.

Devika tasted and then adjusted – by adding even more booze.

'Devika, is that a good idea?'

'Oh, shush. So what really happened with that guy you were seeing for years?'

'Who are you talking about?'

'Was there more than one serious love-of-your-life-type person?'

I shook my head.

'So then you know who I am talking about.'

'Amit,' I said. The name was a kick to the stomach every time. We had broken up well before I met Devika, and I hadn't ever really discussed him with her.

Devika handed me a glass and we found our way to the living room, sinking into plush sofas, legs propped up on an ottoman.

I raised my margarita to my lips, licking a bit of the salt off the rim before tilting the glass. Suddenly my mouth was on fire.

'Devika,' I said, taking a horrified gulp, 'these should be illegal!'

'Potent, aren't they? Haven't I made one for you before?' she asked sweetly.

I thought quickly as I took another sip – this one carefully measured. There was only one subject of conversation that could divert Devika from my non-starter love life. My real troubles.

'I don't know how much longer I can keep my flat.'

'Oh no! Not your flat too! Why?'

'When I had taken it, straight out of college, I thought I would be earning much more. For a while, with all those infidelity cases, it was okay. But ever since I cut back on those, with only the occasional case supplementing my magazine income, it is just too expensive.'

'Can't your CCC gang give you some sort of salary?'

'We have no clients, remember? It's just a bunch of meddlesome people doing their meddling. Nowadays it is all talk. Whatever money does come in is kept in a fund – by which I mean an envelope in DDG's desk – for expenses in cases we choose to take up.'

Devika gave a motherly cluck. 'I don't know why you are wasting your time on all those things when you know the offer at the magazine for a full-time position is always open.'

A solution I was holding out on as the last resort. If I joined, it would be me writing about botox and boob jobs instead of Shweta's other minions.

'I don't want to do that just yet,' I said, hoping I didn't sound too ungracious.

'Well then, why don't you come and live with me?'

'Thank you,' I said, genuinely touched. It was an option I would probably exercise before moving in with either of my parents, but the thought of having to mooch off a friend on a long-term basis was not a happy one.

'I mean it, Reema. We have more than enough space; there are a couple of spare rooms. Vivek travels all the time, and in case I do get pregnant, imagine me being here alone. In fact, you'd be doing me a favour by moving in.'

'Why are you so good to me, Devika? I promise to take you up on that if I need to.'

Devika seemed set to continue her sales pitch, so I jumped in with an effort to change the subject. 'So what's going on with the next fashion week?' I asked.

Fashion was to Devika what food was to me – a passion she would happily let herself be consumed by. Lucky for her, heels didn't send your caloric intake into the stratosphere. They could empty out a bank balance with remarkable speed, but that was not a concern for Devika. Perhaps we picked our poisons with more deliberation than we gave ourselves credit for.

By the time we were ready for a refill, my head was a blur. I quickly went into the kitchen to throw together some nachos and quesadillas before I was too drunk to legally hold a knife. We went through most of our generous platter of comfort food and a second round of killer cocktails rather too quickly. Before I knew it, Devika emerged from the kitchen with a fresh batch.

'No more,' I mumbled.

'Just one!' Devika said. 'This could be my last drink in nine months!'

How could you argue with that?

Devika curled up on the sofa again. 'So tell me about him.'

'Who?'

'Amit.'

No luck, then. She hadn't really forgotten. 'There is nothing to say,' I shrugged.

'You were seeing him forever! Something must have happened?'

I gave it a moment. 'He cheated.'

Devika's perfectly groomed left brow shot up. 'On you?'

'Yes, Devika. Thus my conclusion that you are the only one who thinks I'm irresistible. And it wasn't some little fling, either. He married the girl. All in two months.'

'Oh no,' Devika said, reaching out for my hand. 'And you knew him for years?'

'Since the day we started at the same elementary school. We were best friends and then we started dating in high school. We stayed together when I was away for college in the US, and he broke up with me six months after I got back.'

'Bastard. It's been, what, three years?'

'And a half.'

'Has there been anyone since?'

'There were a few guys who didn't amount to much, and then there was Neil.'

'What happened to him?'

'He was kind of a booty call on loop.'

'When did it end?'

'A few months ago.'

She crinkled her nose in displeasure. 'Why don't you ever tell me these things?'

'What's to tell?'

'I have never known anyone as secretive as you. But I guess that is an occupational hazard.'

'Yes, would you hire a blabber-mouthed detective? But seriously, Devika, I would have mentioned it if it was important.'

'Why wasn't it anything more than a booty call?'

I knew how she would react to what I was about to say next, and I would have known better than to say it at all had I been sober. 'There was nothing going on up here,' I said, tapping a little too enthusiastically at my head, which felt far from clear at the moment.

'What?'

'There was no men-mental chemistry,' I slurred.

How she remained focused with all that tequila floating around her forty-five kg frame I'd never know. 'Silly girl!' she scoffed.

'Huh?'

'Silly girl,' Devika repeated. 'You can't go expecting everything from one package!'

I didn't reply and she felt free to continue delivering judgement.

'No one will ever be able to satisfy all your needs!'

Devika's words made it through somehow, though I had done my best to ignore my own head trying to relay the very same message to me so many times before.

'Do you think Vivek and I have it all?' she continued. 'Our interests are nothing alike. Sure, he's bright as a cracker, but about engineering-type things that bore me to tears. And if I talk to him about fashion, he threatens to take off again on his world travels. And there is the tiny fact that he is never actually here!'

'But it works,' I pointed out.

Devika shook her head. 'Correction: we make it work.'

I let this sink in. It was nothing new, but coming from one of the few happily-marrieds in my acquaintance, it sounded more like wisdom than it did a quote from a beauty-magazine self-help story. (I worked for a beauty magazine – I would have reminded myself had I been sober. It is always prudent to remember which side your baguette is buttered on.)

'But shouldn't the desire to make it work come naturally if it feels right?' I asked.

'Only if you live in a goddamn rom-com, Reema. For women like you and me, the desire to be pinned down to one man doesn't come naturally. We aren't marriage seekers. But at some point, you have to decide. You say there is nothing wrong with Neil?'

I skipped ahead. 'Ergo there must be something wrong with me?'

'No, not you. But maybe your – or his – attitude. And that is where being ready comes in. If you are ready for commitment, it falls into place. And I think you are ready.'

'Really?'

'Not that you'll ever admit it. But you aren't exactly sowing your wild oats here, are you? Don't be a Jane!'

'Huh? Who's Jane?'

'Who's Jane? Only the sister sidekick of your darling Elizabeth Bennett.'

'Since when do you quote from books? That too *Pride and Prejudice*?'

'Ever since you forced me to read it. Might as well put it to some use. You know how she was all stand-offish and composed all the time? That's you! You always seem so self-sufficient that no man will ever make the mistake of thinking that you need him!'

'Well, I don't.'

'Nor do any of us! But they must not know that!'

'I don't know that I want someone that weak.'

'Uff!' exclaimed Devika. 'Even the strongest of men don't mind some ego-stroking now and then. Or stroking of any kind, for that matter!'

She laughed long at her own joke and I joined in, though I couldn't say that I particularly liked Devika's way of suggesting I got a man. But I couldn't deny that there was a kernel of truth in her words. Not about the Jane stuff, though I dare not suggest she *re*-read the book. But about the men in my life. Were they only playing by rules I had unwittingly established?

I very nearly lost myself for a moment. It wasn't Neil I was thinking about; it was Amit. Even after a terrible break-up, the temptation to rose-tint the past was an ever-present threat. And after all we had shared, it was almost impossible to see past the peachy parts to the hard, unrelenting pit that can break a tooth if it takes you by surprise. Particularly when you are as drunk as a skunk.

But there it was – rushing back at me through the haze of time and alcohol. His disparaging remarks about my alleged superhero complex, as he liked to call it. He never could quite understand the impulse behind my career choice.

I suppressed a surge of anger that I hadn't realized I still felt.

Devika continued her lecture about compromise, and how the word shouldn't be confused with subservience, a mistake, she said, often made by people of my generation. I listened without interrupting her, not even breaking in to tell her that she and I definitely belonged to the same generation.

She stopped talking and the moment of silence was enough to prompt my tequila-addled brain to go off on a tangent of its own: there were things I should have said to Amit but I never had. Damn it, I hadn't had the last word!

An hour and another misguided margarita later, I crawled under the sheets in Devika's guest room. But sleep was slow to come.

THREE

I woke up the next morning, too pickled still to be truly hungover. It was Sunday, I told myself, roll over and go back to sleep. I looked at my phone to check the time. 9.57 am. Yup, way too early.

But within seconds of my head touching the pillow again, my eyes flew open. My phone. Last night. Amit.

I groaned as I looked through my recent calls list. The last outgoing call was to Amit, at 1.35 am. Damn those tasty margaritas! I thought I had left my drunk-dialling days behind me!

I tried to recover fragments of what had been said that were still floating around like the dregs of a bad dream. How I wished it were one. I replayed the bits that came most readily to the surface.

'How dare you!' I had begun unceremoniously.

'Is that ... Reema?' Amit had asked, surprise loud and clear.

'Who else would it be?'

'Are you okay?'

'Just a little drunk.'

'Both pissed and pissed off. Winning combination.'

'Save it, smartass.'

'What can I do for you this evening?'

'Why couldn't you just leave me and my mistakes alone?'

'What on earth are you talking about?'

'Your Nancy Drew? That was the best nickname you could come up with?'

'Ah.'

'Ah!' I had scoffed back.

'I think you should get some sleep.'

'I think we should talk.'

'Do you miss me?'

'Yes. No!'

'I'll take that as a yes. It's good to hear from you, Reema. You should get drunk more often.'

Oh no, no, no. Amit, silky smooth with words, had never been at the receiving end of such a sitter as this, and he hadn't squandered the opportunity. How could I blurt out that nonsense about missing him! It wasn't even true! Or was it?

Either way, it was of no bleeding consequence anymore. Even if I could overcome the betrayal, he was now married, which I could never, ever forget, despite his call a few months back. He wanted to be friends again, he said. *He* missed *me*, he said. And like the softy I never knew I was, I had agreed to meet him for coffee. But it hadn't gone well, the old anger, which I thought I had overcome, rising to the surface. He had called a couple of times after that, but I had evaded further efforts at meeting. Now, how he – or his wife – would interpret my midnight call was anyone's guess.

I swung my legs off the bed, took a deep breath and tested the air: miraculously no explosion took place inside my skull. I pushed sluggish feet into slippers and padded my way to the kitchen where I put on water for a cup of coffee as strong as I dared and raided the fridge for leftover quesadillas. Nothing like grease to settle the stomach.

As I heard the water bubbling through the percolator, my mind strayed back to last night. What had happened, exactly? And though I would have loved not to ask, why had it happened? Had I not moved past Amit, or had this all been Devika's doing? Talk of ex-es and alcohol never mixed, even for the allegedly over-composed Reema Ray.

So much for that theory.

Doomed relationship. Doomed career move. The two in my mind seemed inextricably linked. I had wanted to be a detective. Crime fighter extraordinaire. Equal parts Sherlock Holmes and Hercule Poirot, in a fetchingly female frame.

A significant chunk of my parents' life savings had all but gone down the drain when, in the third year of college in the US, I strayed from literature and started taking more and more crime-related courses. It started small with a class in crime fiction and, before I knew it, I had signed up for criminal psychology, photography, cyber crime, criminology and various aspects of forensic science. My parents had been amused more than alarmed till I returned home and advertised my intention of actually becoming a detective. Or investigator – a term I preferred for being a smidgen less smarmy.

But before I could appear for the exams which I had hoped would be my route into a respectable position in the police, my father rang one of his oldest, dearest friends, Sharad Kumar. Uncle Kumar had had front-row seats to my growing-up years and also happened to be deputy commissioner of police in Calcutta.

So green I was still embryonic, I walked into his large, intimidating office upon receiving my summons. Air-conditioned and spotless, utterly unlike the police station I walked through to get there. The stacks of dusty files that seemed to characterize the décor of the rest of the rooms and the stale, cigarette smoke-infused air were noticeably absent. Instead, there was a computer and a phone on the desk, and a large, comfortable-looking chair behind it on which sat Uncle Kumar, dressed in similar spot-free white.

'So you finally made it into my office,' he began with a smile, the hair falling on his forehead making him look younger than his fifty-three years.

I had begged him to bring me here for as long as I could remember, a request he had always responded to with a patient but firm shake of the head.

'Quite an achievement.'

'You never asked why I didn't let you come before.'

'I always figured it was because you were so busy. I have never been inside Baba's office either.'

'Your father is a chartered accountant. I assume he hadn't taken you there for fear of boring you to death.'

My mother certainly seemed to agree with this assessment. But I didn't see where he was going.

'Why do you want to become a detective?' he asked.

'To find the truth,' I replied without hesitation. I was acutely aware of how naïve I sounded, but it was the only answer that made sense to me. And was a little idealism a bad thing?

'That simple?'

'It is one of those things where the answer is rather obvious, isn't it?'

'Is it?'

'I think so.'

'I am not sure I agree. There are numerous other possible motivations – catching criminals, preventing crime, holding people accountable for their actions.'

'Doesn't "truth" kind of cover all of that?'

'I would hesitate before applying a word as weighty as "truth" interchangeably with anything. Yes, sometimes a detective's job is to discover the truth – though the whole truth is seldom required. At other times it is simply to uncover a series of events, which do not necessarily illustrate the true nature of things. Still more often, it is simply a matter of putting available facts together and seeing where they point. The truth – which implies a fuller knowledge of not only the proceedings but also the motivation that brought them about, of all parties – can only emerge, if it is to emerge at all, in a court, where the perspectives of defence and prosecution are held up to scrutiny. Accounts, you will find, tend to vary widely as to how close the criminal justice system ever comes to the "truth".'

'So how would you describe the job of a police detective?' I had asked.

'It is often a matter of merely upholding the law, and a discovery of how it was broken. Once again, truth and law are hardly the same thing. You may find yourself arresting a woman who killed her husband in a fit of rage, having endured decades of abuse at his hands. The law calls her a criminal. The truth of the matter is, however, quite different.'

Yes, yes, I knew the drill. Hadn't I lapped up all the crime and legal shows on TV I could find? What of it? 'Uncle Kumar, I am aware of the ambiguities of the job. The kind of moral dilemmas you are talking about can apply to any number of possible professions, and I am prepared to face them.'

He looked at me carefully and finally nodded his head slowly. 'Then you are far wiser at twenty-two than I was. When I joined the police, I thought I was going to be the next James Bond. A dream fuelled by a certain disregard for reality. And a most definite ignorance of procedure.'

'Procedure?'

'Yes. Every soul-sapping bit of it.'

'I am not sure I know what you mean.'

'I knew there was still something I could teach you,' said Uncle

Kumar with a smile. 'Why don't you stick around the office and find out.'

Uncle Kumar allowed me to come to the police station for a whole week, introducing me as an intern to his colleagues. As soon as he left the room, his men turned away with a sneer and resumed whatever it was they had been doing before the annoying interruption and its lingering subject.

With Uncle Kumar himself spending very little time with me, and most of the others deciding to ignore my presence, I spent the next seven days as a fly on the wall of one of the busiest police stations in town. I was discreet, but I quickly came to realize that my intrusion would not have been felt anyhow. These men and women seemed used to ignoring people; they ignored people everyday with a high level of expertise. Victims, complainants, idlers of all kinds who they seemed to think had nothing better to do than sit about in a police station, waiting for hours before being attended to. It worked well for me: I was at leisure to see all that I needed to. And if this was procedure, I wasn't getting it.

At the end of the week, Uncle Kumar sat me down in his office once again.

'So?'

'I don't know what you expect me to say.'

'Do you still want to be a police detective?' he asked. 'Because if you do, I am sure I can make it happen, even if the exam doesn't go your way.'

For a long moment, I said nothing. I had no idea how to ask him why all save a handful of his team seemed to spend most of their time doing apparently so little. The few times I saw them animated were when I spotted some amongst them counting cash – no doubt received illicitly. Some were a little more discreet about their extracurricular income, and I believed I had identified two or three who seemed to put their heads down and work and only work, though they seemed to be fairly low down in the pecking order.

This had been my re-education, at my parents' behest. It wasn't kind, but perhaps it had been necessary.

Uncle Kumar was prepared for my hesitation, anticipating perfectly its source. 'You are wondering why. As did I when I first joined. I was one of the lucky few who entered through the IPS, guaranteeing me a certain growth path. I could choose to be a part of it or not – I had that option. And to join did not necessarily mean putting my hand out for a share of the pie. It could mean simply ignoring it.

'I don't mean this as an excuse, far from it. But the people whom you see lining their pockets here so brazenly are often the same ordinary people who had to shell out a significant amount of cash for their current positions. They did so knowing full well that once they got where they wanted to be, they would recoup their investment, with interest, through similar means.'

'So it's a vicious cycle?' I asked at last.

'As vicious as it gets.'

'One that can't be broken?'

Uncle Kumar considered this for a moment. 'I would prefer not to be so cynical. But I don't think it can be broken from the inside.'

Cynical, I felt like shouting, no, that wasn't cynical at all. 'And what about the people who come to the police for help – the victims?'

He looked away, staring through the window out onto one of the most bustling thoroughfares of the city. That was his jurisdiction. There walked the people who should hold him and his men accountable. And though I knew Uncle Kumar was personally beyond reproach, shouldn't the buck in his police station stop with him?

Uncle Kumar took his time replying. 'I won't deny that there are victims who fall through the cracks. But it is also incorrect to assume that just because some of our officers are corrupt that they don't also do their jobs as best they can. Quite often, the money they take in bribes is used to investigate cases.'

'Seriously?'

'Would I joke about something so shameful? That our official budgets don't allow for proper investigations to be carried out? Our men often do their best, within the constraints imposed by men and machinery.'

In other words, the system.

I thought of the people I had seen come and go through the department over the previous week. Men and women waiting for hours, helpless, only to be turned away. Officers actively dissuading them from filing complaints. And others, those who arrived in the biggest cars and had called ahead through a 'source', being ushered into empty rooms for discreet, dedicated action.

'Reema, if I didn't see the problems, I wouldn't have gone through this exercise with you. I know how it looks to an outsider. I know that much of what you see with your fresh eyes is true. But there are those of us who are constitutionally able to see past the institutional decay and those of us who are not. You need to decide which category you fit into.'

I left Uncle Kumar's office with the stars snuffed out of my eyes. I was angry: at what I had seen, at my father for calling in his friend to ensure that I had seen it, at myself for having been so easy to disillusion.

I didn't think I'd make it as a cop. But a twenty-two-year-old doesn't have the fight kicked out of her so easily. I had already thought through my Plan B. In fact, at one point, Plan B had been my Plan A.

'A detective agency!' my mother almost screamed the next day at lunch. Her anger quickly found its usual target. 'You had to stop her from becoming a police officer, didn't you?' she yelled at my father across the table. As long as I could remember, that table had never been wide enough for the anger to miss its mark, on either side. If I had thought their divorce five years ago would have been a hindrance, I had been wrong. They still had me in common, after all.

'I didn't know she'd come up with this insane scheme instead!' my father bellowed back.

'Hey, I am still in the room, people!'

They both looked at me, their anger turning into exasperation. 'Reema–' they began.

I quickly interrupted. 'I understand you are concerned and that you both think I am a lunatic. But I have been trained for this. I think I can do this. Can't you trust me enough to let me try?'

I spent the next half hour convincing them that I (in all probability) would not be running around chasing gangsters; that it made the most sense of all the alternatives as all I needed was an office, a computer and an Internet connection; that I had learnt self-defence and even knew how to fire a gun rather well. The last point caused them to cry out in unison, my father saying that he would not give me a single rupee if I bought a gun.

'Baba, I don't need your money. I have enough to get started. And to feed myself. But no, I will not be buying a gun,' I told him coldly.

At least, not till I could afford one, I added mentally.

I left the room in something of a huff. If I hadn't been so annoyed, I might have actually been happy that my parents were finally agreeing on something.

Two weeks later, tiny office rented, computer and desk acquired, name concocted (Steele Securities – I had wanted to invoke a sense of strength as well as an early idol, Remington Steele) and signboard put up, I was considerably less huffy. I was ready to provide all manner of security solutions – private investigation, installation of surveillance equipment, digital security. But no one seemed to want them. I soon began to feel that perhaps inventing my own tall, dark, mysterious, Pierce Brosnan-like associate might swing fortune in my favour. Just as quickly, I assured myself that the clients would come soon enough, no falsehoods needed.

The only weapon required in my arsenal proved to be a healthy dose of self-deception.

The first person to knock on my door was my father, just before my first idle month was through. I couldn't face him, not when I knew the landlord would come for his money the next day and my bank balance was taunting me in a most unrelenting manner. I could scrape through only a couple more months without work, or help.

'Hi, Baba,' I said, trying to project cheer.

'Reema, I've brought someone to see you,' he said with a smile. I could see a lady standing behind him, about his age, wearing a worried expression.

My first thought was that this was the girlfriend. I had done my best to beat down my territorial instinct with reason: this was good, maybe he'd drink less, maybe he'd argue less, maybe he'd even be happy. Hadn't I told him many times that this was precisely what he needed?

'This is Mrs Khanna, my neighbour,' he said.

I noted the formal mode of address and the lack of embarrassment on his face. No, not a girlfriend then.

I stood up to shake her hand and ask them both to sit down. Too late I noticed the layer of dust that covered the visitors' chairs across from my neat, paper-free basic wooden desk. (In those days, I was still keeping up appearances.)

'I think Mrs Khanna might need your help,' my father started, looking encouragingly towards his companion.

Mrs Khanna lifted her uncomfortable gaze from the desk to my face. 'It's my daughter, you see,' she said abruptly, leaning forward. 'She's ... she's found the most inappropriate young man, and she has got it into her head that she is in love.' She stopped, overcome.

My father quickly stepped in. 'The man is a musician with no steady income. Mrs Khanna is afraid that he is after their money. They live in the lovely house next to my building, you know, the one with the lawn and the beautiful dogs?'

If I remembered correctly, Mr Khanna had passed away a couple of years ago. Now it was just the two women, and twin milk-chocolate labradors. But surely Miss Khanna was old enough to render this conversation redundant?

'Mrs Khanna,' I said, 'may I ask how old your daughter is?'

'I know what you are thinking,' Mrs Khanna cried, her voice cracking. 'She may be thirty years old, but she has no experience with men and is very, very innocent and easy to take advantage of!'

My father shot me an alarmed look – this was obvious a potential minefield. I hid my surprise, I hoped, tolerably well. The last time I remembered seeing the young lady in question was at a New Year's Eve party around four years ago, where she had been draped all over a young man who may well have considered himself the party taken advantage of.

'And you would like me to check out this man?'

Mrs Khanna nodded, wiping her tears with the corner of her dupatta. 'Since she won't listen to me, maybe some proof will help change her mind. But you must charge me what you would any other client. Don't think of me as your father's friend. And you can't ever mention it to anybody.'

I nodded solemnly. I needn't tell her that I hadn't had any other client and that I was in no position to offer my services for free. 'Of course,' I said earnestly, picking up my pen. 'Could I ask you a few details about this man?'

***

The case of Miss Khanna's main squeeze was resolved favourably for me and Miss Khanna, though not so much for Mrs Khanna. It turned out that the young musician had a more regular income than had previously been suspected – he had a regular pub gig, composed ad jingles and even had a few students on the side. He had the predictable string of groupie girlfriends behind him but since he seemed to treat them well enough, I deemed fit to keep the full details of this from Mrs Khanna, just as I chose to conceal the dalliances of her daughter.

It was hardly rewarding work, but it paid at least part of the bills. And at last I had lost my detective virginity!

The next month, another paranoid mother, a friend of Mrs Khanna's, came calling. That case too was speedily resolved, only this time it turned out that the man was concealing a former – and still valid – marriage and child. I couldn't help but think my client was a little too happy to learn that her daughter had indeed been duped in the worst possible way. But with two cases in two months, I had been saved the ignominy of declaring my practice stillborn.

My website was ready by this time, and I invested a little on

Internet advertising and through the classifieds, calling myself Calcutta's 'most discreet investigator'. And after a couple of inquiries that went nowhere, I got another pre-marital check, this one from the prospective bride herself. She had met the guy on a matchmaking site and wanted him vetted before moving past the first meeting. I soon established that though the prospective groom was criminally boring, he was otherwise deceit-free.

Over the next quarter, I made enough money to cover the rent for both home and office, and I could even afford a few meals instead of mooching off my parents. Once I had worked my way into the network, the stream of souls looking for love in people they could not trust never seemed to dry up. Sometimes it was the woman, sometimes the man, sometimes the parents. When it wasn't pre-marital check, it was jealous lovers and spouses.

The flow of cases intensified after I came to the notice of a couple of professional matchmakers, and my online ads started getting placed on matrimonial sites. It seemed to be a marriage made in heaven – for a while.

Year One as a detective rolled on. My efforts at finding other kinds of work seemed to never quite take off. Identity verification for companies was something I believed was a natural extension of my existing services, and a couple of cold calls went well till they asked about my set-up and I had to confess that it was only me. I don't know if that was what did it, but nothing quite materialized after that.

In retrospect, perhaps I had gone about it all wrong. Perhaps I should have approached Uncle Kumar and my parents' other friends for help, for references, for a foot in the door. But I didn't, partly because I was reluctant to seek help from those who didn't approve of the choice I had made. And I suppose partly because the idealist in me – yes, she was still hanging on to the edge of a life raft rapidly losing air – believed that the big case that would propel me into the limelight and thus win me a never-ending parade of exciting mysteries was just around the corner.

It was on a slow day about a year and half after I started my business that I got a call from Shweta at *Face*, whom I had gone to school with. 'I have an offer which you may find too exciting to resist,' she said conspiratorially. Her editor, explained Shweta, was looking for a policewoman who could review the latest big-budget catch-the-serial-killer film releasing the following Friday. 'The problem with these cop types is that they are soooo stuffy. Who'd even agree to do something like this? So I thought of you, and Devika just flipped for the idea!'

'What do you want me to do?' I asked, thoroughly confused.

'We want you to write the film review! It adds some masala, no, to say that a private eye – that too, a female – is writing a review for a thriller.'

I didn't see how it could make a difference to anyone, but I was intrigued. I loved writing when I was in school. And reading, particularly detective novels, which is what got me into this mess in the first place.

I wrote my first film review – I can't remember which one it was but I vaguely remember Morgan Freeman being in it – and loved writing it. And the magazine was happy too, apparently. *Face* soon had me writing reviews for just about every film that featured a person being followed, a punch thrown or a baddie nabbed. Fridays became busy for me. And though the pay wasn't great, the extra cash didn't hurt and I enjoyed the excuse to watch films all first day, first show (and expense the tickets).

Then, about six months later, Shweta called with another message from her editor. 'They want to meet you.'

'What for?'

The Masala Murder

'They are hiring, and they want you!'

It made no sense. 'But I am not a writer. I am a detective,' I said at last, as though that settled the subject.

But Shweta dismissed this with an uncharitable snort. 'You are at least as much of a writer as you are a detective. In the past six months, I'd bet you've written more reviews than you have solved cases.'

Point. 'I'll think about it.'

'Fine. Just as long as you've worked it out by tomorrow morning. Your interview is at 9 am, and you'd better be there.'

I went, but only because I didn't want Shweta to lose face. I was sure Devika would realize I was highly inappropriate as a recruit for what was primarily a fashion magazine. I hadn't read one of those in my life, and it showed.

It wasn't that I was badly turned out so much as that I stuck to my uniform. Black T-shirt and black trousers to a formal meeting. Black top and jeans to the pub. When pushed to the limit, black dress for a serious night on the town. But I couldn't remember my last real date, so the solitary LBD hadn't been aired in what must be six months, the matching heels mildewing in the back of my cupboard.

But it didn't go quite as expected.

'You're perfect for the job,' declared Devika about thirty-five seconds after I walked into her office. We had never met before but she had engulfed me in a hug surprisingly wholesome coming from super-toned arms and a breakably thin frame.

'I'm a detective,' I repeated for the third time.

Finally, Devika seemed to hear me. 'I don't want to sound rude, but Shweta mentioned that your practice isn't going so well. So why not give this a shot? You have a flair for it, you know. We barely have to change a word you write. Do you know how rare that is?'

I could honestly say I did not. And though I knew Shweta

adored her boss, I hadn't realized she had shared so much information about me with her.

Devika sensed my discomfort. 'She only mentioned it because I was driving her crazy to find me someone I could hire. And, you have to admit, it makes perfect sense.'

'Far from it,' I whispered under my breath. 'What would I do at a fashion magazine?' I asked aloud.

'We aren't just fashion. *Face*, as you know, stands for "Fashion, Accessories, Cosmetics and Entertainment". Film reviews you already do. We are going through a mini makeover, one which will involve significantly more space devoted to the non-fashion lifestyle space. So you could increase the scope of your writing and get involved with other aspects of the magazine as well.'

I was sceptical.

'Isn't there something that interests you as much as ... detecting?'

My mind had been pushing away a piece of information I knew was critical – the very thing that made me suspect I may not be such a misfit at *Face* after all. 'There is one other thing.'

Devika was watching me hopefully.

'Food,' I said. 'If I hadn't become a detective I would have loved to be a pastry chef.'

Devika's full-bodied laugh filled the room. 'Why didn't you say so before? Don't you know food is the new fashion?'

I left Devika's office with an offer that day, but even before I walked out the door, I began to formulate a way to have my cake and eat it too. What if I could freelance for *Face* for film reviews as well as food, *and* keep my private practice?

FOUR

I owe my love for food to my father. In the evenings we'd be in the kitchen, mucking around with whatever was at hand, while Ma would be off on a shoot, or a rehearsal, or one of those ghastly parties that would invariably end with her coming home well past my bedtime and well past sobriety – or so it seemed from my torn eavesdropping. But even so, her thirst for alcohol had never matched his. Her true poison had been attention, from as many sources as possible at the same time. My father and I alone would never do.

The fights always began in strangled tones – with me straining to hear – escalating into a nocturnal brawl I struggled to shut out. It may have been easier if I hadn't been able to see the storm darkening the sky long before they could. I had become an expert at reading the signs, their patterns of destruction, and expecting it had been worse agony than actually riding it out.

I had devices guaranteed to deliver numbness. I would lie there under my blanket, earphones plugged in and music turned up as loud as I dared, a flashlight trained on the pages of my book, my eyes devouring the words. On those nights any book would do, but the best kind was a detective novel, in which every problem came with a solution. All it needed was an analytical mind to put it all together, to turn every wrong into a right, to answer every question.

My parents, on the other hand, kept asking me questions to which I had no answers – some spoken out loud, others not. Is your father drunk; was your mother with that man at last night's party; will we ever be whole again?

Crime – the solving of, never the committing – seemed infinitely easier.

꒔

'Ma, he's a dog,' I said.

'I know, isn't he?'

'Not Baba! The dog! I am talking about the dog! Of course he jumped on you. Because that is what he does! In fact, that is all he does!'

I had finally dragged myself home, hung over after Devika's tequila fest, to get ready for an interview, and I was going to be late, but I would rather risk that than send my mother into a sulk. She was back with her familiar complaint: my father was mistreating – on the verge of murdering – the family dog. Wrong choice of words, perhaps, for the family that had once claimed Batul as its most precious member had since parted ways. Batul now lived in a state of perennial confusion as to who his true master was, spending time at both the abodes of my warring parents. For years, as I shuttled from one home to another, I had taken up the honorary post of doggy deliverer. When I had jumped ship to my now unaffordable flat, I left my parents to their own disastrous devices and Batul in shared-custody hell.

My father had taken off for a month-long trip around Europe, so Batul was currently in my mother's sole care. And her specific complaint was something like this. 'As soon as I walked in through the door to get him before your father left – and the place is such a pigsty! – he leapt at me. It's like he hadn't been fed in weeks, the poor, poor Snoopy darling.' I could almost hear my mother scratching behind Batul's long retriever ears that looked more copper than they did gold. The drool would have begun to puddle at her feet.

'Have you ever known Batul not to jump on you? Or on anybody else? That's how he would greet a gang of armed robbers.'

My words had zero effect. My mother simply continued in her tirade against my father's negligent over indulgence of poor Batul. It was as though my refusal to become a pawn in their endless battle had caused them to enlist their other, more helpless child for the purpose. It had a heartbreaking effect on the poor pooch, who was already guaranteed to evince sympathy on account of his short stature, looking as though his mother, a fine specimen, had messed about with a dachshund. It was a time-consuming effort to keep the diminutive retriever from packing on the pounds, and the past few years had taken a heavy toll, for in shuttling back and forth from master's house to mistress's house, he had been caught in the crossfire of constant gastronomic warfare. In the doggy world, my parents seemed to have concluded, the master of the year award went to the one who supplied the best and the most food. As a result, Batul, who knew no self-control, would polish off whatever he found in his dish and then, in a fit of eater's remorse, retreat into a corner to sulk.

Batul and I had much in common.

'Ma, have you at least started to do your bit? Have you stopped over feeding him? And started taking him out for real walks?'

'What is the point? Dr Mukherjee says the damage is done. He is now officially depressed. How can I take his treats away now?'

I shook my head, my frustration lost on all but myself. 'And what about you? How are you doing?'

'Oh, I am fine,' said my mother, instantly perking up. 'Busy with a play for the Calcutta Theatre Club.'

'Oh, that's great. Which one?' At my mother's age, interesting roles were hard to find, and she was tired to tears of playing the desolate/avenging mother in small-time Bengali films. So she had withdrawn from the world of cinema all but completely. But I knew she still waited for that call to come.

'*Hamlet*. I'd much rather be a beastly mother than a moaning and complaining one.'

Didn't I know it. 'And what about your plans with Hema Masi?'

'I can't believe she is finally coming to Calcutta! Just the two of us, after all these years!' Hema Masi was my mother's oldest friend who had moved to the US decades ago. A reunion was slated for next week.

She chirped on for ten minutes, her despair over Batul forgotten.

I finally made it to my interview with Mallika Mitra. She was a striking woman – forty-something, tall, slender frame draped in an elegant pale blue silk dress, feet in tan pumps, hair cropped short. Perfect ivory skin that seemed only to be growing more luminous with age, that same distinction in speech, the elegance a certain kind of Bengali woman of that generation seemed to be born with. You could hear the convent education in their voices. These were the women who, on the surface, held up well in matrimonial columns. Thankfully I had eschewed such ambitions for myself early on.

I was seated in Middle Kingdom, Mallika's cosy restaurant on Southern Avenue overlooking the Lakes. 'This is a beautiful spot,' I said. The fifty-seater eatery was high above the bustle, giving it a stellar view.

'Yes, it was quite a find. I grabbed it when the old owners were giving it up before real-estate prices soared. I doubt I could afford a place like this now,' said Mallika. There was something about the warm smile she shot me that reminded me of my mother, and I was instantly sorry I hadn't been more patient with Ma that morning.

'How long have you been running this place?' I asked, taking a sip of perfectly brewed Darjeeling tea from the pristine white china cup.

'Going on six years now. I never thought I would get this far.'

Middle Kingdom had opened while I had been away at college, so it wasn't till more recently that I had discovered how exceptional it really was. Now I was doing a feature on the restaurant and its elegant owner for a series on Calcutta's best eats.

'Do you still enjoy it?'

'Oh yes, as much as the day we opened. Or rather more, for that was a singularly stressful dinner if my memory serves me right.'

'How did you conceive of such a place?'

'I started without really knowing what I was getting into, to tell you the truth. My husband and I had lived in China for a number of years and when we returned I had a lot of time on my hands. I started looking for something to do and toyed with a few other ideas, but eventually I settled on a restaurant. My family had been in the catering business in Calcutta years ago, and I felt comfortable with the logistics. And in those days, there really wasn't any place in town serving authentic Chinese food.'

'There still isn't, is there, apart from this?'

'A few places come close, but they end up heavily customizing for local taste.'

'And you have resisted that?'

'As much as possible. You haven't seen chilli chicken on our menu, have you?'

'Not the Indian variety, at least.' There was a fabulous dish of fried chicken tossed with a mountain of dried chilli and peanuts, but it bore little resemblance to the Indo-Sino khichdi classic.

'Luckily, we found the city was receptive to it, even at our relatively high price points.'

'Everyone remarks on how consistent your restaurant has been. How have you managed that?'

'From the beginning we have had as our chef Abhimanyu Sinha, who worked at a five-star coffee shop in Shanghai. With his exposure to authentic food from across the country, he's been able to train his deputies well.'

'Retaining him hasn't been a problem?'

'He's just become a partner,' she smiled.

There was an interesting angle to be explored there. A chef with an international track record content in a mid-sized Calcutta kitchen? 'I would really like to speak with him. Is he here now?'

'No, he won't be in till later in the evening,' Mallika said. She tapped on the table thoughtfully. 'Why don't you come to dinner tomorrow at my place? Chef will be there too, and you can speak to him then. Nothing fancy, just me and a couple of friends,' she suggested.

'I'd love that,' I said.

We were interrupted by a waiter who brought out tea, this time green, and egg tarts.

'Try these. These are a dim sum classic: Portuguese-inspired treats from Macau.'

I bit into one of the glistening golden discs, smiling like a happy sun in a child's drawing. The tender yet crisp puff pastry crust yielded to creamy, delicately sweet custard filling, with a brown-tinged top providing a burnt sugar bite. I closed my eyes with pleasure brought on by the contrast of sweet and savoury.

'These are fabulous, Mallika.'

'Thanks! We've been trying to get these right for a couple of weeks now as I am thinking of starting a Chinese tea set on weekend afternoons.'

I tore myself away from the food to tell her how wonderful the plan was and to continue with my questions.

'Where do you source your ingredients from?'

'Vegetables and meats have always been relatively easy. We work with suppliers in New Market. It is just a few spices that need to be brought in. And it is all quite simple because of my contacts in China.'

'Some Chinese restaurants are sourcing from a local businessman, Prakash Agarwal,' I said. I had met him for a story as he was considered one of the most important people in the restaurant business, being Calcutta's main importer of gourmet provisions.

'I am not really sure ... I don't think I know him ...' Mallika trailed off, fiddling with her earring. In her big, kohl-lined brown eyes I thought I saw a sudden flash of distress.

The question had been straightforward enough, and I was surprised by Mallika's reaction. It was a small city, and the food circle was even smaller. But it wasn't really relevant, so I moved on.

'How did you assemble such an eclectic mix of dishes?' I asked. The menu was divided by region with a selection from Sichuan, Hunan, Guangdong or Canton, Shanghai, Beijing. It was a comprehensive list of contemporary Chinese classics.

'I thought about all the misconceptions surrounding Chinese food the world over and wanted the menu to be representative of the country as a whole. It was a bit of a gamble but as I said, it has worked.'

As we chatted over the next half hour or so, Mallika described to me the catering venture she had branched into. It became clear that Mallika's business was growing steadily. She was also contemplating a second branch of Middle Kingdom.

'What is holding you back?'

'In part, fear. Abhimanyu and I are quite hands-on in the kitchen and I'd need to hire someone with experience with the same sort of food, which means bringing someone else over from China or Singapore. One wrong step and things can go terribly wrong. Restaurants open and close all the time – it is harder to stay in business than you might think.'

I nodded ruefully. I had had a half-baked dream once, in between breaking up a potential marriage and complete unemployment, of starting a patisserie. Why be a detective, I had asked myself, when food was so much easier, so much more elemental? But then I found out how much money was required and the dream slunk away.

Just then my phone rang. It was Shweta.

'Sorry, I need to take this,' I said to Mallika. 'Hello?'

'Reema, can you come into office?'

'Now?'

'It's kind of urgent.'

'What's going on?'

'Someone you interviewed a while ago has died under somewhat suspicious circumstances.'

I felt a stab of fear. 'Who?'

'The gourmet food importer Prakash Agarwal.'

I looked at Mallika sitting across the table from me, my mouth open in disbelief. 'How?'

'Don't know. He died this morning in hospital. Apparently the doctor recommended an autopsy and called the cops, but by then the body had been released. He was cremated before they responded.'

'So quickly?'

'Exactly the question the police are now asking.'

'Give me half an hour,' I said, hanging up.

'Is everything alright?' asked Mallika.

'Someone I know, in fact the food importer we were just talking about, Prakash Agarwal ... he's dead.'

Mallika's teacup slipped from her hand and shattered as it hit the table.

'Oh my,' she said, grabbing for napkins as a waiter hurried over. 'What a mess.'

'I thought you didn't know him?' I asked, trying my best to help.

'I don't. Not really,' she said, a deep blush spreading across her cheeks. 'But I know of him. What happened?'

'They are not sure yet,' I said.

Mallika scrambled to pick up the slivers of white, her manicured hands trembling.

FIVE

'What the hell happened?' I asked, swinging into the chair beside Shweta's desk.

'They aren't sure. He was admitted to Calcutta Medical yesterday morning with severe diarrhoea and other symptoms. He died in the early hours today.'

'It's so strange – I was just talking about him a few minutes before you called.'

'Really?'

'I was interviewing someone I thought might know him. Do they suspect foul play?'

'I am not sure,' shrugged Sweta. 'What I told you is pretty much all the news guys told me.' *Face* didn't do news, but it had a sister magazine housed in the same building that did. 'As far as I could tell, they aren't sure either and want to know if you have any info that might be useful.'

I had interviewed few people in my brief food writer career who I had liked less than Prakash Agarwal. Mostly people who got involved in the food business, I had found, were nice. They loved food, they loved feeding people. But Agarwal was the exception.

'I really don't know much about him ... But I have to say, he gave me the creeps the one time we met. He was seriously slimy. The whole time during our interview he barely glanced at my face, staring about a foot lower the whole time. And then when I was about to leave, he kept offering me free stuff and saying I was like his daughter.'

'Gross,' said Shweta. She scribbled on a piece of paper and handed it to me. 'This is Paresh Patel's number; he came looking for you. Give him a call and tell him what you know.'

I called Paresh, reporter at *OpenSource* magazine. 'Hi,' I said, introducing myself. 'Shweta told me you had called for information about Prakash Agarwal?'

'Yes, Reema, thanks for calling back. Did you know him well?'

'Not really. I met him once for a profile I did on him.'

'I pulled that from the archives already,' he said.

'Do you know what happened to him?'

'He was ill, apparently. Seemed like food poisoning at first, but he wasn't responding to any kind of treatment. The doctor wanted to bring in the police. He seemed to think an autopsy would be a good idea.'

'Why?'

'The symptoms apparently spiralled out of control when he should have got better.'

'Does he suspect poison?'

'Said it was a long shot, but worth a closer look. They couldn't find anything in the toxicology reports to suggest it, but they thought a forensics team might be able to find out more.'

'Then why was he cremated?'

'The family did not want to involve the police and have a mess of an autopsy, and somehow the body was released without the doctor's knowledge. An outside physician was brought in who issued a death certificate and the family immediately went ahead with the cremation. This is all according to the police, who the doctor contacted sometime in the course of the morning.'

'Unusual.'

'Yes. The hospital is launching an internal investigation to find out how the body was allowed to be released in such a manner.'

It seemed like the cops had responded with their usual sense of urgency. 'What are the police doing?'

'A preliminary investigation is under way to establish if there was wrongdoing.'

'A little late for that, isn't it? How far can they get without a body?'

'I don't know. Not far at all, is my guess. But what I wanted to ask for is your opinion of the man.'

'To be honest, he didn't make a good impression.'

'Why not?'

'He was the unsavoury sort. And a serious lech.'

'Was he?'

'I would have expected some amount of savvy from someone in his line of work, but I got the feeling it was just a business to him, like any other. He could have just as well have been selling ball bearings as gourmet products. No passion for food at all.'

'So how do you explain his success?'

'Lack of competition, for one. And then there aren't many restaurants serving cuisine that would qualify as out of the ordinary. To give Agarwal credit, I think he understood his limitations and took advice from those around him. He also cultivated relationships with some of the best restaurateurs in the city, who must have been quite specific about what they wanted. He learnt the ropes over the years.'

'Did you ever meet his wife?'

'I did, in fact.' She was home the day I visited his office, which adjoined their flat. She let me in when I rang the wrong doorbell and showed me into her husband's office, which was connected to the house as well as having a separate, public entrance. 'She was quite different. Polished yet somehow cold.'

'How did they seem as a couple?'

'Strange. But I don't think it's fair to say more based on my first impression. I really know nothing about her.'

'Would you call me later if something else comes to mind?'

'Of course,' I said. 'And could I ask you to keep me in the loop as the case progresses?'

'Sure thing,' he said.

I hung up. Everything Paresh Patel told me sounded odd – the underhand death certificate, the rushed cremation. The police, I imagined, would be searching his house and office, looking for anything out of place. Perhaps they would question his wife and family, even his business associates. It seemed unlikely that anything would come of it. With so many open cases, how could the police afford to waste time on the unsubstantiated suspicion of a doctor? And the internal hospital investigation would most likely result in nothing more than a wrist-slap. At any rate, Paresh Patel seemed to be my best shot at the story – official and unofficial.

Or was he?

The clock struck 5 pm, a perfectly respectable hour at which to make my departure. I had completed a copy I had to file, chatted with a couple of colleagues about story ideas and researched the specific characteristics of Sicilian recipes versus northern Italian recipes for a senior columnist who had been asked to review a new restaurant very indecorously named The Godfather.

It was all well beyond my freelancer brief and thus, freed from guilt, I set off to pay a visit to Prakash Agarwal's widow.

I found a flower shop on the way, and hopped into the Metro.

Should I be ashamed of my rubbernecking? Wouldn't I just be adding to the poor lady's grief? I knew the Agarwals didn't have children. She would be all alone with her pain and wouldn't I only be compounding it?

But the truth mattered, I told myself.

And wasn't that best left to the cops?

If they bothered to look for it. And besides, this would only be a visit – a common courtesy to a tragedy-struck woman.

It didn't take me long to find the place. I had been there recently, and the long line of cars and groups of huddled visitors on the pavement outside the large, secure compound gave it away anyhow. The scene did away with my lingering compunctions – at least I wasn't the only intruder.

I rode the lift up to the flat. The front door was open, the smell of flowers and incense overpowering me as soon as I stepped into the hallway. Inside, a few people were gathered in the living room; at their centre sat Mrs Agarwal. A strained silence was broken only by a soft word here and there.

There was a moment when I hesitated at the threshold of that room. I could no longer ignore the inappropriateness of my trespassing at such a moment. But I was egged on by a need to know.

I approached the sofa where Mrs Agarwal sat sipping a cup of tea. She looked at me with eyes free and clear of tears. They would come later, I thought.

'Mrs Agarwal, you may not remember me,' I began.

She waved at me to sit down. 'Of course I do, Reema. From the magazine.'

She nodded to the other visitors who then left us alone.

'I am very sorry for your loss,' I said, setting the lilies down on the table and trying my best to smile as I took a seat.

'Thank you for coming,' she said. 'He was very happy with

your write-up. He bought at least 200 copies and distributed them to all our friends. It is up on his office wall. Would you like to see it?'

She didn't wait for my reply. Instead, she stood up and led me to Agarwal's office, the last place I had seen him alive. My eyes immediately went to the article that had been framed and hung on the wall behind his desk. There were still a half dozen copies of *Face* sitting beside his computer.

'He had a party for his friends and handed out copies,' said Mrs Agarwal.

'I am glad he liked it.'

A silence fell between us. I didn't know if I should ask what had happened. Murder seemed like a dirty word to bring up in a house of mourning. But it turned out that I didn't need to.

'You are in the media,' Mrs Agarwal said abruptly.

'Yes?'

'You must get to know things.'

A common perception I had faced through my short career. Journalists knew it all – election outcomes before the votes were cast, bandh dates, party venues. I didn't contradict her.

'I won't lie to you, Reema. My husband was not very well liked. The police came here asking all of these questions about him today, like they thought he had been murdered.'

I nodded sympathetically.

'They asked why we took the body away so quickly. But it was hardly quick! We were in the hospital for two hours waiting for a death certificate. When none was given, we brought in our own doctor. How were we to know they would want to investigate! Dr Mitra wasn't clear on why he wanted us to wait, and when he mentioned an autopsy, I thought he merely wanted to establish the exact cause of death. We – his family and I – didn't see much point in cutting him up because of that.'

'Did you say Dr Mitra? At Calcutta Medical?'

'Yes.'

Hadn't Mallika mentioned that her husband was a cardiologist at that very hospital? 'Would he by any chance be married to Mallika Mitra, owner of Middle Kingdom?' I asked.

Mrs Agarwal's face froze. 'I have no idea.'

'Of course, there could easily be another Dr Mitra at the hospital. He wasn't your regular doctor?' I asked.

'No. Our family doctor was travelling, so we rushed him to Calcutta Medical as it had the closest emergency ward.'

'It would be a curious coincidence if it was Mallika's husband,' I said.

'Not really,' she shrugged. 'We don't know the Mitras.'

'I see.' As another silence fell between us, I looked around the room. It didn't seem as though the police had been through here at all. The desk was neat and orderly, with a computer and phone on top. Behind it was a swivel chair, and to the left was a small chest of drawers, on which sat a tray holding a few opened envelopes. There was the silver snuff box I had seen during the interview. He had been fiddling with it the whole time and I had half expected him to snort away as we spoke. He thankfully had saved me from that final ignominy. Right beside it was a small oblong object, in some sort of white metal and plastic. It looked like a paperweight.

'What's this?' I asked.

'It's a snuff dispenser.'

I took a closer look. 'I've never seen anything like it.'

'Neither had I. It was a gift from – you might have met her – Vineeta Solanki. She runs a restaurant as well.'

'I don't think I have.'

'She was a friend of my husband's,' said Mrs Agarwal.

On the wall opposite was a filing cabinet, a printer, a fax machine and a shelf of products he kept on hand to show clients. His stock was kept elsewhere – he had promised me a trip there to pick up whatever I wanted, an offer I had done my best to sidestep.

I toyed with telling Mrs Agarwal that I could help uncover the truth, if she so desired. But then I felt a stab of familiar self-doubt. I was jumping to an awful lot of conclusions. A man had died. So what? People died all the time and normal, non-detective people didn't go about poking their food aroma-obscured noses into it.

But when Mrs Agarwal spoke next, she swung the door wide open for my morbid curiosity and wild imaginings.

'Reema, will you promise if you hear anything about this case that you will give me a call?'

Not exactly the sort of help I had had in mind. 'I will see what I can do,' I said.

She nodded. 'Whatever else, don't hold back to spare my feelings. Prakash Agarwal was a bastard who deserved to die. But if he was indeed murdered, I would like to know who did it. And why.'

I left the Agarwal residence in a daze. I was relieved to find that the sidewalk outside the home had cleared and that I was steady on my feet despite being thoroughly winded. I walked about aimlessly for a few minutes, my mind racing, Mrs Agarwal's words ringing in my ears.

I walked on till I found myself a few metres from my favourite bar. If ever there was a night to break the never-drink-alone rule, this was it.

Inside Ginger, the Filipino cover band was hard at work in an almost empty room. There was only one table of five foreigners – backpackers by the looks of it – in the corner. It was early yet, though on a weeknight it was possible that this was all the action the place would get. Ginger had seen better days, and that's probably why I liked it as much as I did. I had been a regular when it was the most happening place in town, and after all the fickle folk passed it by, it stood there, battered and bruised, but still beating away.

I bypassed the tables with their slightly faded green tablecloths and headed for the bar. It was far from the band, and I needed to think. I sat on a barstool and ordered a beer and a plate of nachos and tried to focus on what had transpired in the past few hours. For the moment, none of it seemed to make sense. Mrs Agarwal's calm assertion that her husband had been a bastard had been shocking enough, and her request for me to pass on information to her was strange, but too good to resist.

All the years I had played at detective, anything near the adrenaline-activating excitement of a murder had eluded me, and here I was, minding my own business – sort of – when the wife of a murdered man asks me to investigate her husband's death!

Well, close enough.

Was this a sign, one of those cosmic shout-outs that I always told myself I didn't believe in? Was I silly to resist it? Despite all my internal pep talk that I was doing the decent thing, earning an honest wage doing a job I kind of liked, could I deny that getting to the bottom of a murder was more rewarding – and more honourable – than waxing eloquent, on a bad day, about fast-food hamburgers made from a mix of polymer and lard?

Was it wrong to fight it when I could possibly be of use?

I took a long sip of beer. The music from the band hardly filtered through till I heard the familiar tune and the badly pronounced but still recognizable lyrics of 'Dhoom Machale'. I looked up and raised my glass to the band. Luke, the drummer, gave me a little wink. It was terrible, but it hit the spot with the foreign crowd, which now quickly filled the handkerchief of a dance floor.

My mind wandered back to Prakash Agarwal. All I could see were his bulbous eyes screaming his lasciviousness, the tap-tap-tap of the snuff box, his paan masala-stained lips moving around the words that made their way into my article. 'Every restaurant serving Western food has to come to me, at some point. I take care of all *their* everything.'

All except Mallika Mitra. She didn't patronize Agarwal's business. She brought in all *her* everything, down to her chilli peppers.

Did that make sense? It could hardly be economical. Was Mr Agarwal so unpleasant that she preferred to let profits suffer rather than do business with him? Why was she so shaken by the news of his death?

And why did Agarwal's own wife hate him so much? I had no trouble believing that he was capable of all kinds of offences, having left his office myself feeling defiled despite not even shaking his hand. But she had offered no real explanation for her strong words, and I had felt that it was the wrong time to dig deeper.

It was possible that his wife hated him enough to kill him. But then why ask me for information?

Was Agarwal as slimy in business as he was with women? Did he cheat someone? Did someone cheat him?

'This is the third song they are playing for you and you haven't as much as twitched a toe.'

I jumped at the words that came from just behind me. I swivelled around and found myself looking into black eyes dancing with humour. They belonged to a man wearing a navy suit and purple striped tie. Mid-to-late thirties. Six feet tall or in the neighbourhood. Grey just beginning to streak a head of neat, thick hair.

'Not for me; for those white, Bollywood hungry tourist types over there.'

'Are you sure? The drummer looks like he wouldn't mind playing a tune on my head if you so much as dared to stand up with me.'

'I don't dance,' I said, smiling back. I resisted the temptation to look at Luke who, I had to admit, carried an Olympic-sized torch for me.

'I'll drink to that,' he replied, raising his beer and waiting for me to do the same. 'But I hope you're not the band's manager because if you are, I would have to berate you for letting them do what they are doing to Hindi,' he said.

I shook my head energetically. 'No, I'm just a fan.'

'Is that a full-time occupation?'

'Are you suggesting that I am an alcoholic? I usually don't drink alone.'

He smiled. I smiled back.

'Shayak,' he said, putting out his hand.

I took it and received a good, firm shake.

'Reema,' I replied. But I could hardly recognize myself. I never spoke to strangers in bars, no matter how very tall-dark-handsome.

'New in town?' he asked.

'Nope. You?'

'Passing through, as I often do.'

'And what is it that you do as you pass through?'

He smiled again, cocking his head ever so slightly to the right, shedding his distinguished air and looking like that boy in school that almost everyone, even some of the teachers, would have a crush on. 'I am a venture capitalist.'

I wasn't quite sure what that would involve, outside of providing capital for ventures of some sort. I had dozed through the one solitary business class I had taken in college and was certain that any questions would cause me to look irreversibly idiotic. I nodded knowledgably instead.

'And what about you?' he asked.

That was easy. 'I write about food.'

'Enviable job. For a newspaper?'

I shook my head. 'Magazine. *Face.*'

He managed to look like he knew what I was talking about, though he was hardly our typical reader.

My nachos arrived. The platter looked embarrassingly large and I quickly offered Shayak some. He took a smothered chip, and I took an uncharacteristically dainty piece and nibbled. I hated eating in front of strangers. It was a problem I had not managed to overcome, despite the fact that nowadays I made my money doing just that.

'So what kind of food do you write about?'

'Every kind. Preferably global.'

'Ah.'

'I take it you have little interest in such mundane matters?'

'Far from it. You gotta eat, after all.'

'My thoughts precisely.' Though from his lithe frame, I could imagine he didn't eat much. That wouldn't do at all if we were ever to go out.

Not that I was thinking of asking a stranger out.

But what if he asked me out?

I looked at him popping another chip into his mouth. He apparently had no qualms about eating my food, so perhaps I need not worry about out-eating him, if the occasion presented itself.

I was pleased, though I didn't know why.

'Does your knowledge of food extend to the kitchen?' he asked.

'I bake.'

'Cakes?'

'Yes, and anything that can be baked. Cakes, muffins, breads, tarts, quiches, pasta. How about you?'

'I am quite the chef,' he said with a smile.

'And not at all modest about it.'

'I see no need to be,' he said, taking another nacho. It seemed to suddenly occur to him that he was eating up my food. 'Can I get you something else?'

'Not for me but if you are thinking of ordering, I would recommend the chicken wings.' And then a horrific thought struck me. What if he was vegetarian? I had dated one once. A teetotaller, too. It didn't go too well. We only ever met for coffee and I had ended up very, very wired and very, very hungry. 'Unless you are vegetarian, of course,' I said with trepidation.

'I come from a long and proud line of meat eaters,' he said.

I masked my relief by draining my glass.

'Can I buy you another beer?' he offered. 'It's the least I can do after polishing off your nachos.'

I was tempted, but I was also torn. This was a stranger, I told myself. He was good-looking, but I knew nothing about him. I couldn't afford my head to be muddled further than it already was by alcohol. And I had enough to do the next day.

I looked at my watch.

'It's getting late, isn't it?' he said softly.

I nodded and eased off the barstool. I put my hand out and he shook it again. Warm, strong, confident.

'It was nice meeting you, Shayak,' I said.

'Yes, it was.'

I turned around and walked out of the bar. I found a cab and jumped in, wondering why he hadn't given me his number. He's probably married, my cynical PI heart suggested, or had several other perfectly good reasons. I was surprised by how disappointed I felt.

'Reema Ray, snap out of it,' I mumbled.

SIX

My head was still stuck in the bar as I pushed open the small gate to enter my flat, which occupied the ground floor of a tiny house off Hazra Road. But what I saw there drove all thoughts of mysterious, dishy strangers from my head.

There was Amit, sitting on my stoop.

'Surprised?' he said, his smile as sardonic as ever.

What else could I be? The ice in our relationship had hardly thawed enough for him to show up unannounced on my doorstep. 'You sure know how to make an entrance.'

'Sorry for not calling. I wasn't sure that you'd see me if I did.'

'Don't worry about it. The commissioner called on the Batphone to warn me trouble was coming.'

Amit ignored the jibe. 'I hope I am not disturbing you.'

And since when had he cared about that? 'How did you know where to find me?' I couldn't remember telling him where I lived.

'I got your address from your mother.'

'You shouldn't have done that,' I snapped. She too was angry, she still felt betrayed by his desertion. To say nothing of how I felt about the subject. 'I am surprised she gave it to you.'

'I must confess to resorting to subterfuge.'

'You didn't tell her it was you?'

'I had a friend call.'

I was speechless. Why was he saying these things? Why was he here?

'I had no choice, Reema. Believe me.'

'Why?' I asked, my brow making my displeasure known.

'You haven't been watching TV?'

Dread fluttered in my stomach. 'I don't own a TV set. What happened?'

'It's Aloka – they've got her.'

'What do you mean?'

Amit watched my confusion with a disconcerting stillness. 'May I come in?'

I led Amit inside. I picked up the paper, which I had left untouched on my coffee table that morning before heading out.

'It happened too late at night for it to make the morning edition,' Amit said.

'Tell me what happened.'

'It was last night, around 10 pm. Aloka had just left Forum after watching a movie with her friends when two masked men drove up to them, pulled out guns and herded her into a waiting van.'

The truth suddenly dawned on me – while I had been drunk dialling Amit, his wife was being held hostage somewhere.

I continued before I could dwell too long on my shameful behaviour. 'And?'

'And nothing. That's it. That is precisely what happened.'

'No call? No ransom note?'

'Nothing has come to me. But what can I give?'

'To her parents, then?'

'I believe so. But as you know, I am not exactly welcome in that house. One of our friends who has been there since morning has kept me in the loop. The ransom demand is allegedly ₹2 crore.'

'How was it made?'

'Over the phone, I think.'

'When is the payment supposed to be given?'

'I really don't know.'

'What is being done?' I asked.

'Kishan Mohta, her father, has pulled out the big guns – cops, lawyers – to try and track her down. But as far as I can tell, he's not paying up just yet.'

Two crore was a substantial sum for most people, but not Aloka's father, a steel baron. Perhaps the kidnappers had given them time to come up with it.

'Any suspects?' I asked.

'Yes,' he said, putting a cigarette between waiting lips. 'Me.'

'You?' I thought I must have heard wrong.

'According to the police,' said Amit, lighting up and taking a long drag.

'What are you talking about? Why do they think it is you?'

Amit continued in his matter-of-fact tone, as if he was narrating nothing more than the plot of a story. 'When Aloka and I decided to get married, her parents refused permission. They thought I was after her money.'

'And were you?' I asked. Despite myself, despite the situation, I couldn't resist. And it was a valid question if he had come to me for what I thought he had.

He looked at me with an unfaltering gaze, the smoke from his cigarette diffusing. 'You think I would have done what I did to you for money?'

I looked away, watching the tendrils of smoke rise upwards. The truth was that I did not think Amit had married Aloka for her money; I never had, though I had dearly wanted to. Amit had never seemed to have the pressing desire for wealth that I saw in almost everyone else I knew. Money did not motivate him – he wanted to be a poet or, failing that, a writer of some kind. He seemed to know exactly what he wanted for himself long before the rest of us did and that was perhaps what I missed most about him. He used to talk for hours about his dream to earn just enough money to buy a small house with a large plot of land in a village. It would be close enough to the city to ensure he wasn't cut off completely, but for the most part he craved self-sufficiency. If he needed anyone at all, it was me, he used to say. Later, I assumed the honour had passed on to Aloka.

She had also been at school with us. It had been years since I had met her. We had not been part of the same circle – she was the very rich child of very conservative parents. My guess had been that she would be hitched by the time she was twenty-three, with babies not far behind. I had not been far off the mark – except for the babies, and except for the fact that I had never imagined that it would be *my* boyfriend she'd marry.

Amit and I had been living on different continents for the four years I was away at college. Had he come clean earlier than he did, I could have attempted to understand. But instead he started seeing Aloka, who still lived in Calcutta, on the sly. And I, the woman who had made a career – okay, a half-career – out of detecting deceit, had suspected absolutely nothing.

Even when he broke up with me, I refused to believe rumours that he had been cheating. But I could no longer kid myself when, months later, ridiculously young and ridiculously poor to aspire to such a wife, Amit and Aloka got engaged amidst much scandal. We had enough friends in common to fill in the blanks. I had not spoken to Amit for almost three years after that, till he had reached out to me a few months ago.

'So now what?' I asked at last.

'My only hope of getting my wife back is to prove them wrong. They have to see that it isn't me, or else she's gone. I just know it.'

Try as I might I could not see how Aloka's parents – however much they hated their son-in-law – had him pegged as a kidnapper. It was hardly a fitting image – the kurta-clad, idealistic Amit I had known had always been far from menacing – in fact, with his tall, spare frame, his stubble, hair worn slightly long and unkempt, exhaustion showing in every expression, he looked almost ascetic.

'What are the police doing?'

'Very little, it seems, apart from following my every move. They haven't even bothered to question me. You must understand the kind of pull Aloka's father has with almost every crooked cop in town.'

'Why have you come to me?'

'I want you to investigate this on your own.'

'A kidnapping case may be a little out of my league, don't you think?'

'Not really. You see, I think I know who did it.'

'Who?'

Amit paused to take another drag. 'Aloka's father.'

I shook my head as if that would help to clear it. 'What are you talking about?'

'Think about it. A kidnapper would have done his homework well enough to know that relations were strained between Aloka and her father after our wedding. They barely speak, and whatever little contact they do have is at Aloka's mother's insistence. Aloka has been disinherited and she gets no help from him now – in fact, quite the reverse. Why kidnap the out-of-favour daughter when there is a perfectly eligible son to do the job? The only reason someone would want to kidnap Aloka is to harm me.' What Amit said made a twisted kind of sense, the kind straight out of a Bollywood blockbuster. 'Perhaps the kidnapper didn't know about all this. Perhaps this information isn't common knowledge outside the family circle.'

'Hardly,' said Amit with a wry smile. 'You know what these offensively rich people are like. Gossip is their intoxicant of choice. I – and by extension Aloka – have been positively and very publicly shunned. And besides, everything points to an inside job.'

'What do you mean?' I asked.

'No one knew where Aloka was supposed to be that night except the friends she was with, her mother and I. She was supposed to meet her mother for a late dinner at a restaurant, since her father didn't like her going to their home. Her mother's driver was supposed to pick her up after the movie, but failed to show up. Her friends had decided to drop her to the restaurant but before they could find a cab, these men appeared out of nowhere.'

'What about the people she was with?'

'Two of her oldest friends – neighbours she has grown up with, all equally affluent.'

I swallowed my pride to ask the next question. 'So when I called you ...'

'It had already happened, but the friends hadn't bothered to call me – they first contacted Aloka's parents. There I was, thinking Aloka was at dinner with her mother, and then safely home. I only found out when I returned at about 3 am that she hadn't made it back.'

'Where were you so late?'

Again, a pause. 'I work for a newspaper now and had the night shift.'

I barely hid my surprise. Amit hated the media with a vengeance long before it became fashionable to do so. Writers like him, he believed, were reduced to whores in the incessant hunt for stories. Aloka's father must really have worked his influence to reduce him to this.

I still didn't see how I fit in. 'Amit, I'm sorry, but–'

'Please!' Amit exclaimed, finally showing some emotion. 'You know how difficult it was for me to come to you. I can't take back what I did to you, but I also wouldn't be able to live with myself if I didn't do everything in my power to bring Aloka back to safety.'

Amit's anguish filled the room, and I struggled to breathe. I was torn between doing what my head told me – which was to help – and what my heart demanded – which was to run away as fast as I could. This was the man I had once loved and trusted. This was the man who had left me devastated with his lies.

I walked over to the window and opened it, hoping the cigarette smoke would vacate the room and leave me some breathing space. On the street, a boy and girl walked hand in hand down the road in school uniform. A coaching centre occupied the house beside me, and young people left at all hours. I had known Amit – and Aloka, for that matter – since we had been much younger than that boy and girl. And it was for those three children – and not the adults they had become – that I made my decision.

But if Amit was right and Aloka's father was behind this madness, it wasn't Aloka who was in any danger, it was Amit. There was no telling how far Kishan Mohta would go to make his point.

'Give me a few hours to think,' I said. 'I'll call you tomorrow morning to tell you how to proceed.'

Amit nodded curtly. 'I should admit straight out that I have no money to give you.'

'I wouldn't take your money.'

'What do you want me to do in the meantime?'

'Let me know if there is any news.'

'How do I get news?.'

'Stay in touch with Aloka's friends who are close to the family. And keep an eye on the television.'

SEVEN

As soon as I showed Amit out, I dialled Uncle Kumar's number.

'Hi, Uncle Kumar!' I said, happy to hear his voice.

'Reema, hell-o dear! To what do I owe this pleasure?'

I loved to hear him speak. Uncle Kumar had been fantastic on stage, that deep booming baritone of his filling every inch of the auditorium with his clipped Queen's English. It was he who had introduced my father – one of his oldest friends – to my mother, an actress in a play he was in. The friendships had survived though my parents' marriage had not.

'Oh, you know me, always poking my nose where it shouldn't be.'

'Does it smell foul?'

'Acutely.'

'And what can I do to alleviate your suffering, my dear?'

'The kidnapping of Aloka Mohta. You know who she is, don't you?'

'Kishan Mohta's daughter.'

'I don't mean in that way.'

'In which way, then?'

'Do you remember Amit?' A purely rhetorical question, as my parents' closest friend had met my ex-boyfriend numerous times. Lunches, dinners, weddings – Amit had been a fixture on the family scene for years. After it all ended, Uncle Kumar had even threatened to have him picked up and taught a lesson in the lock-up. All talk, of course, but I couldn't say it hadn't helped at the time.

'That ragamuffin you once called boyfriend?'

'That's the one. Aloka is his wife.'

'Oh dear.'

'He came to me, and all I could think of was calling you.'

'You are thinking about helping that scoundrel?'

'Yes, Uncle Kumar. It would be rather spiteful if I didn't.'

'Then you have a more forgiving heart than I.'

'Uncle Kumar! Please!'

'Okay, okay. What can I do for you?'

'I think I need to explain the situation face to face. As far as I know, they have been given three days to produce the ransom money.'

'That was rather generous.'

'But Amit may be in danger too.'

'All the better, I say.'

'Uncle Kumar!'

'Oh well. Why don't you come over tomorrow morning around ten with the nincompoop. But be sure to leave him outside. I might smack him if I see him.'

I hung up, my head reeling. Suddenly there were not one but two cases on my plate. Maybe, all this while, I had been trying too hard. Maybe, if I had just sat still for long enough, the mysteries would have come to me.

*

Less than twelve hours later, I was sitting in the same chair I had sat in as Uncle Kumar disabused me of every childish notion I had regarding the life of a policeman. I repeated to him in detail the story I had heard from Amit the previous night.

Uncle Kumar heard me out in silence. When I finished, he spoke at last. 'How do you expect me to get involved on the strength of this theory?' he asked.

'I honestly don't know, Uncle Kumar. But I had to do something, and coming to you was the only thing I could think of.'

'Do you believe him?'

'He seems so lost, so desperate.'

'That doesn't answer my question.'

I shook my head. 'No, I guess it doesn't.'

Uncle Kumar wasn't about to cut me any slack – he had me squirming in my chair with the unforgiving intensity of his gaze.

'Yes,' I said at last. 'I guess I do believe him.'

'Fair enough,' he said with a gentle smile. 'But you'll forgive me if I reserve judgement till I have seen the scoundrel myself.'

Amit had been waiting outside the police station, and I texted him summons. As he walked in, sweat on his brow yet shoulders squared in the face of Uncle Kumar's evident hostility, I knew that I had been right to put my resentment aside. This was the first man I had fallen in love with, fighting to save the love of his life, and who would I be if I punished him at a time like this?

'So you think the police and your father-in-law are partners in crime?' Uncle Kumar began. He had never been one for chitchat.

'Yes,' Amit said, falling right in with the pace.

'Why should I believe you?'

'Because if it wasn't true, if I did what they say I have, why would I come to a cop?'

'Reema brought you to me as a friend, though I fail to understand why. She knows I'm hardly going to arrest you under the circumstances, much as I'd love to.'

'Even so, a guilty man would run a mile from a uniform. What do I have to gain from this sort of exposure?'

'Who knows? I've seen my share of stupid criminals.'

'And you believe I am fool enough to come to a woman who has every reason to hate me for help?'

I kept my eyes glued to Uncle Kumar's unsmiling face, surprised by how much pain I felt at this statement.

'Explain the situation, as you see it,' Uncle Kumar said. 'Why would a man go to such lengths just to break up his daughter's marriage?'

'Because he has tried just about everything else. In the time we've been married he has had us threatened, chucked out of jobs, followed, spied on, separated. He's even had me beaten up on one occasion. And he has just discovered that we are planning to leave town, to go to Delhi, and he's afraid that he has finally lost his daughter to me for good.'

'One might say that he'd lost her the day you two married against his wishes.'

'Then you don't know Kishan Mohta. There is nothing he hates more than not getting his way, and his daughter disobeying him in such an important decision – marrying someone so wrong, so beneath her – went against everything he believed. His determination to separate us only seemed to grow stronger after we got married.'

'But to put his own daughter in danger?'

'She isn't in any real danger, is she? Whoever has her will ensure that she is afraid, but not at serious risk.'

'I find it difficult to believe a father would put his daughter through the torment.'

'Don't honour killings happen all the time in our country? Isn't that proof enough that parents are sometimes capable of causing the greatest possible harm to their children when they act against the family's wishes?'

I could see that Uncle Kumar was moved by this last statement. What seemed beyond the pale in the air-conditioned comfort of a Park Street office – a father teaching a daughter to toe the family line at dear cost – was all too believable in a different context. Who was to say Aloka's father was above it?

'How do you suppose it happened?'

'Kishan Mohta must have found out where Aloka would be from her mother, and ensured the family car that was supposed to pick her up after the movie never arrived. He hired someone – maybe one of the goons he employs in his factory – to stage the abduction. He probably has her stashed away somewhere, perfectly safe and, I hope, only slightly uncomfortable. And he will be making sure that whoever is in contact with her has left her in no doubt that I am behind the whole thing. In a few days – long enough to ensure she is done with me forever – he will make it look like the ransom has been paid and she will be released. He will win, I will lose and perhaps even get locked up as an added bonus.'

'Sounds a little far-fetched,' said Uncle Kumar, raising a sceptical eyebrow.

Amit shrugged. 'Yes, of course. It's crazy. But no more so than his accusations against me that I have kidnapped my own wife, and those seem perfectly believable to the police. The only difference is the alleged ends – mine, apparently, is cash; his, revenge.'

'If Kishan Mohta is behind this, what are you really afraid of? Your wife is safe and will be released soon. If they have tried to poison her mind against you, she may not believe them.'

For a moment, Amit was at a loss for words. 'That is true,' he said deliberately. 'But if he manages to sell the story that I am behind it, what will become of me?'

Uncle Kumar narrowed his eyes ever so slightly before turning to me and back to Amit. 'You may leave now,' he said abruptly.

Amit stood up, and I followed suit.

'No, Reema, you please stay. Amit, give us a few moments alone, please.'

I watched Uncle Kumar follow Amit's retreating body with his eyes. I heard the door close as Amit let himself out.

'Are you sure about this fellow?'

'What they are accusing him of is ludicrous. And if it is true, why would he agree to come to you if he was guilty?'

'I'd have an easier time believing he was capable of such clear thinking had he not left you for another, decidedly richer woman,' he said.

'Uncle Kumar, you'd hate anyone who hurt me.'

'And with good reason. He'd have to be very greedy – or insane – to leave my Reema for that insipid waif of a woman.'

'Uncle Kumar!' I admonished, though perhaps my outrage would have been more authentic had I not thought the same thing on many an occasion.

'It's true, I've seen the pictures,' said Uncle Kumar, tapping his pen against his desk. 'The whole business stinks, if you ask me. But I have to say that I am inclined to believe him. The entire unit dealing with the case is a particularly unpleasant lot. And a businessman of Mohta's calibre would have plenty of influence.'

'Who is in charge?' I asked.

'Unfortunately, it is my old friend Ravi Sharma.'

'Oh no!' Sharma and Uncle Kumar's fallout had been very public. Though they had once been friends, the origin of their mutual dislike was a murky matter, and one I had never really spoken to him about. 'I don't want you to have to ask him for a favour.'

'Don't worry, child. No favours will be asked for at this juncture.'

'But you'll look into it?'

Uncle Kumar nodded. 'I will make a few calls. I can't promise any more at the moment.'

I walked out to find Amit standing outside the main door of the station smoking a cigarette. Even now, it seemed like he couldn't work up the energy to be palpably anxious.

'He said he'd make some calls,' I said.

He closed his eyes for a fraction longer than a blink, the only indication he was pleased with the outcome. 'Thank you, Reema.'

'Let's go to your place now.'

'Why?' he asked, throwing his cigarette down and killing it with his heel.

'I want to look around, see if I can find anything.'

'Like what? Aloka was taken from the street. Why would there be any clues in our home?'

His discomfort was clear, but I wouldn't budge. Even if I couldn't find anything, I needed a sense of the place, of their life together, to understand something of what was going on here.

We took the Metro into the bowels of north Calcutta and trudged into a building that made my old office premises look like Victoria Memorial. An old wooden staircase was disintegrating. A paintbrush had not touched the walls in years and cobwebs hung from the corners like party streamers. We climbed three treacherous flights up, which felt like six. The lift, of course, was out of order – permanently so.

Once inside the massive wooden door, I was shocked to see how small Amit and Aloka's flat was. It was one big room. The living area had a little cupboard to one side with a small one-burner stove on top of it, the wall above it stained with trails of oil and masala and sprays of dal from an angry pressure cooker. Four wicker chairs were arranged around a small glass-topped table, which evidently served as both dining area and living room. At the far end was an old wooden bed big enough for four, with a lumpy mattress. A small TV stood on a stool at its foot. One corner was walled off and had a cheap PVC door, which I assumed was the bathroom. On the faded turquoise walls, the only embellishments were a Bengali calendar three years old pasted to the wall and a creeping pattern of mould that seemed to have been making itself at home at least as long.

'The landlord's stuff,' Amit mumbled.

He hadn't been exaggerating the depths to which Aloka's father had plunged them. I knew that Amit's own family hardly had the resources to be of much help, so the two of them would have been on their own. And if Mohta had done his best to keep them out of gainful employment, it was no surprise they lived so sparsely.

I looked through the shelves to one side. T. S. Elliot. William Blake. Tagore. Rumi. Amit's books, worn with use.

'What does Aloka do?' I realized I knew next to nothing about her.

'She worked at a bank till about a year ago, when she was asked to leave for no apparent reason.'

'Her father?'

'We think so. Since then, she has been doing some work for a friend who is a fashion designer.'

'And when did you start working with a newspaper?'

'A couple of months ago. I had been working with a small, independent publishing house, but after Aloka lost her bank job, I needed to make more money.'

'Your father-in-law hasn't orchestrated your sacking yet?'

'It's not like he hasn't tried. Lucky for me, my boss doesn't take kindly to his interference in HR matters.'

'You've had a rough time of it.'

'Even more so because we need to support my mother as well.'

'Could I ask why you don't just live with her?' I had been to the house Amit grew up in and, while it was small, Amit and Aloka would surely be more comfortable there then they were here.

For once, my question seemed to give Amit pause.

'Sorry if that's a personal question.'

'No, it's just that my mother didn't take very well to Aloka in the early days. It's better now, but it would be a little uncomfortable for Aloka, for us, to stay there.'

A picture of their marriage – lonely, verging on desperate – was emerging and, despite myself, some of the resentment I had been clinging to was slipping away.

EIGHT

I got home and started work on the Middle Kingdom piece for the magazine, with a self-imposed deadline of tomorrow. If I had any additional questions, I could ask later that night at Mallika's house when I went for the promised dinner. I also hoped to get a chance to speak to Agarwal's doctor, if he did in fact turn out to be Mallika's husband.

I started typing out facts and quotes. But when it came to framing my thoughts for the actual writing, I was all over the place. Mallika Mitra's restaurant. Her attempt to reveal a Chinese cuisine that India seldom got to taste. Her insistence that she knew nothing about Prakash Agarwal's business. Her attack of nerves on learning he was dead.

I finally cobbled together a rough draft at around 6 pm. Then I checked in with Amit: there had been no further developments, no further contact, as far as he knew, from the men who had Aloka. There was nothing else I could do for the moment, so I spent a little more time than usual getting ready, and arrived at Mallika's place shortly after 7.30 pm.

She lived in an apartment above Middle Kingdom and I had

expected it to be small and noisy, but it was neither. Her home was, in fact, as cosy as her restaurant. Large windows overlooked the Lakes and city lights twinkled in the distance. It could have been a scene straight out of a home improvement catalogue, with every throw pillow in place, the coffee table stacked with lusciously illustrated volumes, textures carefully put together for a luxurious feel.

I was the first to arrive, and Mallika and I sat down with our glasses of red wine. Today she was dressed in a becoming black-and-white crepe sari, and I was thankful that I had decided to pull out my solitary dress for the occasion. Black, of course.

'I'm so happy you came,' smiled Mallika.

'Thank you for having me.'

'It's just a small dinner for some close friends. Abhimanyu will be along in a bit. He is looking forward to meeting you.'

'You said your home is attached to your restaurant?'

'The old owners had planned the restaurant as a two-level, but we didn't need such a vast space. So while the restrooms of the restaurant and my office are upstairs, we converted the rest of the space into our home.'

'Are they connected?'

'You can get into the restaurant through the office.'

'It's amazing how quiet it is in here when there is a restaurant down there,' I said.

'We had the entire restaurant soundproofed, even though Middle Kingdom is hardly a boisterous sort of establishment.'

I was just about to ask after her husband when the doorbell rang. Mallika went to answer it and returned to the living room accompanied by a man in his fifties. He looked decidedly put out and, judging from the deep lines in his forehead, it was a chronic condition.

'Where is Vineeta? Will she be long?' asked Mallika.

'Busy with the restaurant, as usual. She said she is just about to reach home, which was about five minutes ago. Given how long she takes to get ready, I would say another couple of hours.'

'Manish!' Mallika chided with a laugh. 'Anyway, I am glad you came on ahead. We may as well get started. Manish, this is my friend Reema, she is a journalist.' As she glanced at me, I saw a hint of discomfort in her eyes. 'Reema, Manish and his wife Vineeta run the restaurant Khana Khazana on Ritchie Road.'

Manish continued to appraise me unsmilingly, without any attempt at a greeting. I had no problem staring back till I sensed Mallika's growing unease.

I picked up my glass of wine. Vineeta. Hadn't that been the name of the woman Mrs Agarwal had described as her husband's friend?

'What can I get you to drink, Manish?' asked Mallika.

'Whisky.'

As Mallika disappeared in the direction of the kitchen, Manish sat down on a sofa opposite me and turned his face resolutely towards the window, head resting on his hand. Thankfully our hostess reappeared soon, armed with a generous pour. I hoped it wasn't the good stuff; it seemed destined to be a waste on this bulldozer of a man.

'How have you been, Manish?' Mallika asked once she settled down on the sofa beside me. 'It's been a long time since we last met.'

'I have been in Assam for a while. Just got back,' he said.

'It's been busy at the factory?'

'Yes, but I am not as much in demand as my wife. It's a surprise if I see her at all these days.'

I glanced at Mallika, and saw she was struggling to keep the conversation afloat.

'Factory?' I asked.

'I have a vegetable oil and lubricant factory in Assam,' said Manish.

'Castor beans,' added Mallika.

'But make no mistake – I'm not as important as my wife,' said Manish.

'The restaurant must be doing well,' I said. 'I've heard good things about it.'

He scoffed. 'Who knows?'

'How long has it been around?'

'About five years.' He paused to take a sip of whisky.

The conversation stopped and started for another ten minutes or so, till the doorbell rang again. This time Mallika brought back Vineeta, looking flustered.

'Sorry I'm late,' she said.

Mallika introduced us.

'Where is Siddhartha?' asked Vineeta.

'Surgery,' said Mallika. 'There was some sort of emergency.'

'That's too bad,' I said. 'I remember you mentioned he practises at Calcutta Medical.'

'Among other places.

'He won't be joining us?' I asked, trying to hide my disappointment.

'I'm afraid not.'

'It's been a long time since I've seen him,' said Vineeta.

'Yes, it's been impossible to coordinate our schedules, hasn't it?'

Vineeta gave a shaky little laugh. 'It's the restaurant ...'

I stole a glance at Manish, but thankfully he seemed not to be listening.

'How are the kids?' Mallika asked.

'Never let them hear you call them that!' said Vineeta, with a hint of a warm smile. 'Hitesh has settled down in his new job, and Himani is visiting after her first semester at Leeds.' She chattered on, and at least while on this subject Manish retracted his claws, preferring a rather disinterested silence to outright belligerence.

Then the last guest arrived – a man in his forties, unusually tall, with salt-and-pepper hair and a slight stoop.

'Chef Abhimanyu,' said Mallika, 'this is Reema Ray, the reporter I was telling you about.'

We shook hands and he gave me a warm smile. My spirits were buoyed by the hope that conversation with Manish would no longer be necessary.

'Sorry I missed you yesterday. When are you coming back for a proper meal?' he asked.

'I already had one before I started research for my story.'

'When?'

'It was about a week ago. It wasn't my first at your restaurant, of course.'

'You should have called.'

'That would have defeated the purpose. We like to do unannounced reviews. It keeps everyone honest.'

'And how did you find it?' Vineeta asked.

'Fantastic. As close to perfect as I expect to get in Calcutta,' I said.

'Come on,' said Abhimanyu with a laugh. 'That's seems rather generous.'

'I mean it. It's been a while since I've had such a satisfactory meal anywhere.'

'So why have we never seen you in our restaurant?' asked Manish.

I cringed. 'How do you know I haven't been there?'

'I would have remembered if you had come by.'

'How could you when half the time you are away in Assam?' said Vineeta, just short of snapping at him.

I smiled politely and glanced at the glass in his hand. It was empty again. He seemed to notice it too and walked in the direction of the kitchen, presumably to help himself.

'But you should come,' said Vineeta.

'I will, certainly.'

'Not for a review, but just to see the restaurant,' she added quickly. 'We've recently redone our menu.'

Manish returned, fortified with a generous volume of amber. 'You write for a magazine?' he asked, glancing at me.

'Yes,' I said, though I would have thought that this fact had been well established in the course of the evening.

'About food?'

I nodded again.

'What a job!'

'And why do you say that?' asked Vineeta sharply.

'All she does is eat and write, eat and write,' he laughed.

'And what we do is so much better – cook and feed?' said Abhimanyu.

Ordinarily I may have agreed with Manish, but that evening I sat there somewhat awkwardly, not wishing to add fuel to the loaded exchange.

'Speak for yourself,' said Manish. 'I am a manufacturer.'

'Of castor oil,' Abhimanyu said under his breath, but loud enough to be heard.

'Yes, not that there is anything wrong with that. And just in case the chef doesn't find that impressive enough, we've just signed a contract with a pharmaceutical company to supply compounds for cancer research.'

'Manish!' said Vineeta.

'What?'

'I thought that was confidential information.'

'I don't expect a bunch of restaurant owners, or a food writer, to sell my secrets to the competition.'

Vineeta closed her eyes and let out a deep breath. A tense silence fell around the circle, till Vineeta seemed to flip some sort of internal switch and shoot me a smile. 'So tell me, Reema, when can you come to the restaurant?'

'Why don't I call you to set a date?' I said.

'But before that, you must come back to Middle Kingdom next week for our dim sum promotion,' said Abhimanyu.

'Dim sum! My favourite!'

'We have a guest chef who specializes in it coming by for a few weeks. If it works, we might introduce it in our brunch and tea menu.'

He started explaining the intricacies of what he had pegged as the highlight of the selection, the Shanghainese xiaolongbao. 'Usually, since dim sum is a Cantonese tradition, the world outside of China only gets to eat dumplings from that region. I thought it would be interesting to have a representation from elsewhere.'

'I don't think I have had that one,' I said.

'It is a pork dumpling with soup inside.'

'Soup! How does that get in there?'

'Come and try it and I will tell you.'

'I must! I have to include this in my story.'

Mallika disappeared into the kitchen, returning with a tray laden with crackers with bleu cheese, walnuts, fig and balsamic drizzle, baba ganoush and homemade pita and lamb and vegetable skewers. Not only was the food delicious, I was grateful for the distraction it provided from the strained conversation. But the reprieve did not last long. Manish kept drinking, and rather rapidly seemed to lose whatever control he had over his tongue.

'So when will the good doctor return?' he said.

Mallika shrugged slightly, her pretty earrings bobbing up and down. 'Later tonight.'

'Is he ever here?'

'He works with so many hospitals. You know that, Manish,' said Vineeta, urgency creeping into her voice.

'But how can he bear to leave you alone so often, Mallika?'
'Manish!'
'What, Vineeta? A man with a wife like Mallika should stay home more.'

I concentrated on my food as silence descended over the coffee table, the only sounds coming from the cutlery and Manish's glass clinking as he set it down.

Manish's performance over the next half hour was enough to leave the rest of us squirming. Abhimanyu, clearly used to the drill, drew me to a corner where he continued to tell me about the regional variations of Chinese food. We shortly relocated to the dinner table, where I would have been more than happy to not say a word and savour the grilled haloumi with vegetables and lamb tagine with mint-and-lemon scented couscous. But that was too much to ask for.

'Reema, do you ever write about Indian food?' asked Manish.
'Yes, of course I do.'
'But you just aren't as interested in it as you are in Chef Abhimanyu's pig dumplings.'
'Dim sum is unusual for me, for Calcutta, so yes, I would say that I find it more intriguing than chicken tikka masala. And more newsworthy.'
'I would say that is the same for your new friend here, Mallika. See, she never cooks us Indian food, though I am sure she knows I hate anything else.'

This stretched even the impeccable Mallika's hospitality to the limit and she tried her hardest to pretend she hadn't heard.

But Manish was relentless. 'Isn't it nice how every cook in a western restaurant gets called "Chef"? Nothing else. Just Chef. Like Doctor. Ha!'

I waited for Abhimanyu to rise to the bait but when I looked at him, he was watching Mallika anxiously.

'Will you be coming to the restaurant tomorrow morning? I wanted to show you some samples a new vegetable supplier has brought in,' Abhimanyu asked Mallika.

If he thought shop talk would deter Manish, he was wrong.

'Mallika,' he continued. 'We are all a little beneath you, aren't we? Me, my wife, the rest of the Indian restaurant owners. You stay far away from us all. But then, I suppose it's not just us. You seemed to stay furthest away from Prakash Agarwal, who made every last rupee by selling imported trash from across the world to every substandard restaurant in the city. What was it about him that you just couldn't stand? Especially when he was so popular with everyone else! My wife seemed to like him very much!'

'Manish!' exclaimed Vineeta, standing up, sweat beading her brow. 'I think it's time we went home.'

'Yes, we may as well. What does it matter anyway, now that he's dead?'

And yet Manish Solanki showed no inclination to join his wife. 'And isn't it strange,' he continued, 'that the good Dr Siddhartha Mitra was the one who treated him at the end? He was on life support for a while, wasn't he? Was it Mitra who finally pulled the plug?'

'Now, look,' said Abhimanyu, standing up.

Mallika sat absolutely still, staring at the wine, blood red, in her glass.

'Don't worry, Chef. I am leaving. I wouldn't dream of making any of you uncomfortable with the truth,' Manish spat out, rising from the table on unsteady feet. 'Hypocrites, the whole bunch of you are hypocrites!' he slurred as he stumbled out of the room, jerking away from his wife as she tried to lead him by the elbow.

On my way home, any reluctance I had about looking into the death of Prakash Agarwal seemed to slip away. After that little performance it was hard to remain aloof, especially since Agarwal seemed to inspire enough hate all around to harbour half a dozen motives for murder.

There was only one way I could think of proceeding: if I was going to investigate this matter on my own, I would need resources and I would need some access to information.

I dialled Santosh da's cell.

'Bolo, Reema,' he said cheerily. 'How can I be of help?'

'There is a matter I would like to discuss with the group and I thought you might be able to call a meeting.'

I outlined the suspect circumstances surrounding the death of Agarwal, the role of the doctor in the whole business and Mrs Agarwal's remarks.

'It is very strange indeed,' Santosh da agreed.

'Yes. I thought perhaps the group might be able to get involved, provide some support.'

'Why not? Why don't you call them?'

'Santosh da, you know that they don't take me seriously.'

'If that is the case, then why not do this on your own? I can help.'

'There is no client here. I need resources. I am broke,' I admitted. I didn't need to remind him that so was he.

Santosh da let out a deep breath. 'Okay, Reema. Let me call them to my office tomorrow. Does 9 am suit you?'

'Sure.'

I hung up, and thought about what I had just begun. Not one but two cases were now on my plate. I felt a thrill of excitement, marred by a mild but undeniable vein of panic.

NINE

The next morning, I was woken up way too early by my phone.

'Hello,' I said, groggily.

'Sorry, did I wake you?'

'Yes, who is this?'

'Paresh Patel. It's 7 am, I thought you might be awake by now.'

'I clearly wasn't,' I said. I was surprised myself. I must have turned my alarm off. As I sat up, I felt like a lorry had driven over my head. I hadn't drunk enough to blame it on the wine. I remembered tossing and turning most of the night.

'Sorry,' said Patel, without sounding like he was.

'Tell me.'

'There has been a development in the Agarwal case that I thought you'd like to know about. The police have dropped the investigation.'

That woke me right up. 'What? Why?'

'The doctor changed his statement. He said it seemed to be a routine case of food poisoning after all, and the police are taking his word for it.'

'They are probably just happy to have one less case to work on.'
'Could be. Who knows.'

And then I remembered Manish's accusations last night. 'What was the doctor's name?'

'Siddhartha Mitra. Cardiologist.'

I closed my eyes. 'Who took the call to drop the case?'

'It must have been Ravi Sharma. It was his case.'

Why wasn't I surprised that in both my cases it was Sharma I was dealing with? 'Thanks, Paresh.'

'I'll let you know if there is any change in status.'

I got out of bed and homed in on the coffee maker. Everything seemed awry: doctors changing their minds overnight about the possibility of foul play; the police dropping a murder investigation based on such a fickle opinion. And if the involvement of Ravi Sharma wasn't enough to convince me something was amiss, everything seemed to hinge on the doctor, who in fact was Mallika Mitra's husband, who in turn had a severely strained relationship with Agarwal. Now the question was, why?

Far sooner than I expected, I found myself staring at the uncooperative faces of the CCC once again. They listened as I explained how Agarwal had died, how the case had been picked up and dropped, how, according to Mrs Agarwal, they hadn't been exactly thorough with their investigation in the first place.

'Has the wife asked you to investigate?'

'Not exactly,' I said.

'What do you mean?' asked Terrence.

'She wanted information from me in my capacity as a journalist. I don't think she even knows I am a detective.'

Terrence started to laugh and, as he saw me glare at him, converted it into a cough behind a discreet hand. Not discreet enough.

'The question is, can we take it up as a case?' I asked.

'What case? The police have said it is not a murder,' said Terrence.

'On the strength of a verdict from a doctor who is connected to the victim.'

'Have you established motive? A doctor just knowing the victim is not enough. Half of Calcutta must know Agarwal.'

'Worse still, half of Calcutta knows each other. That is many motives for many murders,' said DDG with a condescending smile.

'I said there *might* be a murder here. I think it is worth looking into. The doctor seemed suspicious enough to involve the cops in the first place. What changed his mind? No autopsy was performed.'

'If the doctor did it, why would he call the cops in the first place?'

'I am not saying he *did* it. I am simply saying it is strange.'

'What else?' asked Santosh da.

'The wife's attitude. She called him a bastard to my face. Just straight out like that.'

'It sounds like you are going on instinct alone,' said DDG.

'I wouldn't say that.'

'I agree,' said Ojha. Words – any words – were unexpected from him, particularly if they contradicted DDG. 'When it comes to murder, the police should have taken action of some sort even on the basis of the initial call from the doctor.'

'Reema,' said Santosh da, 'why don't you make some preliminary inquiries, and then we can discuss the outlook in a few days?'

I looked around at the others. I knew resources were tight, and if I suddenly asked them to cough up money I would be shot down. 'Sure. I'll start by visiting the doctor. And Mr Ojha, could you try to find out from your colleagues precisely why the investigation was dropped?'

The Masala Murder

He hesitated for a moment, but then nodded.

I wouldn't have asked him to do even this much if it hadn't been for Ravi Sharma. I didn't want to involve Uncle Kumar in this. But without my ears and eyes inside the police, my position as an outsider posed a problem. While I had a toehold in the kidnapping of Aloka, thanks to Amit and Uncle Kumar, in the matter of the suspicious death of Prakash Agarwal, I was on shaky ground. There, the CCC network might be required to produce results.

*

I went back home, pondering all the way how I should proceed. First, I thought I should call Mallika to see if she could help me contact her husband. She didn't answer the phone.

Then, I considered that since the police had abandoned the matter, Mrs Agarwal might be more willing to be proactive. Perhaps I could even tell her my background and offer to ask some questions.

I picked up the phone. 'Mrs Agarwal, this is Reema,' I began. 'I hope I am not disturbing you.'

'Not at all,' she said.

'I just heard that the police have dropped the investigation into Mr Agarwal's death.'

There was a long pause at the other end.

'Mrs Agarwal?' I said at last.

'Yes, Reema. Thank you for the information. I suppose that settles it, then.'

'You are satisfied that he died of natural causes?'

'I don't see why not. If the police feel no need to look into it, they must have good reasons.'

'I understand that, but don't you think–'

'I don't feel there is any reason to make this more than it is. I appreciate your call, and your help, Reema. Thank you very much.'

'No problem,' I mumbled, hanging up.

I gnawed at my bottom lip. Mrs Agarwal's blow hot-blow cold routine might be another hindrance, but it left me even more determined than before.

I turned on my laptop and found the file that contained my work material. In it was an audio folder of the Prakash Agarwal interview.

I had developed the habit early on of recording all my conversations. I had been the victim of too many people claiming that they had not said what I wrote they had said, and decided that backup was the only way to battle it. Yes, even a food writer could find herself in the midst of a war of words and retractions, fragile egos not being able to withstand the post-print heat that often resulted from stray insults traded by chefs and restaurateurs.

I hit 'play'.

'Sit down, beti,' he began. All the time, I remember, staring at my breasts. It still gave me the shivers. More so because that voice now belonged to a dead man.

'Please, have some tea,' he said. I had called him after his name had repeatedly emerged in my conversations with restaurant owners. His company, Gourmet Express, was, in a sense, their lifeline – connecting their kitchens with those across the world. I had thought he'd make an interesting person to profile but within five minutes of entering his office, I had changed my mind.

'I usually go in for my tea around this time but since you were coming, I decided to have it in my office instead.'

'It is a pity your wife couldn't join us,' I said. I had hoped this reminder of his marital status would help him focus his eyes on a more appropriate part of my body.

To no avail. 'She is busy.'

I could hear the sound of my teacup hitting the saucer with a little more force than necessary. 'How did you get started in this business?'

I listened to his raspy breathing, and the tinkling as the snuff box he was fiddling with brown-stained fingers hit the metal frame of his chair. 'It was about ten years ago. We started by importing one particular brand of chocolates from a supplier who had his regional office in Hong Kong. Then, when they branched out into other products, so did we. They are still our partners.'

'Which items move the fastest?' I asked.

'Italian ingredients do well: dried herbs, pasta, olive oil, vinegar. Then the cheeses and processed meat have great demand.'

He continued to give details about their most successful offerings. 'Japanese and Lebanese ingredients are also doing well these days.'

'You also supply to a few of the city's best bakeries.'

'Yes – flours, flavours, colours, chocolate. You women must always have your chocolate, after all,' he said, breaking out in a raspy, paan masala-stained laugh. I remember the force with which it had struck me at that point that even a relatively good-looking face could be rendered hideous by an expression.

'When you started out, you were the only one doing this sort of work. Now there is competition.'

'All the others in Calcutta are small-time operators and charge huge sums for such small, small quantities. No one covers as many products as I do, so every restaurant serving Western food has to come to me, at some point. I take care of all their everything.'

'Any plans of expanding your business?'

'Not in the existing form, but we are working on a revolutionary concept.'

He had said the word 'revolutionary' to rhyme with 'mercenary'. 'And what is that?' I asked.

Here he had edged forward in his seat, bending towards me

conspiratorially, finally addressing my face. 'A gourmet spice chain to be started in Hong Kong through our partner, and then to be taken across the world! Stores stocking the finest Indian spices, with packaging and service to match. It doesn't exist anywhere, I am sure. All spice merchants sell cheap plastic bags filled with the best of Indian spices. It is a problem.'

'It is?'

'Yes. Many people are now interested in cooking Indian food, but they have no idea what they are doing. Even so many young Indians, like you, living abroad and without their cooks for the first time! We will help them!'

I remember fighting the feeling that his words made sense. That a man such as Prakash Agarwal could actually have vision is not something I had been prepared for. 'How will your products be different from those already available in global gourmet supermarkets?'

'The variety and authenticity of the spices. The freshness. We will sell in small quantities, in combinations required to make particular dishes, so the spices do not sit on a damp kitchen counter somewhere getting spoiled. Indian curries, not British ones. It is time to remind the world where curry is from!'

'How will you be marketing this?'

'We will make convenient packs with a booklet on how to use them, with recipes. It will be linked to a website, which will have some more recipes as well as videos. We will sell spice kits – not only pre-ground masala, which has a shorter shelf life, but also the whole masalas that consumers can grind on their own with clear instructions. And then there will be high-quality premium products such as saffron and vanilla. And morels, too. And items that Indian homes abroad often miss – kasuri methi, sattu, besan, posto. You Bengalis must always have your posto.' Then that laugh again.

There was a pause as Agarwal left his desk to walk over to the cupboard. I could hear the sound of his footsteps on the tile floor of his office, and the gentle creak of the cupboard opening. Footsteps again and then a soft thud. He had put a cardboard box on his desk containing the prototypes of his packaging. I had found myself even more impressed. And then there was the dal starter kit – with different kinds of dals and pouches of the masalas needed to make them with complete directions. Similarly, pulao.

'In select stores in premium locations, we will also have fresh and frozen produce. But that will depend on the franchisees.'

It was simple and elegant. No salt or oil had been added, so you could be as healthy or not as you desired. I could see myself using such products – a happy compromise between time-consuming preparation of from-scratch cooking which required a fully stocked pantry of spices you might use only once before they took on the charming aroma of dirt, and the guilt of greasy, sodium laden pre-packaged meals and takeout.

I closed the audio file. What I re-heard didn't seem to provide any additional insight, really. I already knew that Agarwal was an unpleasant man, but a good businessman. That he was slimy in some respects yet slick in others. But still no motive came to me.

So I would have to go searching for it.

I rifled through my drawer to find the notes from my interviews with various members of the culinary community who I thought might give me a better sense of the man and his universe. Flipping through pages of my hurried, near illegible squiggle proved more time consuming than informative but finally I reached a name I thought might be helpful: Manoj Chakravarty, owner of Taste of Punjab. Not my favourite restaurant in town, but Chakravarty was an enthusiastic talker and, if I remembered correctly, he had also had a brief tryst in the spice trade.

I gave him a call. 'Mr Chakravarty? This is Reema Ray,' I said tentatively.

'Oh yes, beti! How are you?'

'I have been fine, Mr Chakravarty. And you?'

'Very well, very well,' he replied. 'I saw you at Mr Agarwal's house the other day but before I could say anything, you had gone inside. Very sad, very sad.'

I leapt at the opening. 'Mr Chakravarty, in fact that is why I was calling you. I wondered if you might be able to answer a few questions I had about Mr Agarwal.'

He paused. 'Questions?'

'Yes, for an article I am working on.' I dared not say anything more as he seemed to ponder my query. I could picture him frowning, his lips pursed, duckbill-like, in concentration.

'Why don't you come over to the restaurant?' he said at last.

'Right now?' I asked, looking at my watch.

'I don't trust cellphones, you see. Embedded technology.' With that somewhat cryptic remark, Mr Chakravarty hung up.

*

Taste of Punjab was the unimaginative sort of establishment that dotted the Calcutta food scene. North Indian staples that held no surprises, served in a kitschy dining room meant to remind patrons that tandoori chicken is indeed a Punjabi dish. If the fare at Taste of Punjab had been a colour, it would be food-dye red.

The smell of cheap booze, old oil and pickle rushed at me as I opened the glass door. Mr Chakravarty came forward with a smile, his face as impish as his body was round. It was almost a wonder that he did not keel over when he stood up, for his barrel-shaped torso seemed an impossible weight for his spindly legs to support. But, remarkably, he usually stayed upright, and did so again as I walked in, rushing forth with quick, short steps that would do a dancer proud.

He put one chubby hand on my shoulder and stuck the other

out towards me. Then, mid-handshake, he seemed to think it a rather inappropriate greeting and tried to get both his ample arms around me as I stood there rather awkwardly.

'How are you, beti? You have become so thin! Aren't you getting enough to eat?'

I had shed a kilo or two since I saw him last – I better have, for all those hours I had been busting my gut kickboxing. But I could hardly be considered *too* thin.

'I eat all day, Mr Chakravarty. That is my job!'

'True, true. Then you must have worms.'

Before I could even sit down, a liveried waiter arrived with a tall steel tumbler full of lassi, a thick layer of malai floating on top. I took a sip. Too sweet, but otherwise quite pleasant.

'Very nice,' I said, smiling at my host sitting across the table.

He nodded. 'Namkeen lao,' he told the waiter. 'Just you taste it, Reema beti. Made from shudh ghee.'

The waiter returned in a moment with a bowl of bhujia and another of nimki. They were both superb. 'Why don't you sell this? They are fantastic!'

'I will, I will. I plan to start export also. And now with Agarwal dead, I may actually have a chance.'

I squirmed in my seat. Mr Chakravarty, however, seemed without any sort of discomfort till he saw my face.

'This business, very sad, very sad,' he mumbled.

'Yes,' I said.

'But I have to say, someone up above,' he said, pointing a porky fistful of nimki towards the heavens, 'saw his bad deeds and decided to put an end to it.'

I tried to keep the new wave of shock from my face. 'You and he ... were you not friends?'

Crumbs flew out of Mr Chakravarty's mouth at the force of his scoff. 'Friends? With that badmaash? Never.'

'Why? What has he done?'

'What has he done? What hasn't he done!' Mr Chakravarty's Pekinese eyes seemed ready to pop out of his face. 'Because you are like my daughter, let me tell you. Agarwal was a cheat, a crook and a liar. A liar, I tell you!'

Mr Chakravarty stuffed the nimki into his mouth. 'Before, I had a small side business supplying imported foods to restaurants. He saw my business and decided that this was what he wanted to do. He told me his family was spice trader in New Market and he wanted to continue the family tradition in modern way. All lies to play on my sentiments, you see. I have people there, too. I found out his family is cloth trader, and at that too they had failed.

'But this man came here, and I don't know how he did it, that shaitaan, he brought in products from Hong Kong and started selling them much cheaper! Can you imagine what that did to my business? Thankfully I had restaurant otherwise what I would do I don't know.'

I was puzzled. 'How did he undercut you so much?'

'I don't know! Just to steal my customers I think he paid from his own pocket. His products must have been bad, maybe past sell-by date. Or cheaper brands. And these people also, I tell you, they will take anything from anyone as long as it is cheap!' Mr Chakravarty lunged at his own glass of lassi and tossed it back. 'And then,' he continued, wiping a hand across his mouth, 'when he started raising prices, he still made it a point to keep all rates a little lower than mine. Within three months, I shut down. There was no point continuing to incur loss.'

'So all of the restaurants in town serving foreign cuisine sourced from Mr Agarwal?'

'All the big ones. Apart from Mallika Mitra, I believe.'

'Oh?' Though I knew this already, I wanted to hear what he had to say. 'Do you know why?'

'No, but what I do know is that they were not good terms. I saw them come face to face at a food festival once a few years ago, and Mallika looked like she had seen a ghost.'

'And then?'

'Then what? She walked away and I tried to get her some food. It would make her feel better.'

'What about him? How did he react?'

'He seemed fine, smiling and all. But then his missus called him away.'

Mr Chakravarty would not let me go without feeding me a full-on meal. But he also steered clear of saying anything more about Agarwal. When I left his restaurant, I knew little more than when I had walked in – except for the fact that the dead man seemed to be universally disliked. And that perhaps Mallika Mitra knew him a little better than she had admitted to me.

But while Mr Chakravarty may have hated Agarwal enough to not bother to edit his ire despite the tragic turn of events, I didn't think he had motive enough to sneak into his home and poison him.

What I needed now was some evidence. Rusty though I was – and utterly inexperienced at investigating anything at the scale of murder – I knew I had to have far more real information and less hearsay if I was going to scratch even the surface of this business.

TEN

Motive, means and method.

In theory, I knew how to solve a murder. In practice, I had never come close, never even had the chance.

So that left me with book knowledge, and gut instinct. My biggest problem was that, usually in a murder investigation, there was something to start with – most often, the means. How was the murder committed: bullet, sharp object, violent beating, *poison*. In this case, I had only the doctor's original statement, since retracted, to go by that the victim died under suspicious circumstances.

Assumption #1: Dr Mitra's initial assessment was the correct one. Without a body or a postmortem report, I was still working blind.

Assumption #2: Death was delivered via poison.

Without knowing either of these things for sure, it seemed unlikely that I would first be able to uncover *how* Agarwal's life ended. I would have an easier time, I felt, trying to discover *why*.

Which brought me back to Rule #4 of the Pastry Principle: Nothing is ever as simple as it seems.

※

Day Two of my (unofficial) investigation, first stop: Calcutta Medical Centre. I stood outside for longer than I'd like to admit. I had an appointment with Dr Mitra, but it had been obtained through borderline fraudulent means. I had got the number of the hospital public relations officer and had told her that *Face* was doing a piece on cardiac health. I had called to set up an appointment, and the doctor asked me to come over immediately as his schedule was packed for the next two weeks.

If he knew of my connection with his wife, I could not tell from his reaction. It was possible Mallika had not mentioned me, and I was happy not to have to bring it up.

Now came the hard part. I would have no choice but to lie to his face. This was not my strong point, but I could see no way around it so I squared my shoulders and went into the building, navigating my way through disinfectant-scented hallways to his office.

After a ten-minute wait, I was greeted by Dr Mitra, an attractive man in his forties, wearing a button-down navy shirt with a designer label that even I recognized and beige flat fronts. A smattering of grey at the temples set off his distinguished features. I could just see him with Mallika on his arm, oozing urbane class, the very essence of middle-aged success and poise.

'Good morning, Reema,' he said. 'How can I help you?'

I smiled as best I could. Even his impeccable bedside manner couldn't put me at ease now. 'I am working on a story about how health problems can be reversed by weight loss.'

I had chosen my subject with care. A Google search had revealed that the topic was close to Dr Mitra's heart. He was a frequent speaker on the need for lifestyle modification in managing early signs of cardio-vascular disorders.

As he set out detailing exactly how it all worked, I took diligent notes. I also stole glances around the office. I could find no personal touches: no photographs, no certificates, no books, nothing to tell me more about the man. It was probably an office shared by other doctors during their clinic hours.

I asked a few more questions – hell, I thought I might even get a good piece out of this for the magazine after all – while I tried to think of the most discreet way of getting to my real point. Eventually I decided I had to employ brute force.

'Doctor,' I began. 'There is also another issue I would like to discuss with you.'

He smiled at me. Quotes were always good for business, and Mitra didn't look like he was new to the sound bite. 'Of course.'

'I am also a food writer and I am doing a follow-up story about the death of Mr Prakash Agarwal for the magazine. I was told that he was your patient.'

After a brief moment of confusion, Dr Mitra's face arranged itself into a mask, giving away nothing. 'Yes, he was my patient. But why is a magazine like yours concerned with his death?'

'He was something of a lifeline for all of the restaurants in town that served international food.' I made no mention of the doctor's wife's own restaurant, which was notable as the exception.

'Okay,' he said deliberately.

'Our police sources said you had contacted them shortly after his death as you believed his symptoms were suspicious.'

'At the time I thought so, yes.'

'But then you changed your mind.'

'Yes. I was called in during the final hours of his treatment, after the attending doctors in the emergency ward were alarmed by his rapid decline. He suffered from asthma and also had a pre-existing cardiac condition, having had a heart attack three years before. To begin with, it seemed to me that the illness had moved very fast, from food poisoning to respiratory distress and cardiac failure. It was unusual, but when we ran a toxicology screen, we came up with nothing, and in the light of his existing illnesses, it made sense.'

So it would seem that Dr Mitra had suspected poison, and had ruled out the common ones. But even my basic knowledge of forensics told me that there were many other compounds that would be outside the purview of the usual hospital diagnostic tests.

'Did you have a theory as to what may have caused the symptoms?'

'Not really. All I can say is that it was unusual. But it could have just been that his general ill health had been compounded by the food poisoning.'

'Isn't that strange?'

'Reema, contrary to the picture presented by TV shows, very little about medicine follows a script, particularly in the emergency ward.'

'But you yourself said that it was odd, which is why you called the police in the first place.'

'Yes, and then I spoke to his family and the emergency-room staff and learned that he had been ill for two days before they came to us. The food poisoning he suffered had severely compromised his system by that time. If they had brought him in earlier, I am confident we would have been able to save him.'

'And so you told the police that you were mistaken in your suspicion?'

'Yes, after I received the last lab reports which convinced me that the death, though possibly preventable had he received more timely treatment, was natural. I saw no reason to cause the family additional grief.'

I could, of course, think of no further questions to ask within the framework of my deception. 'Dr Mitra, thank you for your valuable time,' I said, getting up.

'You're welcome,' he said, giving me a curt nod.

I had been dismissed. And should I ever need a cardiologist, I would do well to look elsewhere, judging from the temperature of Dr Mitra's parting smile.

Everything the doctor had said had sounded reasonable. Then why was it that I didn't quite believe him?

I left the hospital and got into a cab, all the while grappling with a growing unease. Overwhelmed – yes. Out of my league – yes. Two crimes – a murder and a kidnapping. One client, in a manner of speaking. One vague request for information, since recanted. I had no trouble believing there was plenty of potential for damage to self. But wasn't it preferable, in a matter of life and death, to overdo it rather than under-do it, to choose action over inaction?

In my hunt for real clues, I had to venture once more to the scene of Agarwal's death. Of course, once the cab had pulled up outside the complex, I asked myself what I had been thinking. Had I really believed I could waltz into the Agarwal residence and start filling up evidence bags?

I called Mrs Agarwal.

'I am in your area and was wondering whether it would be okay if I came by?' I said.

Once again, she surprised me with her response. 'Actually, I was hoping you would call. Please come over any time.'

'How about now?'

'Of course.'

The Agarwal household had reverted to tranquillity, as had Mrs Agarwal's demeanour. She wore a lovely blue-and-yellow floral crepe sari, her meticulously set hair forming a frame for her face which had been painted on with an artistry born of experience. She wore no jewellery and, at least before me, she chose to rid herself of the adornment of sorrow she did not feel.

We sat in the living room, where there were no more flowers or incense tingeing the air.

'I have arranged hotel rooms for all the guests. I couldn't bear to have them around, it just felt so unnatural – all that dripping grief.'

'You need your space.'

'Yes. I always have.'

Given her lack of artifice, I saw no need to further delay bringing up the point of my visit.

'Mrs Agarwal, I have been thinking a good deal about what you said to me,' I began.

'Yes, Reema, that is also why I wanted to meet you. I feel I should apologize for my abrupt behaviour the other day during your visit, and also over the phone.'

She paused to weigh her words. 'I was upset, naturally. And later I realized how unfair it was of me to ask you for information about this case. After all, you write about food, am I right?'

No apology for her hate-filled words about her husband. 'You don't have to worry about that. I understand your need for information, under the circumstances. In fact, I wanted to ask you whether you are still satisfied with the police having dropped the case.'

'I think I am. Why?'

I considered telling her about my training as a detective. But something told me that the only reason she was confiding in me was because I had nothing official to do with the investigation. So I decided to stick with one lie instead of inventing a second. 'My editor wants me to do a follow-up story, since your husband was so important in the local restaurant scene.'

'I see.' She looked marginally unsettled by this.

I ploughed on. 'Can you think of anyone who may have wanted your husband dead?'

A grim little smile twisted her glossed lips. 'How about almost everyone who knew him? You will be hard-pressed to find a woman he hasn't offended, a friend he hasn't betrayed and a business associate he hasn't cheated. In fact–' she broke off.

'Yes?' I prompted.

'Speaking of business associates, I find it very odd that I haven't heard from his partner, Mayank Gupta, yet. He is based in Hong Kong and from what little I have seen of him, he is a decent man. He called immediately after he heard the news but that was the last contact, despite the fact that he must have numerous business matters to tie up. My husband ran a one-man operation. In his absence, they would have to contact me.'

'But you weren't involved in the business?'

'I am a partner on paper. And I know enough to be of assistance in this situation.'

Agarwal had mentioned his Hong Kong partner during our interview, but hadn't gone into detail about the nature of their association. 'Perhaps he is giving you time and space before intruding on you with work?'

'Perhaps.'

'Will you be taking over the business now?'

'Oh no. I have never really worked before.'

'Could you give me Mr Gupta's contact details? I would like to know more about his plans in Calcutta now – whether he will be continuing with a new partner or wrapping up operations.'

'Certainly.' Mrs Agarwal walked to a small writing table at a corner of the living room. From the silk rug under my feet to the chandelier above my head, it was clear that a great deal of money had been spent decorating this room alone. And with taste that could only belong to Mrs Agarwal. This was a woman who had enjoyed the benefits of her husband's wealth. Could that explain why she stayed with him despite detesting him? Or did it point to motive most foul?

Mrs Agarwal returned with a sticky note in her hand.

With more questions on my lips, I was surprised by a sound at the door to an adjoining room. A young man opened it and came in.

'Memsa'ab, chai?' he asked.

'Reema?' asked my hostess.

'Yes, please,' I said.

'That's Dhyan. He's been with the family for years.'

'He lives here?'

'In a room adjoining the kitchen.'

'There is a service entrance?' I asked.

Mrs Agarwal seemed to sense where my mind was moving. 'We've known Dhyan since he was a child. His father has been with Prakash's family since he was a young man. I can assure you they are all above suspicion.'

I nodded, and couldn't help wondering at the disparity between the husband and wife. Agarwal I had to try hard to tolerate; his wife I had to try just as hard to dislike.

'And trust me when I tell you that the police checked all of us out that first day when they had come. As they did Dhyan's room and that entrance.'

'Could you tell me a little more about the events leading to your husband's death?'

'We were gone for most of the evening my husband took ill and when we came back, I ate dinner and went to bed. He fell asleep, or perhaps unconscious, at his desk in the course of the night.'

'You didn't realize he had taken ill?'

'Not till morning. My husband and I stopped sharing a room

years ago. Dhyan and I had to force open the door to the office when we realized his bed had not been slept in.'

'In what state did you find him?'

'Barely conscious.'

'But you didn't take him to the hospital till the evening?'

'On Prakash's insistence. He was diabetic, and thought it was blood sugar fluctuation.'

'He didn't say anything about food poisoning?'

'He complained of indigestion, nothing more.'

'Mr Agarwal didn't come out of his office for dinner either?' I asked.

'No, he had a heavy tea and often ate very late. So Dhyan had left his dinner on the table and had gone to bed.'

That seemed unusual, but I reminded myself that this was not a happy home with its comfortable rituals.

'There is a second entrance to the office from outside the apartment?'

'Yes, for official visitors.'

'Mrs Agarwal, could I ask what the police asked you when they came for questioning?'

'About our relationship, primarily. They were suspicious about my claim that I hadn't heard anything and hadn't noticed that my husband had not returned to the room all night. Once it became clear that we did not share a room, the obvious questions followed, particularly as I stand to inherit almost all of my husband's ill-gotten gains.'

'Ill-gotten?'

'Oh, you know what I mean. He was not involved with anything necessarily illegal – or if he was, I didn't know about it – but Prakash Agarwal was hardly known for playing by the rules.'

'Did they indicate what they believed had killed him?'

'When I asked, they said they couldn't be sure.'

'What about the timeline?'

'What do you mean?'

'Did they say anything to give you an idea of when they felt the poisoning – if that is what it was – occurred?'

'No, but they did ask if I knew who his visitors were in the two to three days before his hospitalization.'

'Could you share that with me?'

'As I told them, his visitors mainly used the other door that leads directly to the office, so I don't really have any idea of who came and who went.'

I didn't linger much longer after that. By the time I left, I was happy to have a better idea of what happened that night. But I was also convinced of one more thing: Mrs Agarwal was trying to play me. Her openness, charming and useful though it was, could not be explained otherwise. I just needed to figure out why. But as of now, she was also my only point of access into this sordid business.

On my way out, I observed what I could of the building. There was only one entrance into the building itself as far as I knew, and there were two entrances into the complex. There were surveillance cameras in the lobby and the elevators.

It wasn't likely that an intruder would have been able to hide behind a discreet disguise given the amount of security. It was just as possible that the murderer was known to Agarwal and hadn't required a disguise to enter. Or had managed to obscure his or her face from view. Or that he or she lived with him. And if Agarwal had indeed been poisoned, there was no telling when the event had occurred. The police had asked about Agarwal's visitors in the days preceding his death, so for the moment, it was impossible to establish a timeline for when a poison may have been administered.

Just as I was leaving the building, I saw a police car on its way down the driveway. I was quite certain that an upmarket area couldn't have two crime scenes at the same time. I approached as the policeman stepped out of the car. But as the uniformed man came into view, I wished I had walked away instead: it was Ravi Sharma. But he had already seen me.

'Reema Ray, what a surprise!' he said.

I had met Sharma at Uncle Kumar's annual New Year's party, when things were still pleasant between them. I was shocked he remembered me at all.

'Hello, Uncle Sharma. How have you been? It's been years.'

'The last time I saw you, you were still at college in the States. You decided to come back?'

'Yes.'

'What are you doing now?'

So he didn't know about my ill-fated PI stint. And why should he? 'I write about food.'

'How lovely.'

'In fact, I had done an interview once with a man in this building, who died just the other day.' I gave a theatrical gasp and covered my mouth. 'That's not why you are here, is it?'

'What makes you think that?'

'I had heard that the police were investigating it as a possible murder.'

'My, my, you stay well informed,' Sharma said, his eyes narrowing.

'I work at a magazine.'

'Yes, you are right. We were looking into the Agarwal death. But we have dismissed the notion.'

'Could I ask why?'

'Of course you could. But that doesn't mean I'd tell you.'

'Oh, Uncle Sharma!'

'Believe me, it is nothing exciting. There is simply no evidence that a crime was committed.'

'I just met Mrs Agarwal, in fact, to pay my respects,' I said. 'Such a tragedy.'

'I'm on my way up there now to conclude some business,' he said. 'It was nice seeing you, Reema.'

*

I had been waiting for a cab for a few minutes when I spotted Dhyan, the Agarwals' help. He seemed to be watching me from a distance.

'Hello,' I said.

He didn't reply.

I noticed a bag in his hands. 'Going to the market?' I asked.

'Mrs Agarwal and you are friends?' he asked by way of response.

I was unsure of how to react. 'Yes, you could call me that.'

'I have never seen you before.'

'No.'

'And Agarwal sa'ab?'

'I met him only once. I am a journalist. I wrote an article about him.'

'Is that why you ask so many questions?'

I felt a rush of blood to my face. I nodded.

He watched me with intensity burning bright in his small face. He hardly looked over fifteen. It then occurred to me that he had come out here with the hope of speaking to me.

'Is there something you want to say to me?' I asked.

'You shouldn't believe everything memsa'ab says.'

I couldn't help but show my surprise. He had obviously been listening to our conversation. 'Why?'

'She and sa'ab were ...' he trailed off.

'Always fighting?'

'No, but ...'

Mrs Agarwal may have been willing to give Dhyan a glowing endorsement, but it was not a favour her employee wished to return.

'What will you do now?' I asked.

Dhyan shrugged. 'Will you be writing about sa'ab again?'

'I hope to.'

'About the murder?'

'So you think he was murdered?' I asked.

He nodded his head slowly, and then held his hand out towards me. At first I thought he wanted to shake hands, but then I saw he was holding something. I put my palm out and he dropped a small object into it. It was a pearl-and-silver earring.

'This was found in sa'ab's office the morning we found him unconscious. I saw memsa'ab pick it up and throw it into the dustbin in the kitchen.'

'Are you sure it is not Mrs Agarwal's?'

Dhyan nodded. 'Maybe you could give it to the police? I saw you speaking to Inspector sa'ab just now. Memsa'ab was in the room the whole time they were speaking to me, so I was too afraid to give it to him myself.'

'Did Mrs Agarwal say anything to you about it?'

He shook his head. No.

'Do you know who it belongs to?'

'No.'

'Did your sa'ab receive any visitors the night before he got sick?'

'There were a couple of his men who work in the warehouse.'

'Anyone else? Someone who may have worn this earring?'

'There was a lady. She came to the house at night.'

'Who was she?'

'I don't know. She was waiting for sa'ab – he was out – in his office. But then I went to the store and by the time I came back, the door to sa'ab's office was closed. I didn't see anyone leave.'

'Could you describe her?'

He shrugged. 'Memsa'ab let her in, and then she sent me away. I didn't get a good look at her.'

So Mrs Agarwal was lying about not knowing any of her husband's visitors. 'Could she have left by the outside door after you came home?'

He nodded. 'She could have. Don't know. She could have left before I got back also.'

'Did you remember finding any food or boxes of any sort when you cleared the office the next day?'

'No, nothing like that.'

I looked at the earring again. It was very pretty, though probably not very valuable. It was a little silver cone from which peeked out a pearl. The kind of thing you could get at any number of stores in New Market. I didn't know what kind of a lead it was, but what it did tell me was that a woman had visited Agarwal the night before he was ill, and her presence was something Mrs Agarwal wanted to hide. Why?

'Thank you, Dhyan,' I said.

He nodded his head and walked away, bag in hand.

ELEVEN

I was in a rattling, incense-filled cab headed home, trying to block out the sensory assault to process what I had learned that evening. But before long, I was interrupted by the shrill peal of my phone.

It was Amit. 'Someone's been in my apartment,' he announced without preamble.

'What do you mean?'

'Things have been moved around.'

'Don't touch anything. I'll be there in half an hour.'

After a brief stop at home to pick up my evidence collection kit, I was at Amit's house. I walked in to find Amit pacing the room, things strewn everywhere.

'What happened?'

'I have no clue. I was at work and when I came home I found this mess.'

Amit had severely understated the situation over the phone. The place had been trashed. 'Did you touch or move anything?'

'No, I don't think so. The door was closed, so I pushed it open as I always do. The moment I stepped in, I called you.'

I first took a look at the lock on the door. It was a standard deadbolt. There were a few scratches around the keyhole. I examined it for trace evidence, and then dusted it for prints. Then I began looking around. There were clothes everywhere, books had been tossed to the floor, even the tiny fridge looked as though it had been rummaged through.

'Do you know what they might have been looking for?'

'No.'

'Are you sure?'

'What do I have that anyone might want?'

'Don't think in terms of value. Think in terms of information.'

'I still don't see what a kidnapper might hope to gain,' Amit said with a shrug. 'Unless they wanted to take something from here to incriminate me, to plant at the place where Aloka is being held.'

'You think he would go that far?'

'He has enough thugs and fixers on his payroll to get the job done. Maybe he's decided that casting suspicion on me and ruining my marriage isn't enough. Maybe now he wants me in jail as well.'

'That still doesn't explain why whoever broke in felt the need to make such a mess. It seems personal.'

Amit merely shrugged. I started to take photographs of the wreckage and dusted around for prints. Then we started clearing things away. When order had at last been restored, Amit still could not say what may have been taken. It was certainly nothing of monetary value – they had nothing of value to take.

I thought through the implications of the break-in. I still couldn't understand the long silence from Aloka's abductors but the way it was looking now, it was Amit who needed my protection, not Aloka. For if the Mohtas were about to escalate events, then the next target would be him.

'Do you have somewhere you could stay for a few days?' I asked.

'Why?'

'Whoever did this might be back for more.'

'Then wouldn't it be a good thing if I were here?'

'What would you do faced by an armed attacker?'

'I think I'll take my chances.'

'And what if the cops swing by with an arrest warrant?'

'Then it's all over, isn't it?'

'You're ready to give up so soon?'

'What choice do I have?'

'Lie low for a couple of days. Go somewhere inconspicuous. How about a hotel? There are plenty of holes in this city to burrow in.'

'No money, Reema.'

I bit the inside of my cheek. 'Ditto.'

'I can hardly go to my mom's place.'

'No, that's the first place they'll look.'

'Then here is fine; it has to be.'

'No, it's not.'

'Well, there is nowhere else I could go.'

There was an edge in his voice. I knew that after he had broken up with me, a lot of my friends – who had been our friends – stopped speaking with him. But I hadn't realized he had become so isolated.

'How about my place?' I offered.

For once, Amit's face registered shock. 'No.'

'Why not? If I am okay with it, what problem do you have?'

At last, Amit was speechless.

'Can you think of a better solution?' I said, challenge loud in my voice. I didn't stop to think what my bravado was attempting to cover.

He looked at the ground. It might be evil to feel satisfaction under the circumstances, but I couldn't help it. I felt pleased to be the bigger person. 'Just till Uncle Kumar comes up with something. Or they go public with a new demand.'

'You think they'll do that?'

'It's possible. They have to make it look like a real kidnapping for the cops to take them seriously.'

'What happens if the cops already know exactly what is going on? That they are all acting in this charade?'

'I know you've always been fond of your conspiracy theories, but I doubt it. And we have Uncle Kumar on our side, remember? Come on, Amit, pack your things. Two days, maybe three, tops.'

Amit, looking frustrated, ran a hand through his hair.

'Relax, I won't bite.'

'I might feel better if you did. You're too good to me.'

'That's true. So just remember not to push your luck.'

The auto ride home was a silent one. From the moment we walked in, my flat felt way too small for the two of us. It was one floor of an old house that was built till the very edge of the land it stood on yet was still tiny. A bedroom, a bathroom and a large room that packed in a seating area, a small table where I usually worked and an open kitchen that was little more than a counter and stove with a chimney over it. When the urge hit me to cook properly, I'd go to one of my parents' homes to muck around in their kitchens. Then I'd bring home the fruit of my labour and reheat. It was the fridge and my teeny toaster oven that saw the most traffic.

'It's not much,' I said. 'You can have the futon. It's not too uncomfortable.'

'It's actually quite charming,' said Amit.

The furniture was functional at best, but I had attempted to make the space my own with prints of photos from my travels, happy cushions and cheap rugs on the floor.

I rummaged through the fridge but didn't find anything inspirational for a quick meal, so I opened to the freezer and found some lasagna I had made a couple of weeks ago at my dad's place. I had frozen it in individual servings; I took out a couple and also discovered a log of cookie dough that I had stashed away. I put the lasagna in the toaster oven and left the dough to soften a bit.

'Are you always this well stocked?' Amit asked.

'I was a Girl Scout, remember? I'm always prepared.'

'Seriously, where do you find the time?'

'When I get busy, I don't feel like cooking. So when I have the chance, I get innovative.'

'And do you always have cookies at hand?'

'You never know when the craving might strike.'

Amit gave me a strange sort of smile, part rueful, part sad.

'What's the matter?'

'You were always good at managing.'

'Managing what?' I asked, pulling out some veggies from the fridge.

'Everything. Always on top of things.'

'I don't know about that. I'm organized about the cooking because I don't have the money for a cook or to go out all the time, and while I would love to subsist on chicken rolls, I try to avoid the treadmill as much as possible.'

'Via cookies?'

'Merely an occasional treat.'

'See, you think of everything. And you have self-control. While the rest of us are prepared to roll around in our fat and filth and mountains of empty Maggi packets.'

I cut up some cucumbers and carrots, calling it a salad, and carried it over to the coffee table.

'Have a snack,' I said, sitting down.

'Once again, most people would have opened a packet of potato chips.'

'I would have thought you'd approve. What happened to your dream of growing your own vegetables, rearing your own chickens and living off the land? Where do Maggi and potato chips fit into that?'

Amit looked at me with his eerie intensity, as though he were remembering the day he first told me his dream. I remembered, too. It had been a different living room; my mother had been out of town, and he had come over. We had spent a lovely, awkward afternoon with each other, testing the boundaries of our relationship, which had only recently deepened beyond the friendship we had shared so far. That afternoon had told me I wanted more from Amit. We were seventeen.

I felt as though Amit could hear the memory hum through me, like the notes of an old song. I stood up, impatient to break the moment, to change the conversation that I had led to this precarious place.

'I have a bottle of wine that I purloined from my mother. Would you like some?' I said. Only this urgent need to fill the silence could have prompted me to offer up the Bordeaux which I had been saving for a far more special occasion than this.

'Sure.'

I opened the bottle and checked on the lasagna, which was ready. I brought them both over to the couch and went back to cut wheels of chocolate-flecked cookie dough and pop them into the oven.

As we ate and sipped our wine, once again I felt compelled to speak. 'You said that you and Aloka were planning to move to Delhi. What are you two planning to do there?' I asked.

'I have some friends in the media there for whom I have been freelancing a bit. They said they could help out with some sort of job. Aloka has an aunt in Delhi who is not on talking terms with Aloka's father. She was willing to give her a job in her business. It wasn't much but it would have given us the security we needed to get out of this place and away from her father's influence.'

I was sure I hadn't been able to keep the flash of pity off my face. I quickly got up to clear our plates.

'Very filmi, I know,' Amit said with a wry smile.

'You never lacked for drama,' I replied, pulling the cookies out of the oven. The room filled with the aroma of buttery goodness. 'And this business has finally given the rebel a cause.'

I looked up just in time to see the smile drop out of Amit's eyes, and then a flash of anger.

'Here,' I said, walking over to him. 'Have a cookie.'

Amit didn't move, sitting still on my blue sofa. 'You must think I've been a fool.'

I took a cookie and put the plate down on the coffee table. 'I didn't say it.'

He let out a half laugh, and stood up. 'You didn't have to. Here I am, with no one to help me but you.'

'I don't know what you are talking about.'

'Don't play stupid.'

'You're being ridiculous.'

'I was crazy to let you go,' said Amit, turning to look down at me. His eyes were filled with sadness, and I closed mine to shut him out. And then, I found myself on my feet and in his arms. I didn't know how it happened; I had had no intention of letting it. But there were his hands, cupping my face like the old days, lips on mine like they had never whispered to another. Despite every cell of my brain telling me to pull away, the rest of me was instantaneous in my betrayal. His hands homed in on all their favourite places – the small of my back, the nape of my neck, the leaping pulse at my wrist – and I let them as though they had never strayed.

'Amit,' I said, as his lips wandered to where jaw gave way to soft, responsive skin.

'Hmm?' he murmured.

'Amit,' I said again, this time more insistent. 'We can't do this.'

And yet he seemed to disagree. As his mouth showed no sign of stopping, I pushed him away.

'Reema ...' he began.

I could see the desire in his eyes, could see the words spinning in his mind; I jumped in before he could justify what had just happened, what was about to happen.

'No.'

'But–'

'I don't want to hear it. I don't want to hear that you still want me, that you need me to get through this. You made your choice and when you did, you lost me for good.'

'But you reached out to me even before all this.'

'I don't owe you anything because of a drunken phone call!'

'Can you say you've got me out of your system?'

Whatever he had done to me, I found I could not lie to his face. I could not answer.

'I still dream of you, Reema.'

'A dream is just a dream.'

'You can't really believe that.'

'What if I don't? I am allowed to lie to myself, to you, seeing as how you left me for someone else. That is far more real than any dream.'

Desire fled Amit's face, replaced by a haughty smile.

'The Reema I remember didn't believe something as frivolous as a piece of paper should get in the way of love. As I remember, you had little time for marriage.'

'I didn't. And I don't. But I had assumed that you did, since you went through with it in an awful rush.'

'That was a mistake, I know that now. Aloka's father had been raising hell about us every chance he could, and I think it was my way of trying to protect her.'

So he had stomped on me to save another. He had thought me unbreakable. Well, I could certainly act the part.

'Now you need my help to protect her, again.'

Amit said nothing, standing there with his mask back in place. He had given me all that he would. Now it was up to me.

'I agreed to help you, didn't I? I haven't changed my mind – yet. You might want to do your best to keep it that way.'

Amit turned away and I tried my hardest not to flee the room. I retreated as far as the kitchenette to clear up. Just as I was finishing up, my phone rang. I answered gratefully.

'Hello, sweetheart,' purred my father.

'Baba! Where are you?'

'Sweden. Off to Finland tomorrow.'

'How has the trip been so far?'

'Fabulous! I wish you'd come.'

In that moment, I wished I had as well. He had offered to take me on his two-month tour of Scandinavia and east Europe but I had turned him down, pleading work commitments. I had been terribly tempted, but even if I had been able to clear my schedule, how could I pay rent for the time I was away if I wasn't working? I couldn't touch him for the trip as well as my landlady's monthly pound of flesh.

'I wish I was there too, Baba.'

'Tell me how you've been.'

'Oh, same old, same old.'

'That's not what I hear.'

'And what is it that you hear?'

'That you've been busy with a new case.'

'Then I suppose I need not ask who you've been talking to.'

'Kumar called, but only because he was concerned about this whole Amit situation. I wish you had told me yourself.'

'You're on holiday. There was no reason to disturb you.'

'There was every reason.'

'We can talk about this when you are back.'

'We will talk about this now. It's happening now, isn't it?'

I was silent. I looked at Amit, who was browsing my bookshelf. If only my father could have seen us five minutes ago, he would have been on the first flight back home with bloody murder on the mind. I went into my bedroom and closed the door behind me.

'What is going on?' Baba continued. 'Why is he back in your life?'

'You heard about the kidnapping?'

'Yes.'

'Then you know why he is back in my life.'

'I didn't realize you were in touch.'

There was no reason to conceal the truth anymore. The old wounds had already been reopened, and they weren't mine alone. 'He got in touch with me about three months ago. He wanted to see if we could be friends. We've talked a few times since then. That's the extent of it.'

My father didn't ask why. He knew well enough how close we had been, and for how long. When we broke up, I had lost more than a boyfriend. There was a lifetime of memories that had nothing to do with our love, and with it all suddenly out of bounds, I had been bereft.

'How did you feel about that?' asked my father.

'I can't say that it went well. But we were trying – him more than me. Then when this horrible thing happened, Amit came to me.'

'What are you doing about it?'

'It's slow right now. There isn't a lot to go on at this point.'

'That's not what I mean.'

'Baba, Aloka's safety is more important for now than my feelings. She used to be a friend too, once upon a time. Don't you remember that lovely weekend her family took us on for Aloka's birthday?'

'Of course. Near Digha somewhere. You were so excited. But you still haven't answered my question.'

'I'm over him, Baba.'

'Don't give me that bullshit.'

'Baba–'

'I know that you are over him – that's not my point. But I can still see the scars, even if you try to hide them.'

'I won't give him anymore than I need to. I have put him behind me. He has no power over me.'

'Then why haven't you let any man come close to you for the past three years? You have become so guarded.'

'I was a teenager when we got together! Maybe I have just become more cautious with age. People change, don't they?'

'I know you believe that. That's what I'm most afraid of.'

TWELVE

I was up at what most journalists would consider the crack of dawn the next day, no alarm clock needed. I made my coffee and retreated to my bedroom. Amit was still asleep on the futon in the living room.

I turned on my laptop and searched the news sites for any developments on the kidnapping. It was still making headlines but, from what I could see, the content of the articles was largely speculation than fact. And the police seemed to have revealed precious little though they did confirm that after the first ransom call, there had been no further contact from Aloka's captors.

Time to change track: I fished through my bag and found the scrap of paper Mrs Agarwal had given me with her husband's business partner's information.

I searched for Mayank Gupta's company online, as well as Agarwal's company, Gourmet Express. It became clear that Gupta's operation was much larger and diversified than Agarwal's, but I learned nothing about how the two were connected.

It was time to make another call to Paresh Patel.

'Still interested in the Agarwal case?' he asked. 'I'm afraid I have no fresh information to share.'

'Not strictly about the case itself. I was wondering whether you had dug up anything about Agarwal's business?'

'Not much, except what I read in your article. But before the case was dropped by the police, I contacted the Calcutta Restaurant Association. They keep track of local entrepreneurs, and told me they did have a file on Agarwal.'

He gave me the number of the local representative: Vineeta Solanki. 'She owns a restaurant as well,' Patel told me.

'Yes, I have met her. Thank you.'

I hung up and dialled Vineeta's number.

'Vineeta?' I said. 'Reema Ray.'

There was a brief pause and I wondered whether she remembered me. 'Yes, Reema,' she said at last. 'How are you?'

'I'm fine, thanks. I was looking for some information on Prakash Agarwal's company, and I have been told that the Calcutta Restaurant Association keeps track of restaurants and allied businesses, and that you are the person in charge there.'

Another pause. 'I would have to check if we have anything on Gourmet Express.'

'It is a little urgent,' I said. A small lie again. 'I am writing a follow-up piece on Mr Agarwal's death and how it will affect local restaurants.'

'Why don't you give me a bit of time to pull up the file? I should have something for you by afternoon,' Vineeta said finally.

In the meanwhile, I focused my attention on Manish Solanki. I wasn't sure why he seemed so resentful of Mr Agarwal's strained relationship with Mallika and the congenial one with his wife.

But I knew I would get nowhere by interviewing him without any ammunition, so it was for this that I went in search.

Solanki's office was on N. S. Road, and there was one person I knew who had his tentacles in every inch of Dalhousie Square's office para: DDG.

Instead of calling, I decided to drop into his office for a visit, to give him less of an opportunity to spurn my request.

DDG's business card led me to an old building behind the high court. His offices were large, but cramped with books and files which lined every inch of the wall. I wondered how he found anything in here. What floor space was left was full with a big wooden desk and his hearty frame.

DDG was dictating notes to his harried assistant and didn't look up as I entered the room. I stood waiting as he finished. Finally, it was his assistant who noticed me.

'Saar?' he bleated.

DDG looked up as saw me. 'Reema ji?'

'Sorry to disturb you like this.'

'No problem, no problem. Please sit.'

I sat down on one of the wooden chairs placed in a neat row across from him.

'Kamal, bring us some tea.'

'Saar,' he said, rushing from the room.

'Tell me, how can I help you, Reema ji,' he asked.

'I need to find out about a man in connection with the Prakash Agarwal case. I thought you might know him through your work.'

'Who is this person?'

'He is a businessman by the name of Manish Solanki. He lives in Calcutta, but is in the lubricant industry with a factory in Assam.'

'What kind of lubricant?'

'Castor oil. If I am not mistaken, you had mentioned that you had some contacts in Assam?'

'Oh, I know many people in Assam. Many of my clients in tea and other sectors are there.'

'So you might have some common acquaintances?'

'Castor oil, you said?'

'Yes.'

'I think I may know someone. How is he involved in the case?'

'His wife is a business associate and a friend of the deceased.'

'You suspect that there was some hanky-panky going on?' he snorted.

I ignored this and he didn't press for more information, picking up the phone and dialling.

'Satish ji,' he said, drawing out the 'ji', 'this is Dutta Gupta. Yes, yes, I am very well. Thank you, thank you. Do you by any chance know someone by the name of Manish Solanki from Assam?'

I watched as he took out his handkerchief to wipe the beads of sweat dripping down the side of his face, despite the mouldy draught blown into the room by the clattering old air-conditioner. My eyes moved towards the remarkably black moustache hanging above his upper lip, jutting out like the stiff bristles of a shoe brush, bobbing up and down like a single entity.

'Haan, haan. Sounds like same person. Can I send my friend Reema ji to meet you? She needs to know about this Solanki.'

He nodded and scribbled on a piece of paper in front of him. 'Thank you, Satish ji. She will be there.'

He hung up and tore the slip of paper from the notepad and handed it to me. 'Satish Gandhi. This is his address. He is expecting you any time today.'

'Who is he?'

'My wife's sister's neighbour's brother-in-law.'

'And he knows Manish Solanki?'

'Same community, you know. And he is also accountant and handles books for many tea gardens in Assam. He knows most people there.'

I thanked DDG and immediately headed over to meet Satish ji. It turned out that his office was just a couple of buildings down, with the same smell of dust and the same rickety old staircase. When I walked into the office, however, I was surprised at how modern the interior was – all laminate and glass.

The receptionist waved me through to Satish ji.

'Mr Gandhi?' I said, presenting myself in the small but neat office.

'You must be Reema,' he said. 'Please come in.'

'Thank you for agreeing to see me.'

'Dutta Gupta ji said you wanted information on Manish Solanki.'

'Yes.'

'May I ask why?'

I hesitated. I had expected this, but I still wasn't sure how to tackle it. I finally decided to go with a version of the truth that didn't involve implicating him in the murder. 'I am a private investigator, and he may be a person of interest in a case I am looking into.'

'What case?'

'I'm afraid that is confidential at this point.'

Satish ji's eyes narrowed. But he either seemed to conclude I was harmless enough, or he was not the kind to turn down the opportunity to gossip, and launched into his story. 'Manish Solanki is a man who is well known among business circles in Assam.'

'Why?'

'There aren't many people who he is on good terms with. And in a close-knit community, particularly those with Calcutta roots, word gets around.'

'Could you be a little more specific?'

'He has stolen land from his own community's people. Slowly, slowly encroaching. Then he sabotaged one of his other neighbours, who he knew he was financially vulnerable, by contaminating his land and then making an offer to buy him out. The poor man had no alternative but to sell.'

'Why didn't he go to the police?'

'With what? It was all rumours. What could they have done?'

'Any reports of violence?'

'Not that I know of.'

'Is he doing well?'

'Very. That is why he is even more hated. Now, he's hired agricultural scientists to improve yield and create by-products from the castor oil production process.'

'What about his wife?'

'In the community here, she has a good reputation. But she hardly goes to Assam. Before you came in, I called one of my relations to ask about them so I could give you correct information, and he said they see her once every few years. She was there a few weeks ago, though, for a family wedding.'

'And she and her husband ...' I trailed off.

Satish ji looked at me blankly.

'They have a good relationship?' I concluded.

'What do you mean?'

I thought I had been plain enough, but I stumbled on awkwardly. 'I have heard suggestions that they may have had ... er ... problems.'

'I would be surprised if they didn't. Solanki has a bad name when it comes to the ladies, as well.'

'Manish Solanki is having an affair?'

'Not one, but many. I assumed that's why you were here. That maybe the wife had hired you.'

'Oh no, that's not it.' This time, at least, Solanki's philandering wasn't my primary concern. If he was having an affair, however, was he trying to paint his wife as a possible cheater amongst their circle as a means to an easy divorce?

'Do you know if Mrs Agarwal may have any similar ... interests?'

'Not in Assam. But what she's up to when her husband is away for months is anyone's guess.'

*

The compact dossier on Gourmet Express at the offices of the Association left me impressed once more with Agarwal's achievements. In the absence of virtually any competition, there were few restaurants in Calcutta that weren't his clients, and he had also expanded to Siliguri, Durgapur, Jamshedpur and Guwahati. But there was one thing notably absent from all the literature – financial data. The office did not have it. Not a surprise, given that Gourmet Express was a privately held company and such information was not in the public domain. But there was a brief bio on Mayank Gupta from a press release given out the year before during a symposium on business opportunities for Indians in China. Gupta, based in Hong Kong, catered through orders made online to all of China. With the growing presence of South Asians in the country, his timing had been fortuitous. He was also involved in the trade of carpets and gems, and had been consulting with a few top Indian designers and a lifestyle brand that had since opened up shop in the Far East, businesses with which Agarwal did not appear to be involved.

Agarwal seemed only to be associated with the eastern Indian operations. Perhaps he would also have marketed his new line of gourmet food kits through Gupta. I was left wondering why an apparently respected businessman of international repute would join forces with one as questionable as Agarwal, no matter how well connected he was.

I left the office and called Vineeta once again.

'Thank you for the file,' I said.

'I hope it was of use.'

'It was, but I do have some more questions.'

She hesitated for a moment before finally asking me to come around to her office at 4 pm.

Vineeta's office was way too cold, and I sat shivering there for nearly half an hour before she saw me. Sitting in front of her, I felt the chill even more. In her own territory, Vineeta seemed far more formidable than she had at Mallika's home, in the shadow of an unruly husband.

'Thank you for seeing me,' I said, hoping to induce a thaw.

She said nothing, watching me with a rather fixed gaze. Was she still embarrassed about her husband's behaviour during our first meeting? Or had I merely caught her at a bad time?

'I was hoping to gather some financial data about Gourmet Express,' I explained. 'I didn't see anything on that in the file.'

'I don't think I am the right person to talk to about that. Since I run an Indian restaurant, I wasn't even one of Prakash's clients.'

'And in your capacity of secretary of the restaurant association?'

'That really is more of an honorary position. I am a volunteer whose job it is to make sure things are running smoothly,' she said.

I persisted. 'But you were friends with Mr Agarwal.'

'Yes.'

'Close friends?'

'I don't know about that.'

'You must have some idea about the business then.'

'All I do know is that his will be a hard void to fill.'

'What do you mean?'

'Many restaurants in town depended on him.'

'Are you acquainted with his business partner Mayank Gupta?'

'Only with his business credentials. He has a business based in Hong Kong.'

Vineeta was doing her best to give me information she must know I already had. 'Mr Chakravarty felt that he was undercut by the prices Gourmet Express offered when they entered the market.'

'Yes, they did discount, but that would not have been enough to get most people to change suppliers. Gourmet Express had a far more comprehensive range, better quality and service.'

'How did you two become acquainted?'

'I don't know, Reema. It was years ago. Maybe through common friends.'

'Does Mallika know him?'

Vineeta's eyes narrowed. 'You should ask her about that, I think. Not me.'

'I have been trying to contact her, in fact,' I said, trying to sound unconcerned. 'Would you happen to know if she is out of town?'

Vineeta looked taken aback. 'No,' she said. 'I don't know, actually. I haven't seen her since ...' she trailed off. She hadn't seen her since the dinner during which her husband had created that memorable scene.

I nodded. Just then a large group of tourists came in, with a flag-bearing tour guide.

Vineeta stood up.

'I guess I should get going. I wouldn't want to keep you from work.'

She walked away, and as I turned to leave I took a quick look around the restaurant floor. That is when my eyes found his. Coal-black eyes, watching me from across the room, set in the impassive, inscrutable face last seen finishing my nachos. Shayak Gupta.

Then the crowd of tourists, ever growing in number, converged to conceal the wall against which my watcher had been leaning. A moment later, when the wave had passed, he was gone.

I quickly exited and looked around. But darkness had descended suddenly, and I could see no one. I felt my cheeks flush, and asked myself why Shayak's presence – or absence – bothered me in the least.

※

I was already home when I saw the missed call from Santosh da. In an effort to keep his phone bill to a minimum, he would never, ever complete a call or even send a text. It was a good thing Santosh da was such a nice man, or else I would never have bothered to call back. But as always, I did now.

'Reema, I think I've found something,' he said. 'It might be nothing but I think you should know about it. Can you come to my office?'

I felt like I had been shuttling across town like a public bus for the past few days, and didn't feel like making the trip. 'Could you tell me over the phone?'

'Of course, of course. I forget that you have given up your office and are no longer my neighbour. As I said, it might be nothing. But for some time, since you have told me about this whole business, I have been wondering why the name Prakash Agarwal sounded so familiar. It is a common name, so at first I didn't think anything of it. But it kept nagging at me. So I looked through some of my old files and found something in one of my ActNow documents.'

ActNow was an NGO that worked with women who had suffered violent crime; Santosh da consulted for them from time to time.

'It was in a case study I had gone through when I was drafting the PIL for stronger police action against sexual harassment last

The Masala Murder

year. It mentions a number of cases on public record that were categorized as eve teasing, which should be regarded as sexual assault. It goes back about thirty years, and is quite an extensive document. One case was about a young girl in Calcutta who had complained that she had been assaulted about twenty-five years ago. The matter was reported, but the girl finally backed down when the police told her charges of attempted rape wouldn't stick. They told her that, at best, she could get him for eve teasing. The man's name was Prakash Agarwal.'

I felt a kick to my stomach. 'Are you sure it is the same man?'

'That is the problem. This was all so long ago that there is nothing that might identify him conclusively. No photographs, no biographical details.'

'Where did this incident occur?'

'New Market thana area.'

New Market? Didn't Chakravarty say something about Agarwal's family having a business there once upon a time?

'Santosh da, wait for me, please. I'll set out for your office right away.'

Santosh da's minuscule chamber was in a garage off a crowded street a couple of blocks away from the high court, not far from where my office had once been. It was deserted now, long past court hours; cars had left their parking spots, making the roads passable for a change. I went by the tea shop that must be open this late only to keep Santosh da fortified and opened the rickety old wooden door.

Santosh da had his back to me and was rummaging through his cabinet.

'Good evening,' I said.

He turned around. 'Hello, hello,' he said with a shy smile. If he were about twenty-five years younger I don't think I would have been able to resist that expression; his kindness would have made me his willing slave. Luckily, his well-greased grey hair and obliviousness to the ways of the world were constant reminders to me not to even joke about it.

Santosh da handed me a thick file filled with yellowing A4 sheets, opened to the document that had brought me here.

Looking over the solitary sheet, I felt my little balloon of hope deflate. It contained little to go by – only a brief outline of the account from unnamed sources two-and-a-half decades ago. A teenaged girl had been molested in a store in New Market, in the makeshift trial room. A complaint had been filed against the shop owner and a case lodged. Shortly after, the matter was dropped as the family had been convinced the charge was not worth the trouble. But that too sounded like speculation on the part of someone at ActNow. Significantly, the girl had not been named, probably in the interests of protecting her.

'Is this all?' I asked.

'I'm afraid so. I called ActNow to find out if there was any further information, but I am afraid there isn't.'

'It's not surprising. Three decades is a long time for details to get lost.'

'That is exactly the problem! If this happened now there would be so many media reports – but then you wouldn't know what to believe, would you?'

'Santosh da, do you think you could call Prashant Ojha and ask him if he could check the national crime database for any further information?'

'On this case? But it is so old!'

'It is worth a try, no?'

Santosh da saw the dismay on my face and relented. 'Okay, let me see.'

He picked up his phone, but I knew that this was one of those times a missed call would be a waste of time. 'Here, use this,' I said, handing him my phone. 'But call his landline. It's better if he doesn't know that I am here.'

Santosh da made the call. So far, when it came to the CCC's 'investigations', Ojha preferred to take his orders from DDG. I wondered whether he would give either of us any time at all. I hadn't heard back from him with the input he was supposed to gather about why the police had dropped the Agarwal case.

'You haven't heard anything new about Agarwal's death?' asked Santosh da. 'No? But I think I may have something. This man, Agarwal, may have been the accused in a sexual harassment case some time ago.'

There was a pause as Ojha spoke.

'It was twenty-five years ago. And, yes, it might still be relevant,' continued Santosh da. 'Could you please just run a search in the database?'

Another pause.

'But Mr Ojha, we have nothing to lose, isn't it so?'

Santosh da hung up.

'He said he'll call back.'

After a couple of minutes of waiting, Ojha had an update for Santosh da. It wasn't good news. 'I am sorry, Reema, it appears that the case is too old. The electronic records go back only till 1995.'

Though I had no real expectation of success, I couldn't help but feel disappointed. 'That's okay, Santosh da. It was a long shot anyway.'

꒰ ꒱

I reached home, and found that Amit was out. For the moment I was in no mood to face him after last night's debacle, and couldn't care that he was potentially at risk.

I tried to get through to Mallika Mitra again. Still no answer.

I sat down on the sofa to think. It had become clear what I needed to do, what perhaps I should have done in the first place. I picked up the phone and called Uncle Kumar.

'Good evening, dear,' he said. 'I was just about to call. It would appear that Amit is right about one thing at least: he is being treated as the prime suspect in his wife's kidnapping.'

'I feared as much.'

'And there is more. The kidnapper's deadline was allegedly yesterday. It didn't happen and Sharma is advising the family against paying.'

'Has there been any contact by the kidnappers?'

'E-mail, apparently.'

'So much easier to fake an e-mail than a phone call,' I said, exasperated.

'True. They are trying to trace it.'

'Is Sharma coming after Amit now?'

'I don't know. And you know how things are between us. I could speak to the commissioner, but–'

'No, not yet. Maybe if this thing escalates to the next level.'

'If Amit is right and Aloka is in no real danger, it might be wise to wait for them to make their next move. This charade can't continue indefinitely.'

'I agree. And Uncle Kumar, would you hate me if I asked you for another favour?'

'Try me.'

'Would it be possible to run a check on a man? He is recently deceased, under suspicious circumstances. I have just learned that he may have been accused of assaulting a young girl some years ago.' I gave him a sketch of what I knew, and then hesitated. 'The death was being looked into by the police – by Ravi Sharma's team, in fact – but they dropped it, claiming there wasn't enough evidence of foul play.'

'And you think they are wrong?'

'I think they might be.'

'Do you have this man's last known address?'

'Yes,' I said, giving it to him. 'And I do happen to know where he lived twenty-five years ago.' Luckily, that was a conversation we had during our solitary meeting. 'Lake Road, near the Best Rolls stall.'

'Oh, those are tasty devils.'

'Yes,' I said. It was the one point I had bonded over with Agarwal. 'And I also believe that his family owned a cloth store in New Market.'

'That should help,' said Uncle Kumar. 'I will do this on condition that you promise me you are not going to use the information to get into any mischief.'

'On the contrary, I will use it only to get to the bottom of mischief perpetrated by others.'

'That sounds like trouble.' Uncle Kumar's words were only partly in jest.

'Trust me. I am not going to do anything dangerous.'

'Never have any words sounded less deserving of trust.'

'And, Uncle Kumar?

'Yes, dear.'

'There is another name. Mallika Mitra.'

'Also dead?'

'No, but unreachable and possibly associated with the case somehow.' I bit my lip at the fib. Well, she could be, right? I gave her Mallika's current address. 'She used to live in China for a while and before that, she was in Jadavpur, till about ten years ago. Next to Sharma Sweets.'

'Trust Reema to give addresses according to her favourite foods nearby. How is it that you aren't obese, my child?'

'Uncle Kumar, sometimes I feel I am.'

'Nonsense. You are as bewitchingly beautiful as your mother. And a fair bit less unhinged in the upper quarter.'

'Enough,' I laughed.

'Give me a few days.'

*

I found some leftovers of questionable provenance in the fridge and as I scoffed them down in front on my laptop, I hit Google once again. I was certain that some more information must be available about Agarwal and his business.

I began by trawling through pages of references to Prakash Agarwal, thinking I may have missed something the first time around. Nothing relevant. I went back to the company website but found little more there.

Then I decided to key in a new query: Mayank Gupta.

Up popped the same social-networking links. I ignored most of them, opening a few here and there to make sure I wasn't missing anything. It wasn't till I opened the second page of results that I spotted something promising. I clicked.

It was a news story regarding an awards ceremony held in Hong Kong, organized by the Indian chamber of commerce there. It named a number of local businessmen of Indian origin who were being honoured; amongst them was Mayank Gupta. 'Gupta has for over a decade been the ambassador of Indian food in China and beyond, bringing the full gamut of South Asian flavours to the Far East. But this is not why he is being recognized today – it is his new business ventures, including the introduction of the highest grade of Indian jewellery and lifestyle products, that has earned him this award from our association.'

On the right side of the page was a picture of the consul general of India in Hong Kong giving an address. I followed the link to the picture gallery, scrolling through the pictures as fast as my Internet connection would let me. The captions popped up before the images. 'Mayank Gupta accepting his citation from the CG,' it said. I waited for the picture to open.

It did. And if I wasn't completely mistaken, it was Shayak Gupta!

I took in every detail. Could my eyes be lying? The man in the picture had greying hair and the man I met at the bar – and thought I had just seen today again – had predominantly black hair. It hadn't looked dyed to me, but it was always possible. This picture had been taken from an awkward angle, as the two men shook hands. The man called Mayank here seemed to have a bit of a belly, which had been notably absent from the lithe frame of the man I met at Ginger. But once again, nothing a couple of months at the gym couldn't fix.

Yet why would a random stranger give me a fake name? If he was married and looking to get lucky? I wracked my brains for a mention of Mayank Gupta's family in the bio I had read earlier that day, but came up blank.

If the man I met was Agarwal's business partner and had been in Calcutta for the past few days, why hadn't he visited Mrs Agarwal yet?

There was another possibility, of course – that Shayak and Mayank Gupta were related. Perhaps the picture made too much of a strong family resemblance. Shayak may even be involved in the company for all I knew, and might have been sent here to follow up on the Agarwal business – or worse, take care of it.

THIRTEEN

In the bustle of the previous day, I hadn't had the time to review the evidence I had collected from Amit's house, and I finally got down to that the next morning. I had taken Amit's fingerprints to exclude them from the lot, and had lifted a couple from Aloka's hairbrush in the hope of doing the same with hers. It didn't take me long to realize that the only prints I had collected belonged to the two inhabitants of the house.

I turned my attention to the photographs, examining each one for anything that might seem out of place or unusual. At the end of it all, I was still as confused about the break-in as when I began.

I decided that I would have to return to try and learn more. After all, it was the only lead we had at the moment. It had happened in the afternoon and it was possible that someone had seen something.

The night before, after Amit had returned, we had gone over all the places Aloka might be. The company guesthouses and factories were all out, as was anything else that Aloka would be able to identify as her father's property. But I was getting the feeling that there was something staring me in the face that I wasn't quite seeing.

I found Amit awake and on my battered blue sofa. He had folded his blanket neatly and placed the pillow on top of it. He was reading the paper and sipping a cup of coffee, which he took, like me, strong, black and sugarless.

'There's a cup for you.'

'Thanks,' I said, walking over to the counter I called the kitchen to retrieve it.

'Have you heard anything from Mr Kumar?'

'He's working on it,' I said. 'I need to get back into your flat.'

'I'll come with you,' said Amit, folding the newspaper.

'I don't think that is a good idea.'

'Reema, don't be silly.'

'There is nothing silly about it. Why go back and put yourself at possible risk?'

He brooded over this for a while.

'Have you heard anything new from your friends?'

'Only that there has been no news from the kidnappers, and the family is beginning to get restless. Aloka's mother is inconsolable.'

'Do you think she knows?'

'I am not sure. Even if she does, I doubt she has much say in the matter.'

'I don't see what we can really do either. Without any evidence, your theory is just a theory.'

'Can't we try to find her?'

'Based on what? Do you have any idea where they might be holding her?'

He shook his head.

'Then till they make some sort of contact again, our best hope is that your intruder did something stupid.'

At Amit's flat, I looked for anything that might give away what the trespassers were after. Amit believed that Aloka's family was looking for evidence to plant in order to frame him. If he was right, it could be even the smallest thing – a sock, a dirty tissue, a book.

I looked around the small area which passed for a bedroom. Beside the double bed was a small rickety table with teacup stains and dust that seemed to be embedded in the peeling paint. On it was a simply framed photograph of Amit and Aloka. I hadn't seen her in years but she looked exactly how I remembered her. There was no way to say when the photograph had been taken; it could have easily been when Amit had been seeing Aloka while I was studying in the US. In fact, it was the probable explanation, for they had the glow of new love, and Amit lacked the gaunt look that seemed to stick to him now like a hungry leech. They stood in front of a one-storey white-and-green house, fringed by palm trees. It might have been the old beach house I had been to in Digha.

I forced myself to put the photograph down and move onto the little chest of drawers on which a mirror had been propped up. Face cream, deodorant and perfume. A lipstick. But where was the hairbrush I had left there the last time? The one I had taken the prints from?

I checked the bathroom and didn't find it there either. I opened the cupboard. No hairbrush, of course, but surely there had been three pairs of jeans, not two, hanging there amongst Aloka's clothes?

I surveyed the rest of the house carefully, but it did not seem as though anything else was out of place. I turned off the lights and slipped out quietly. Then I noticed the floor mat. I bent down and picked up a corner for a look underneath. Nothing there, apart from a thick layer of muck.

I straightened up, dusted off my hands and turned in the direction of the stairs. But who I saw as I did so made me stop dead in my tracks.

'Uncle Sharma,' I said shakily.

His face was decidedly humourless. 'What are you doing here?'

'I had come to meet my friend,' I said, ignoring for the moment that he had caught me elbow deep under the doormat.

'She is not at home. Haven't you heard? She's been kidnapped,' said Sharma, face taut.

'Yes, I know that! I meant her husband, Amit.'

His eyes narrowed. 'He's not at home. I've been looking for him for some days. You wouldn't know where he is, would you?'

'Me?' I asked. 'No.'

I tried to move past him, but Sharma blocked my way quite comprehensively. 'What were you looking for?'

'I told you – Amit.'

'Under the doormat?'

'No, of course not!' I said with a laugh. 'I thought I had dropped something.'

'What?'

'An earring,' I said. There were quite a lot of those being dropped nowadays, which may have been why it was the first thing to come to mind.

'You aren't wearing any.'

Oh. But it wouldn't do to back down. 'Precisely, but I thought I had been, you see,' I said.

I must have managed to confuse him just enough, for he didn't stop me as I slipped past him. I had made it as far as the staircase when he caught up with me.

'I don't know what you are doing here, but if I find you hanging around here again, I will take action. These premises are now part of an ongoing investigation into a kidnapping.'

I was about to protest that I had every right to be there, but decided it was wiser to cut my losses and make a dash for it.

As I left the complex, I saw Prashant Ojha about to walk into the building.

'You! What are you doing here?' he said.

I looked at him rather triumphantly. 'I am working on a case.'

'This kidnapping?' He looked incredulous. 'Why didn't you mention it when we met?'

'It, er, came up after that. But why are you here?'

'They are closing in on the kidnapper.'

'The husband?' I asked.

'Yes.' And then he seemed puzzled. 'Who are you working for? How many private investigators do they have on this thing?'

'What do you mean, how many? Who else is there?'

'Never mind. I just assumed ... I must be wrong.'

I heard footsteps and turned around to see Sharma exiting the building.

'Listen, Mr Ojha, I have to go now. I'll call you later and explain everything.'

He nodded.

It wasn't for another fifteen minutes, when I had made it as far away from the apartment building as possible, that I felt safe. I had walked as fast I could, and found myself in the neighbourhood of New Market. I was parched, so I stopped to buy a cup of bubble tea from a stall. I stood there sipping my drink, the globes of tapioca popping into my mouth, each as unexpected as the next.

The din of traffic – both two-legged and four-wheeled – shut out everything else blissfully for the moment.

The white noise was interrupted by a distant rumble of

thunder. A flash of electricity ripped through the sky. I walked slowly towards the Metro, and it was within sight when a man in a black trench coat stepped out from a shop between it and me. Tall, handsome, unmistakable, and I nearly choked on one of the bubbles in my tea. Shayak or Mayank or whatever!

It didn't appear as though he had seen me, and my body did an about-turn without consulting my brain on the subject, getting ready to walk with all the speed I could summon to put as much distance between myself and the man as possible. But I hadn't made it much farther than the bubble-tea stall when I felt at least a dozen heavy drops of water assault my body from all sides.

I thought of braving it through the rain but it came down faster and harder, forcing me to step under the awning of the tea stall again to grope around in my bag for an umbrella with one hand, clutching my teacup with the other. No luck. And then I saw Shayak – whatever his name was, for the time being it would have to be Shayak – standing before me.

'What are the chances?' he said, a small smile at his lips.

'Not as slim as you would think,' I said wryly.

'And why do you say that?'

'I seem to run into people I know on an almost daily basis. Something about Calcutta, I guess.'

'Really? The city of fourteen million people is too small for you? Well, you are a journalist. You must meet loads of people on a daily basis.'

I returned his smile. 'So what brings you here?' I asked.

'Business,' he said. 'And you?' I paused, feeling a trace of panic. I was an out-of-practice private investigator, but this shouldn't be hard, I reassured myself. 'I had a spot of shopping to do, and then I stopped to get some bubble tea.'

'Bubble tea?'

'Well, actually tea with pearls, if you are getting technical about it. You've never had it?' I asked, grabbing at the distraction. I turned around and asked the young girl behind the counter for another. All too soon the drink was ready and I handed him a sealed plastic cup, identical to my own, with a thick green straw sticking out of it. 'Try it. It's huge in the Far East – Hong Kong, Shanghai, Korea.'

I watched Shayak's face for a reaction to Hong Kong, though I couldn't detect one. But it didn't take long for a look of disgust to register on his face. A mouthful of smooth, somewhat slimy pearls of starch was clearly not to his taste.

'What are these things?' he scowled, thrusting the cup at me. I shook my head. One was quite enough.

'Tapioca beads.'

'Drowning in sugary milk?'

'That's the tea.'

'Yech.'

'Yech?' I repeated with a smile, as he tried to take another sip and rejected it in quite the same manner.

'Sorry, but I am a black-coffee person,' he declared, chucking the cup unceremoniously into a waiting bin.

'At least we have that in common.'

Mischief flashed in his eyes. 'I am sure that is just for starters. Why don't we find out over lunch?'

I looked up into his smiling face, unsure of what to say, surprised and pleased – without the time to ask myself why. But this man was the enemy now, and I wouldn't give in so easily.

'Now, if we could only find a cab.'

It seemed as though Shayak, or Mayank, had assumed that I was accompanying him for a meal.

'Impossible,' I said. 'Impossible to get a cab in this weather, in this area.'

Shayak was just about to dash out from the shade of the tea

stall when he turned around to look at me, raising a questioning eyebrow.

He bounded out with long, sure strides, hands in his pockets. In two minutes, sufficiently damp but victorious, he waved to me. Even in the rain, he held the door open, waiting for me to scramble in.

Perfect, I said to myself, unable and unwilling to resist. And then I told myself that Shayak was a person of interest in the Agarwal matter so it was my job to get to know more about him. I got in at last.

'So where are we headed?' he asked.

'If you're taking me out, shouldn't you choose the place?'

'I'm from out of town. And besides, aren't you the food expert?'

'Fair enough.' I gave the cab driver directions. 'Since the tea I just subjected you to was from the Far East, I'd like to stay with the general theme and redeem the culinary traditions of the region.'

As long as I was being railroaded into lunch, I could at least kill two birds with one meal. We reached Middle Kingdom and I headed first for the restroom upstairs, grabbing the chance to look around. Mallika was not there, and if Abhimanyu was, he must be in the kitchen.

One look in the mirror and I was appalled by what the rain had done to me. I looked in a state of apparently irreversible dishevelment. And of course, it was too much to expect me to have carried a comb.

When I emerged, I found that Shayak had evidently also visited the men's room, and looked as unruffled as ever. His hair, neat and just damp, curled above his nape. There was definitely some grey there, and it didn't seem as though it he would have dyed it. His tall frame was so trim that it was hard to imagine him carrying additional weight. Face to face, it seemed impossible that this man was the Mayank Gupta from the photograph so I would have to go with the relative theory, though that hardly exonerated him of suspiciousness.

Shayak flashed me a grin.

'What?' I asked as I took my seat.

He tilted his head, which transformed him from distinguished to devilish in under two seconds. 'You don't look like a food writer,' he said.

'And what is a food writer supposed to look like?'

He examined me carefully and unapologetically. 'More frothy, maybe? Not to mention a little less ... athletic.'

'Athletic?' I could hardly contain the joy that touched my self-loathing heart. I would take 'athletic', I told myself, sucking in my tummy and sitting a little more upright.

But then I saw a hint of a smirk and bristled. 'What do you mean by 'frothy'? Don't take me for one of those goth-chic clichés just because I wear black,' I said.

Shayak looked thoroughly entertained by my delayed outrage. 'I don't even know what "goth chic" is. All this jargon young people use nowadays ... I must be getting old.'

The waitress arrived before I could ask him just how old 'old' was.

Shayak handed me the menu. 'All yours. I won't get between a woman and her area of expertise.'

With this I happily complied. The dim sum menu Abhimanyu had told me about was there, and I ordered a plate of Shanghai's soup dumplings, xiaolongbao – 'These come highly recommended,' I told him – barbecued pork pastries, sautéed bok choy, spare ribs, soy-garlic-tossed cucumbers and a bowl of dan dan noodles, split in two, and a couple of bottles of beer.

'You certainly do know your way around the menu,' he said.

'I've been here before. And it's my area of expertise, as you put it. If you receive a business plan from a company that you are interested in, you know exactly what to look for, right?' I hoped like hell that was what venture capitalists did.

'Right,' he said.

'So, I know what to look for on a menu, and I do my research. Leave as little to chance as possible, except when I want to leave everything to chance.'

'It seems like a lot of work.'

'Really? How many times do you eat a day?'

'Five.'

I raised my eyebrows.

'Small meals,' he said with a shrug.

'And how long do you take over each meal?'

'Fifteen minutes if I am eating alone and the meal is ready, up to two hours if I am cooking.'

'So that is anywhere between seventy-five minutes and multiple hours a day. A lot of time to spend over an activity worth no thought at all.' I was surprised to find myself on the defensive. Usually, I was the last one to take my writing job seriously. The PI stuff, however, was personal.

'Did I say it wasn't worth the effort? I am sorry if it came across that way,' he said. 'I simply meant that the process seems far less off the cuff and requires more homework than I would have thought.'

I busied myself pouring out our beer, which had just arrived, silenced by the thought that I might be encountering the perfect man, except for the fact that at the very least he was a liar, and at the very worst a murderer.

Our food and drink arrived in a flurry and demanded our undivided attention for a few moments. I quickly went for the dumplings.

Now I knew these parcels were supposed to be filled with soup, so I scooped one up with chopsticks, placed it gently on my spoon and made a small incision with my teeth. I then gently sucked out the soupy goodness within. Insides more or less drained, it came down to a reasonable temperature, and it was safe to put the rest of it into my mouth.

Shayak stifled a smile. 'You seem to have that figured out.'

'You need a lesson?' There was that edge again.

'No.'

'Can't use chopsticks? Go for it with your spoon.'

He shook his head. 'No, I'm fine.'

'Don't tell me you aren't having any?' I asked suspiciously.

'Of course I will.'

'Then why are you smirking?'

'I object to your terminology. I was merely noting the difference in our mode of attack. I love xiaolongbao but I prefer to wait for the dumpling to cool slightly so I can put the whole thing in my mouth at once.'

I felt self-conscious enough to put down my next dumpling altogether.

Shayak didn't hide his amusement anymore. 'Please, eat. It is interesting to watch you talk about and eat your food with so much ... zest.'

I suppressed an angry 'hmph'. He was diverted by my food talk, but what else was I expected to say to a complete stranger? That I believed he may be mixed up in a murder? That I never spoke to men I met in bars, on principle? That my hand blazed from where he had touched it while I was getting into the cab?

I managed a well-mannered though evasive 'hmm' instead and popped a dumpling into my mouth as a distraction. As I bit in, the still-too-hot liquid exploded and left me breathing out in the futile hope of saving my insides from permanent damage. Damn him. This was a dangerous activity that required the utmost care!

Shayak clucked sympathetically and poured me some more

beer. I drank it gratefully, the cold liquid smothering some of the protest.

'Are you okay?' he asked, seemingly genuinely concerned.

'Fine, fine,' I lied.

There was a brief pause while we both concentrated on some of the non-scalding dishes on the table.

'Why don't you ask me what it is you want to know?' said Shayak.

'Huh?' I seemed out to prove the limited range of my vocabulary to this man. Not only did he make me feel like I was in high school again, he had the unhappy ability to constantly take me by surprise, and I didn't like it one bit.

'I don't do this either. Strike up conversations with people I meet in bars. And then offer to save them from the rain. But I did it this time. So ask what you want about me.'

'For the record, I did not require saving,' I said.

Shayak put down his chopsticks to give me his undivided attention, his intense black eyes showing no trace of discomfort. How was he so unfazed all the time? I, on the other hand, clutched at to the cutlery as though I could will them into nunchucks if the occasion so demanded.

'How old are you?' Inane, but it was a beginning.

'Thirty-six,' he said.

A decade older than me. 'Are you married?' Bolder, better.

'No.'

Relief. But how would I know if he was lying? 'Have you ever been?'

'Yes.'

Which led me to believe his previous answer.

'Do you have kids?'

'No.'

Mild relief. 'What brings you to Calcutta?'

'I thought we'd covered that already during our first meeting at the bar.'

So I was likely to make no real headway in that department. If there was indeed any to be made.

'What were you doing in Vineeta's restaurant yesterday?'

'I don't know who Vineeta is but if it was a restaurant, I must have been having a meal.'

'An Indian one. Around dinner time. You saw me there, didn't you?'

'I had an early dinner. I was hungry. It was in the neighbourhood.'

'Why did you disappear?'

'Without talking to you? You looked busy; I was done and had some place to be.'

I was silenced by the questions I couldn't ask him. For instance, 'Why did your marriage end?' or, 'Are you a wife beater?' In short, roundabout ways to reach the answer to my real question, which was, 'Why are you single?' This was a conundrum that I could make as little sense of as the other, unmentionable riddle about how this completely unreadable man sitting before me could have anything to do with the life or death of Prakash Agarwal.

Could I be wrong? Could my eyes be playing tricks on me? Perhaps the man in the picture I saw online had nothing to do with the man sitting across from me now. Just a bizarre, coincidental resemblance. Stranger things had happened, right?

Having run out of safe territory, I offered a role reversal. 'The questioner is now prepared to become the questionee.'

Shayak broke his gaze at last to examine his beer glass briefly. 'I think I'd rather take my time to find out,' he said at last.

My stomach dropped down to my feet.

By the time we left the restaurant, the rain had grown into a deluge and the road resembled a fast-flowing stream. Not a cab in sight.

'Wait here,' said Shayak.

'In this weather–'

But he was gone. In less than five minutes he reappeared seated in a cab, and jumped out. Now there was no doubt left – anyone who could get me a cab in the worst downpour of the season was nothing short of Prince Charming in a rather greasy charger.

He held the door open for me and I stood there, rain pouring down my face, like a schoolgirl staring at her first crush.

'This was ... unexpected,' I said.

'Yes, it was,' nodded Shayak.

I didn't have his number and he didn't have mine, but I didn't want to be the one to bring it up. 'Well, goodbye.'

'Don't be silly. Get in,' he said.

I sat down.

He looked at me expectantly. 'Well? Scoot over! You aren't getting the only cab left in Calcutta to yourself.'

I quickly scuttled across the seat and he got in and closed the door. I told the driver where to go amidst intense internal confusion. Did he expect to come to my place?

It was a ten-minute ride home, and my feeble attempts to make conversation were not at all memorable. I was relieved when the cab finally pulled up outside my gate. The rain had slowed to a drizzle but the damage had already been done: there was ankle-high water all the way to my stoop.

Shayak stepped out of the cab to let me out. I climbed out after him and stood there, all but soaked through, still without a clue about what to say next.

'Well, bye!' I said, hearing a rather unattractive, high-pitched note creep into my voice.

Shayak smiled. 'In a city of fourteen million people, expecting more than one coincidental reunion may be a bit optimistic.'

'Of course,' I said. I dug a piece of paper and pen from the depths of my bag, scribbled my number on it and handed it to him. He took it and slipped it into his pocket.

'Goodbye, Reema,' he said finally.

I walked away, knowing he stood there in the water, soaked to the bone, waiting for me to enter my little flat. It took every ounce of my paltry willpower not to look back. As I opened the door, I chanted one line over and over again in my head: 'Please don't let him be a murderer. Please don't let him be a murderer.'

It wasn't too much to ask for, was it?

FOURTEEN

I walked into an empty house – Amit was out. After my run-in with Sharma that morning I had texted to inform that it was better he didn't go to work for a few days, as it would be easy for the police to track him down there, so I wasn't sure where he was. I only hoped he had sense enough to stay out of trouble.

I changed into dry clothes, mind racing, and not just because of the lunch with Shayak. I had to organize my thoughts, to get a handle on two disparate cases and what I needed to do next. I opened a notebook and began with the Agarwal case. I wrote down what I knew – and what I thought I knew – before calling Mallika again. Her phone was now switched off. I called Mrs Agarwal who confirmed she still had not heard from Mayank Gupta. I wondered if I had made a mistake in holding out on Shayak; perhaps if I had just asked him I would have had some answers by now. But what reason did I really have to trust him? There seemed nothing to do but wait to hear from Uncle Kumar about the case histories and any possible link to what Santosh da had dug up.

I then moved on to Aloka's kidnapping, and became even more frustrated. I had, at the end of the day, nothing more to go on than Amit's word and some vague intelligence about the police investigation. I was getting nowhere.

But then I remembered the items that had been moved. And it wasn't during the break-in; it was sometime *after* it. I went back to my crime-scene photos and confirmed my suspicion – I had definitely left the hairbrush on the makeshift vanity. I didn't have photos of the inside of the cupboard, but I was fairly certain about the jeans going missing – they had been hung in order, left to right, of increasing blueness. It was the middle pair which was gone.

I made myself a cup of coffee. An idea was just forming in my mind, almost like a forgotten dream that comes back more as a feeling than a narrative. But then my phone rang, shattering the amorphous thought.

'Hello, baby.'

'Hi, Ma.'

'Dear, Hema is coming tonight! I am so excited!'

'Yes, Ma, I remember,' I said, whacking myself on the forehead. How could I forget? 'What do you two gals have planned?'

'Oh I don't know. I'll see if the old lady is tired and needs to rest. But I am sure she'll want to see you soon.'

'I want to see her too. Call me when she is up and about tomorrow and you know what you are up to.'

'Yes. We have to show her a good time, Reema. I can't have her leaving with the idea that Calcutta is dead.'

'But it *is* dead, Ma.'

'Yes, but there is no reason for her to know that.'

🌶

It was about 8 pm by the time Amit got home.

'Where have you been?' I asked.

'Don't you sound like the jealous wife?'

'Don't be absurd. I thought I told you not to go to work.'

'I wasn't at work. I was at a friend's place.'

'Amit, you need to lie low.'

'Yes, I know. This is a person I can trust.'

I let it go. If Amit wanted to expose himself that was his business. But I needed to up the ante of my investigation if we were to do anything more than wait around, for which Amit certainly didn't need my help.

'We are getting nowhere with this strategy,' I said.

'I don't understand.'

I felt my exasperation rise. 'If this is a ruse on the past of Mohta, why has there been no further effort to make it look real? There have been no more calls, letters, videos, nothing.'

'Suppose for a minute that it is someone else, a real kidnapper, wouldn't you have to ask the same question? Why hasn't the money been paid yet? In fact, seen in that light, doesn't it seem more likely that Mohta is behind it since there *has* been silence?'

'I don't know, Amit. We have nothing to work with. I need to speak to the family.'

'What would they say anyway?'

'The ransom deadline has come and gone: that would have been the ideal time to end this without arousing suspicion. Pretend to pay; bring Aloka home.'

'And you think you can waltz in there and ask them why they didn't conclude their fake kidnapping according to your neat script? All you will do is put yourself on the radar and possibly blow my cover.'

I let out a deep breath. I hated to admit it, but Amit was right. 'Then how do you expect me to help?'

'Is Uncle Kumar in touch with the officers in charge of the investigation?'

'Yes. And they are still focused on you. If they come for you, I don't think there is much Uncle Kumar can do.'

'If they had found a way to pin this on me, I expect they would have done so by now. Since they haven't made their accusations public, maybe they are having second thoughts about their theory. I can only hope that now they'll see reason and start investigating alternatives.'

'Your wife is gone. Are you seriously satisfied waiting around?'

'What choice do I have?'

'Let me do some actual detective work. Let me speak to the family; maybe her brother, or the friends that were there at the time of the abduction.'

'Uncle Kumar will warn you if they are coming after me?'

'He might. I really don't know. This is a big case, and he may not be able to stall if it comes to that.'

'Then let's wait and watch a couple more days. Something's got to happen, right?'

'Amit, I don't get this. Why did you come to me if you didn't want to do anything?'

'Reema, believe me, you've done enough.'

I shook my head.

'Trust me, Reema. I know you are a woman of action, but I don't think any action is required here. The way to get to these people is by not playing their game.'

'Alright. For now, I guess I'll do this your way.'

✦

The next morning, when my calls and messages to Mallika still went unanswered, I finally called Chef Abhimanyu.

'Reema, lovely to hear from you! When are you coming to try the dim sum?'

'Any time you're ready for me.'

'Why not today, around noon?'

'Sure,' I said. He didn't need to know that I had already been there the previous day, and that food was the last thing on my mind.

At the restaurant Abhimanyu rolled out one exotic dish after another, and despite myself, I enjoyed them. Char siu bau, or barbecued pork buns, shrimp har gao, deep-fried pastries stuffed with turnip, steamed lotus leaf-wrapped sticky rice with chicken and red bean paste pancakes. And of course, more xiaolongbao. He talked me through each as I revelled in the flavours and textures, some new, some familiar. The secret to the soup dumplings, he finally revealed, was aspic, which melted into a delicious broth on steaming, encased by a dangerously thin wrapper. By the time we were through, I was so happily satiated that I almost forgot why I was really there.

'Why did you leave China?' I asked.

'I had been living away from India for so long that I thought it was time. It was a chance to do something on my own. Had I started in China, I would have been committed to living there for at least as long as the restaurant was a success.'

'Why did you choose a partnership?'

'I am too risk-averse to go it alone. I don't think I would have had the balls, quite frankly,' he grinned. 'And as romantic as it all seems, the restaurant business can be cruel and competitive and difficult. You need someone to watch your back. If Mallika or I weren't here at all times, I doubt Middle Kingdom would have lasted as long as it has.'

'So are you on round-the-clock duty now that Mallika is out of town?'

'Out of town?' He seemed confused. 'I don't know anything about that.'

'Maybe I'm wrong,' I said. 'I have been trying to reach her and when I found her phone off, I assumed she must be travelling.'

'Mallika ... she sometimes ...' he began, before trailing off with a shake of the head.

I waited for him to resume, hoping my silence would prompt him to continue. 'She tends to zone out sometimes, particularly when she is under pressure.'

'I hope everything is okay.'

'Yes, I think it is. It's just that ... it's just this whole business with Agarwal has got her a little wound up, I think.'

Bingo. 'How so?'

'It started the day the news came. I remember hearing that you were the one who told her?'

I nodded.

'Well, after that, she just seemed very distracted. Then three days ago, she said she needed some time off.'

'Do you remember when she told you this?'

Abhimanyu looked confused. 'When? It was sometime after the lunch service.'

That would be soon after I went to meet Dr Siddhartha Mitra at the hospital. 'Do you know where this is coming from?'

'What I tell you will be completely off the record?'

'Of course.'

'It is no secret that there was bad blood between Mallika and Agarwal. So I can't understand why his death should have got her so rattled.'

'You've known her a long time, Abhimanyu. Do you know what the source of the animosity is?'

'That's just it. Mallika is so bloody self-contained that she has never mentioned it to me or, as far as I know, to anyone else. Even more surprising, Agarwal, not generally known for his discretion, doesn't seem to have talked about it much – or at all.'

'Have you spoken to her about this?'

'No. You aren't the only person who has been unable to get through to her.'

'And her husband?'

'What about him?'

'Have you spoken to him about it?'

Abhimanyu looked away with a smirk. 'Siddhartha? No, I think I'd rather not. Even if I did try, he'd probably tell me to make an appointment at the hospital to discuss it.'

'What do you mean?'

'He's so busy he doesn't have time for Mallika's friends.'

'Their relationship ...'

'Oh, the relationship is fine. Fairly solid, I'd say. It's just everyone else the doctor has no time for.'

'Does Mallika confide in anyone?'

'I think Vineeta and she are quite close, but I didn't want to call her about this.'

'Why?'

'It's just that – these are only rumours – but, I heard that she and Agarwal, well, you know.'

'They were involved?'

'It is possible.'

That would fit right in with the hateful Manish's implications during the dinner at Mallika's place.

I thanked the chef and got up to leave. He walked me out of the restaurant, and on the way out, I stopped to look at the wall behind the hostess's podium on which hung the various awards won by Middle Kingdom over the years. And there, at the centre, was a photograph of Mallika at one such ceremony. In clear view was her right ear, and from it dangled an earring startlingly similar to the one Dhyan had given me.

'She looks lovely in this picture,' I said.

Abhimanyu returned my smile.

'I love those earrings.'

'She wears them all the time, so I guess so does she.'

I hurried out of the restaurant as fast as I could.

There could be no doubt about it now – Mallika Mitra had been to see Agarwal the day before he had taken mortally ill. But why? And why did Mrs Agarwal, of all people, feel the need to hide the evidence of this visit?

But I had no time to be with my raucous thoughts, or to follow up on them just yet, for my mother had been calling throughout the lunch. I had ignored the silent ringer, but I had to call her back now.

'Darling,' she gushed.

I had tried hard to get her to drop the 'darlings', the air kisses, the kitty-party conversation in my presence, but I had failed. I had at last decided that it was wise to accept that which was beyond my control.

'How is it going with Hema Masi? When do I see you?' I asked.

'Right now! We are coming over!'

'I'm not home right now.'

'That's okay; I have my emergency key to your place. We'll let ourselves in and wait.'

'No!' I said, my voice coming out too sharp.

'What's the matter?'

Amit was there: no way could my mother meet him. And even if I managed to get him to clear out in time, if there was one thing my mother could sniff out with unerring accuracy, it was a man.

'I am at the other end of town and have a ton of work; can you meet me somewhere this side?'

'Okay, but we're hungry! And Hema says that the only reason she is here, apart from to meet me, of course, is to eat.'

I heard the laughter of the two ladies and thought quickly. Though Hema Masi would be too nice to say it, my mother's cooking would be the last thing she – or any sane-minded person – would want to consume. 'Can you meet me at Park Street in half an hour?'

I reached the Middleton Row-Park Street crossing. 'Reema darling!' said Ma, throwing her arms open, without making any move towards me. Same old Ma, she always made you do all the work of loving her.

On her heels was Hema Masi, who had last seen me on my graduation day – the sole voice of sanity telling my parents what a great decision it was for me to become a detective. She, having been my closest thing to family on foreign shores, was the only one in the know beforehand of my career choice and, unable to dissuade me, had become a reluctant co-conspirator.

'I knew you would finally grow into that face of yours!' said Hema Masi, enveloping me in her soft arms.

'What is that supposed to mean!' I laughed as I hugged her back.

'Growing up, you were so skinny! All angles, I used to think. You now have the softness of a lady, my dear, with the cheekbones of a ramp model.'

You had to love Hema Masi. Bless the woman for not having watched a fashion show since the 1980s.

My mother pushed her sunglasses to the top of her head. This was enough of a compliment to my presence as any other she could have paid me.

'Darling, you couldn't find something a little brighter to wear?' she said after she finished her appraisal.

'It's not like all the clothes available in the shops are black, Ma. It's just that I happen to choose all the black ones I can find,' I said, winking at Hema Masi.

'It is just so depressing. And it makes me feel so hot!'

'I have a few white tops. I can wear one of them the next time if it will make you feel better.'

My mother shook her head, pursing her lips enough to make her displeasure known without disturbing her scarlet lipstick. She herself was dressed in all white – a white top that dipped at the cleavage, set off by a solitaire hanging from the thinnest chain of platinum, with earrings to match, and white capris. Thankfully she had dispensed with white when it came to footwear, opting instead for peacock-blue sandals revealing scarlet toes. Perched on her head were Gucci sunglasses.

We walked into Flurys and took our seats by the window.

'So,' said Hema Masi, flashing me a smile bright enough to dispel my mother's frown, 'fill me in. What have you been up to?'

'Work, mainly, Hema Masi. Writing for the magazine,' I said.

'I've been reading your links. I feel I can almost taste what you have eaten the way you write about it all so vividly.'

'Maybe while you are here, you can teach my mother how to use the Internet, too.'

'Why bother, dear,' my mother said with a dismissive wave. 'I read your magazine in print.'

'You might keep in touch with me more,' smiled Hema Masi.

'Oh, writing is such a bore.'

'You obviously didn't get your talent from your mother here.'

'You should know; you went to school with her.'

'That's true. I don't recall she had much time for writing then, either.'

'It was a bore then, it's a bore now. I must have had that attention deficit disorder thing they are talking about nowadays.'

'And yet you never seemed to lack attention when it came to chasing after the boys.'

My mother nodded, taking on a philosophical air. 'I wish my

daughter had inherited something from me. She wouldn't have been single now.'

I did my best to ignore her. Today I would not allow anything to go wrong. No matter what my mother said about whoever she chose to say it about, it would not affect me. And the best way to ensure we all remained buoyant was sugar – lots of it.

I ordered a round of coffee and pastries. I put the menu down and took a cursory look around the restaurant. Just then, Shayak Gupta walked in with two companions!

I quickly picked up the menu again and did my best to hide behind it, hoping they would be seated far away from us. What were the odds? How was it possible that we kept landing up at the same place at the same time!

With my run of luck, it shouldn't have surprised me that they were seated three tables down. Looking businesslike and, somehow, better than ever in a pale blue shirt and grey trousers, Shayak was accompanied by a young man and woman.

Trust my mother to notice. 'So there are some good-looking men in this city after all!'

I studied the menu with unflagging concentration.

'Did you see him?' 'Yes, Ma. He's probably from out of town.'

'That's true,' my mother said sadly.

'When did that ever stop you?' said Hema Masi.

'I don't mean for me, silly goose. I mean for Reema!'

'Hush,' I said.

I put down the menu and the power of the ladies' joint attention must have attracted Shayak's attention; he turned, saw me and smiled. Despite myself, I smiled back. Then, to my dismay, he rose and approached our table.

'Good afternoon, Reema,' he said.

Two heads swivelled towards me. Even Hema Masi couldn't resist the meaningful looks. I had no choice but to introduce them.

'We keep bumping into each other, don't we,' said Shayak, still smiling.

Hema Masi pointed to the empty seat beside her. 'Why don't you sit down?'

I glared at him again but this time he chose to ignore my silent entreaty, happily making himself at home at our table.

'Yes,' I finally managed to stammer out, 'quite ... quite a coincidence. Ma, Hema Masi, this is Shayak Gupta'

'So, what do you do, Shayak?' my mother asked, getting straight down to it.

'I am a boring businessman,' he said, looking at me. 'I find Reema's work fascinating, though.'

Hema Masi nodded enthusiastically. 'She has always loved food, and poking around in other people's business.'

I cringed.

'But she never seems to put on any weight. That runs in the family, of course,' giggled my mother.

I suppressed the urge to run. My mother advertising my genetic health to every man she fancied for me was all I needed. I tugged at my top, and my mother's hand shot out to slap my wrist.

If I hoped the little performance would distract Shayak, I was wrong.

'What do you mean when you say Reema loves poking around in other people's business?' he asked.

'Just that I like interviewing people, finding out about their lives,' I said quickly, shooting Hema Masi a razor-sharp look, and was relieved when she didn't feel the need to launch into a detailed CV of my PI career.

And then, thankfully, the conversation slipped away from me. Seldom have I seen a couple of fifty-three-year-olds so flirtatious. Did they think that by turning on the charm they would succeed in chasing him into my arms in abject fear?

The Masala Murder

Shayak, predictably, handled it all too deftly. It was as if wherever he went, mothers did nothing but try to pimp their daughters out to him. By the end of it, I was the only one in the cosy foursome who seemed flustered.

'Did you two really have to do that?' I hissed as soon as I saw him safely seated at his own table.

'Do what?' they both asked, eyes round with deceitful innocence. This was why they were friends.

'Pounce on him like he was the second course?'

'Nonsense,' said Hema Masi.

'Did I bring you up to be such a prude?' said my mother with what I hoped was mock outrage.

'Far from it, Mother,' I said.

'Oh, don't call me that. I feel like I am eighty with breasts down to my knees when you call me "Mother".'

'But tell me, Reema,' said Hema Masi, 'what was so wrong with that perfectly delightful young man that you refuse to even consider him?'

I shook my head. 'You've been here for all of seven minutes and already you've ambushed me!'

'Don't be so dramatic. We are merely wondering why my splendidly beautiful daughter is still single.'

I was speechless. My mother had called me beautiful. Splendidly so.

'Is he married?' asked Hema.

'No.'

'Gay?'

'Never,' my mother interjected.

'Then? Have you thought about asking him out?'

What could I say? That I had, but that I also thought about the fact that he may be a murderer? How pleasant that would be. Ma, meet my boyfriend. He is a venture capitalist and a murder suspect.

But knowing my mother and her selective perception, my saying the word 'boyfriend' would render irrelevant all else.

'Can you let it go, please?' I pleaded. 'And don't you think he's a little old for me?'

'You are hardly a typical twenty-six-year-old, my child,' said Hema Masi. 'I can't see you with one of those young, silly boys of your own age, anyway.'

Luckily, our second round of coffee arrived just then. We sat there like the three witches, stirring and sipping, two of us hatching plans of alchemy of a human kind, the third wondering how to counter every spell cast. If I had any hope of finding a man, it would definitely require keeping my mother and all her friends away from them.

'Such a nice man,' my mother intoned.

'You are women of easy virtue. Having exchanged all of a dozen words, how could you possibly know what he is like?' I said.

'But you seem to know him quite well,' said Ma.

'And you are all defensive. So that means there is something there!' said Hema Masi, wagging her finger at me, no doubt the same finger she had wagged at her own daughters while they were growing up. They had both got married before they hit twenty-five; by the look of it, Hema Masi hadn't left them with a chance.

However close their maternal instincts had led them to the truth, I didn't respond. I tended not to bandy the details of my love life about, and my mother headed the blacklist ever since the Amit wreckage. 'So in less than ten minutes, you have found a man who is absolutely perfect for me. That's impressive, even for you guys.'

'Who said anything about perfection?' said my mother, her smooth brow creasing ever so slightly. 'But would it kill you to date? Try on a couple of guys for size – you may just like it!'

'Ma, I've had boyfriends, you know.' No need to mention that one of them was currently living in my flat.

'Well, how am I supposed to know when you don't tell me anything?' she sulked.

Of course she knew perfectly well that I had had boyfriends in the past. Shalini Ray was simply fishing for information – and grabbing every excuse she could find to pout.

FIFTEEN

Home after tea with the ladies, I called Ojha in the hope that he might have some leads.

'Anything new in the Aloka Mohta kidnapping case?'

'Ravi Sharma told me to keep an eye out for you. Why would he do that?'

'Maybe he thinks I am meddling in his business.'

'I see,' he said. He sounded like he wanted to know more but if he did, he'd have to ask.

'What happened at the apartment after I left you there?'

'Not much. We looked around the place, didn't find anything. There seems to be no sign of the boy. He hasn't even called his office. Didn't get anything from the mother, either.'

'Did you take anything as evidence?'

'No,' he said.

So they hadn't been the ones to take the hairbrush or the jeans.

'But Sharma did ask the forensic team to collect prints, and we found the place had been wiped clean.'

Oops, that had been my doing. 'Now what?' I asked.

'There isn't enough evidence to arrest the husband as yet, but from what I've heard, Sharma is working on it.'

'They aren't considering any other suspects?'

'Reema ji, there are no other suspects.'

'But why?'

'If this was a professional kidnapping, why has there been no more contact after the first call? It's been a few days, and that is quite unusual in a kidnapping, you see.'

'Perhaps there has been contact but the family hasn't mentioned it?'

'But they are cooperating fully with the police. Mohta and Sharma are friends. And then there is the security consultant from Mumbai who has also been brought in.'

'Security consultant?'

'Yes, I haven't met him myself, but Sharma seems to know him from some other case.'

'Have the police considered the father may have a role to play?'

'Kishan Mohta? Reema ji, why would he try to kidnap his own daughter and extort money from himself?' I could hear the impatience in Ojha's voice.

'You're right,' I said quickly. 'What about the Prakash Agarwal business? That's Ravi Sharma's case too?'

'I am not involved in that, but I did ask around. There is no interest in pursuing the case from the side of the police.'

'Do you know why?'

'Lack of evidence,' he said rather smugly.

'Would it be possible to try and see the file they had opened? If I could see the doctor's reports that might be very helpful.'

'I can try.'

As I hung up, I was hardly hopeful. But clearly my queries had inspired interest from other quarters because half an hour later, I got a call from DDG.

'Hello, Reema ji.'

'Yes, Mr Dutta Gupa,' I said.

'Prashant told me that you were somehow involved in the Aloka Mohta case?'

'Yes,' I said.

'But this is a serious matter. Why didn't you discuss it with us?'

'I am still working on it. If I need any help, I will be sure to contact you all.'

'Okay. But see, Reema, some of us feel that you might want to keep this to yourself because it is a high-profile case.'

'You seem to forget that I do have a private investigation agency of my own. Why should I share every case with you?'

'So you will only come to us with hopeless cases, like that Agarwal business?'

'It is in the spirit of the group that since I didn't have an actual client in that matter that I brought it to you. Here, my services have been sought out.'

'You have been hired – to find the girl?'

'Yes.' Did it matter that I wasn't getting paid?

'Oh. I assumed it was one of your extra-curricular projects.'

'Well, it's not.'

'Who has hired you?'

'I'm not at liberty to say.'

'Okay, Reema ji, but just one request. Remember us if you ever get the chance to speak to the media. A mention on the news might do us some good.'

'But what about preserving our anonymity, to help us work better, as independent agents?'

'Oh, you know, hehe. Sometimes having paying cases helps also, no?'

I mentally counted to five and reminded myself that I needed the CCC now. I recognized that a time might soon come when I would need to delegate. 'Mr Dutta Gupta, I can assure you that your help may soon be needed, and I will not hesitate to ask for it when it is.'

'Of course, Reema ji, of course.'

It was an afternoon of phone calls but the next one, from Uncle Kumar, proved to be the most important.

'I just spoke with Ravi Sharma,' he said.

'Oh?'

'Your friend is on the verge of big trouble.'

'What did he say exactly?'

'It seems the family is convinced that Amit is unscrupulous enough to cause Aloka serious harm, and Sharma is inclined to believe them.'

'Does he have any evidence to make it stick?'

'I think that is the problem. They don't seem to have much more than Kishan Mohta's theory.'

'This is exactly what Amit said would happen.'

'Yes, but are you sure it is not true?'

'Why would he come to me if it were?'

'I'm not sure, Reema.'

'Are they ready to make an arrest?'

'I think they will start a manhunt. Do you know where he is?'

'Uh, no.'

'I'll pretend for the moment that I believe you.'

'What next?' I said quickly.

'I would say that you should tell your friend to turn himself in.'

'I don't think that is advice he would follow. He distrusts the system enough as it is. On top of that, he is convinced that his father-in-law's influence will be enough to see him behind bars regardless of the truth.'

'I can't say I blame him – he's probably right. But I do also have some good news for you. My men have finally dug up some records about your man Agarwal. They stopped kissing up for long enough to express displeasure at having to wade through waist-high layers of dust to find it, but they managed to locate a few documents.'

'Could you fax them to me?'

'Sure. I have them here. Give me your number. I hope to have some information on Mallika Mitra soon.'

In five minutes I was holding the contents of the file that had been put together in 1983 – the start of an investigation.

Records of the Agarwal family's shop in New Market – Sri Krishna Cloth Merchants. Father and brother listed as partners.

Mutation documents for a flat near Burrabazar.

Marriage registration certificate, dated 27 April 1976.

Complaint filed by wife's family regarding dowry demand, 10 March 1983. Complaint subsequently dropped.

The next year, a report indicating that police from the local thana had visited his office in response to a complaint filed by a young girl, whose name had been withheld, on an allegation that he had molested her in his garments shop.

That's where the paper trail on Prakash Agarwal's life ended.

Dowry torture? Molestation? It had all been so long ago. Could these allegations be mere coincidences, long forgotten offences the scars of which had faded? Or did that make Mrs Agarwal and this unknown victim suspects in Agarwal's death, a quarter of a century later?

I called Uncle Kumar.

'What do you think?' he asked.

'This is very useful, Uncle Kumar. This molestation business, I still don't know whether this has anything to do with his death.'

'In my experience, my dear, everything is connected. You just need to look hard enough to see how.'

Amit had specifically warned me off visiting Aloka's family but I decided that a trip to her home, just to look around, wouldn't hurt. A big black gate stood between me and the three-storey building that was Aloka's childhood home. It was a grey block of a building. I had never been inside it, but it didn't look to have a lawn or any kind of open space.

Of course, with an eight-foot-high boundary wall, there was only so much I could see. I crossed the relatively quiet, narrow lane and watched the house. Someone who looked like a servant left, but that was about all the action I witnessed before I saw a police van approaching. I started to walk casually away from the house, till the van rounded the corner and into a narrow alleyway. I stayed there, more or less hidden. Another car approached, this time a black sedan. But the windows were tinted so dark that, in the dying light of day, I couldn't get a view of the driver from my angle.

My phone rang again; this time it was Devika.

'Hey, how's it going with the hubby in the love nest?' I asked.

She laughed a little. 'It's been good. Fingers crossed.'

'How long is Vivek in town?'

'A couple more days. Then I'm off to Delhi for couture week on Friday.'

'Great. I won't disturb you till then.' 'Actually, I need to see you. Can you come to the office now?'

'Can it wait? I'm a little caught up.' 'I'm afraid it can't.'

'On my way.'

It was seldom that I got called into office, and even more rarely by Devika. She was no longer my boss at *Face*, having been shifted to only fashion at her request some months ago. But as the seniormost staff member in the Calcutta office, she was called in to troubleshoot. I knew this meeting could only mean bad news of some sort. I feared that perhaps word of my fraudulent claims to be writing a follow-up piece about Agarwal had got back to the office.

I got in and Devika rose to give me a tight hug which did nothing to alleviate my growing feeling of dread.

'How have you been?' I asked.

'Busy,' said Devika with a smile. But I could see that she was uncomfortable.

'What is it?'

She took a deep breath and closed her eyes. 'You know that I love the work you do for us, right?'

'I think I do.'

'The point being that this isn't about you. It is about the company and its bullshit HR policies.'

'Spit it out, Devika.'

'Mumbai has flagged a number of local expenses at the Calcutta office during the last audit. Revenues from here are at an all-time low and, as usual, instead of putting pressure on the marketing guys to perform they are squeezing editorial to cut costs.'

'And?'

'They have raised questions about your fee.'

'I could hardly charge less per word. If I did, I'd end up paying you guys to carry my work.'

Devika didn't even crack a smile. 'They are saying that for the amount you are getting paid on a monthly basis they should have a full-time employee, not a freelancer.'

But I am more productive than most of your staff here.'

'Exactly what I said. But predictably, management doesn't see it that way. They are saying that in that case there is a productivity problem in the Calcutta office.'

'Jesus. So what do they want?'

'For you to join full time.'

'Or?'

'Or scale back your contributions to no more than two small pieces a month.'

'They have no problems with my work otherwise?'

'No.'

'Great. What kind of sense does that make?'

'Reema, I don't like it any more than you do. This kind of baseless meddling makes my blood boil. The arrangement works and that should be that.'

'There is no way to change their minds?'

'I can't seem to find one. But you should take the job. You know I've felt that you belong here for some time.'

'How would it work?'

'It won't be much more than your take-home now, but you'll get considerable savings in the form of provident fund, and don't pretend you don't need that. Plus, there are other perks too – outstation assignments, health benefits, office cars. Overall, you'll be the winner.'

'What about time?'

'Five-day weeks. Fairly relaxed for the first fortnight after the issue's release. More pressure the rest of the time.'

'I don't know, Devika.'

'I'll tell you how I see it. If I was getting all my money from one job, that is where my loyalties would lie.'

'I know. But an inflexible work schedule will kill my practice altogether.'

'You've been saying it has been dead for a while anyway. And that voluntary stuff you do with your superhero squad can continue on weekends.'

'What of my college education? Was it all for nothing?'

'Plenty of people study engineering and go on to marketing jobs. This is almost the same thing. And who knows, your detective skills could come in handy. You might eventually want to make a switch to hard news, maybe even investigative journalism.'

It's not like I hadn't considered that option in the past. But somehow it had never appealed to me. I wanted to solve crime, help people in distress, make arrests. I didn't want to conduct hidden-camera sting operations, which was all I had seen by way of 'investigative journalism' in the past.

'How soon do they want a response?'

'As soon as possible.'

'What about the stuff I am working on now?'

'Submit those. I'll get the payments processed. But I need a decision soon.'

'Can I have till the end of the month?'

Devika looked at the calendar. 'Two weeks?'

'Yes. I need to think.'

'Okay, I can buy you that much time. But once I'm back from Delhi, I'll need to set things in motion.'

I was about to leave when Devika stopped me. 'Oh, and another thing,' she said.

'What is it?'

'We got a call from the PR officer of Calcutta Medical.'

I froze. 'What did she say?'

'Dr Mitra had some unpleasant words for her after you left. He said he was thinking about filing an official complaint to the editor.'

'Oh no.'

'What did you do to rattle him like that?'

'I have no idea.'

Devika's brow told me she didn't believe me. 'The PR managed to convince him against it, but she says the piece you were working on better be good.'

'I'll send it to you ASAP.'

Another one for my overflowing plate: an article about reversing cardiac problems through lifestyle management. If my suddenly elevated blood pressure was anything to go by, I might have to start taking some of that advice myself.

*

All I wanted to do was go home, but I knew Amit would be there and I wasn't equal to seeing him in my current state of mind. I decided to walk through the perennially open door of Santosh da's office first. There he was in his tiny garage, steel desk and overflowing racks all around him. 'Reema! How nice to see you!' he said, standing up.

Crow's feet fanned away from his always twinkling eyes. Always curious. That must be the secret to Santosh da's inexplicable optimism, his ability to weather hardship and disappointment with a smile on his face.

'I hope I am not disturbing you,' I said.

'Of course not. Have some tea.' Santosh da sat down and opened the flask that seemed to be always at his side. He pulled out a small white battered ceramic cup with pink flowers from a drawer and filled both it and his own cup. Then he pulled out a tin and held it towards me. 'Have a biskut.'

I arranged myself with care on the worn black chair across the desk from him. Hard bits of coir stuffing emerged from all angles and I tried to avoid being poked as far as possible.

'Having luck with your sleuthing?'

I couldn't help but smile. 'I am still waiting for a few specifics, but the Prakash Agarwal mentioned in the ActNow files seems to be the same one who is dead.'

'Good work, Reema!'

'I still have to see if it is relevant. I hope it gets me somewhere. What about you?' I asked, breaking a biscuit to dip it into the small cup.

'I'm working on a very interesting case now. It is a case filed by an NGO against a brothel owner from Sonagachi. Two teenaged girls were rescued from there a few months ago. Evidence is strong. The girls too are willing to testify,' he said.

Contentment spread across Santosh da's face and I was filled with wonder. 'Santosh da, could I ask you how you have stuck to this sort of work? Weren't you ever tempted away by money?'

'It isn't so bad. I do get paid. Not as much as my colleagues who do corporate cases, or civil cases. But I make enough for my needs.'

'And you never wanted more?'

'Reema, let me tell you how I live. I eat simple food at home. I don't drink, smoke or have any other bad habits. I travel in buses. I live in the house my father built thirty years ago. It is small and I don't have the money to paint it, but it puts a roof over our heads and I don't have any loans and I don't have to pay rent. My wife teaches and tutors and her salary is enough to help. My daughter is in a convent school where the fee is very low. What do I need money for?'

'What about retirement?'

'I don't intend to retire. I have managed to save a little over the years, for when I can't support my family anymore. But I hope never to be idle.'

I envied his simplicity, but I knew that no one's story was ever quite so straightforward.

'Why did you become a lawyer?'

'My father was a lawyer. At first I took it up because it was expected of me. And then I realized that it is also what I love doing, in my own way.'

'What do you love about it?'

'The same thing I think you love about your job.'

'Which is what?' From one infidelity case to another, I had lost track of my motives.

'It helps me make sense of the world, Reema. To understand it. To set things right where I can. And to help people who are helpless.'

It sounded so noble coming from Santosh da, who had stuck to his convictions. He was too good to see that I had hardly remained as true. Even when I was practising full time, I was busy breaking up more marriages than I cared to count. Hardly the kind of help Santosh da was talking about.

'But tell me, why are you worrying about all of this now?' he asked.

'I have been given a choice. I either join the magazine full time, or I cut back so much that I more or less lose my source of income.'

'I see.'

'So now the question is: am I willing to give up on being a detective altogether?'

'If you don't take the job, what would you do?'

'Either I could continue to write and freelance for a larger number of publications, but that is likely to be so time consuming as to amount to the same thing as joining *Face*. Or I could put in everything into one more effort at making my agency a success and take every case that comes to me. But either way, the uncertainty will force me to give up my flat.'

'And you don't want to do that. Can't you move back in with your mother?'

'Santosh da, you haven't met my mother.'

'No, no, that's true,' he said with an endearing earnestness.

'So that is where things stand.'

'It is a hard choice. But I think there is one other option. You could look for a job with an established detective agency. It would give you a platform to do the work you enjoy for sometime and then, later, when you have more contacts, perhaps you could start on your own once again?'

'I had tried that when I first came back to India. I didn't have much luck.'

'But now you've had a few years of experience. Why don't you send out some applications once again? You could speak to Terrence.'

I did not relish that particular thought. 'There are others as well.'

'In Calcutta they are the best.'

'Perhaps it would make sense to look outside Calcutta.'

'It would be very bad to lose you.'

I smiled and drained my teacup. 'Thank you, Santosh da, for the advice.'

'Reema, just remember that you have too much intelligence to waste it doing something you don't love. And if you follow your instincts, it pays off in the long run.'

'I hope you are right.'

I pondered and fumed through the four-kilometre walk home. Either way, the choices before me were not happy, but meeting Santosh da helped pull me out of myself for a moment. It also gave me the calm to put into perspective the other piece of news Devika had delivered: Dr Mitra was not at all pleased at my digging around. In my experience, that was evidence enough that I was onto something.

I entered my living room to find Amit sitting on the couch reading Dylan Thomas.

'How was your day?' he asked.

'How very domestic of you,' I said, handing him a bag with two chicken rolls that I had picked up, mine long since tucked away. 'Egg-chicken. Just like the old days.' I heard the edge in my voice. I needed to relax. 'Want a drink?'

'Why not?' he shrugged.

I walked over to the cupboard where I stashed my liquor. My supplies were dwindling, and it seemed unlikely that I would have the spare cash to replenish them soon. I poured myself a vodka tonic.

'What do you drink nowadays?' I asked.

'Not particularly fussy.'

'I guess you have abandoned your opposition to intoxicants.'

'I guess I have,' said Amit, coming up behind me.

I turned and found him standing a little too close. 'Here you go,' I said.

He took his glass and raised it in a salute. We sat down at the dining table.

'Have you heard anything new?' I asked.

'No.'

'And you still don't want me to try to make contact?'

'Not yet. Anything from the police sources?'

'Not much. But I don't think we should expect anything good to come of this. We're waiting around for something to happen. When it finally does happen, believe me that it will be bad.'

Amit narrowed his eyes at his ice cubes. His glass was empty.

'Help yourself,' I said.

He stood up and poured himself another drink.

'I need to get back to work. I can't afford to lose my job,' he said.

How ironic that Amit and I had ended up in virtually the same position after all these years. Both of us practically penniless. Both of us with dreams that had betrayed us.

'Why did you give up on your poetry?' I asked.

'Why do you think?'

'Money?'

'Of course.'

'You used to say none of that mattered.'

'I used to not know what put food on my plate.' He stood up and leaned against the wall, glass in hand. 'When I realized there was no market for poetry, I thought I would write songs. I told myself they were the poems of today. But then I lost my words somewhere.'

'You didn't lose them, Amit, you gave up on them.'

'True, perhaps. You were always so uncompromising in your honesty. Some of us aren't so strong. We need stories to hide behind. The best stories we even believe ourselves. Then we run out of luck one day and discover our subterfuge. That is a bad day. Leaves us with nothing. Nothing but the poverty of broken hope.'

'The truth, Amit. When the lies are abandoned you are left with the truth. And that is something worth building on.'

He tilted his head and watched me, refusing to drop his gaze. 'How is that you haven't changed at all?'

'Who says I haven't?'

'You didn't sell out.'

'Who says I haven't?' I repeated.

'You may be writing to make ends meet, but you never stopped being yourself.'

'That's not how it looks on the inside.'

'Then you aren't seeing straight. Just look at us. I have come to you and you have let me in. You are helping me but you won't bullshit me. No empty platitudes out of your mouth. And no accusations.'

'I thought you might prefer it that way. So why is it that you sound angry?'

'Don't get me wrong. I am grateful for what you are doing. But just once, it would be nice to see you crack. Just once.'

'Funny way to show your gratitude.'

'How can you even stand to look at me?'

He watched me with eyes suddenly angry. I stood up and refilled my glass, gathering myself with my back to him. When I swung back around, I was ready for his gaze.

'How can you not hate me after what I did to you?' he continued.

'I've moved on, Amit. It's quite simple.'

'Why are you helping me then?'

'Would you prefer it if I didn't?'

'Answer the question.'

'I don't see why I should.'

'Because I need to know. How are you so able to forget when I can't?'

He backed me into a corner, blocking out the light. I couldn't breathe. He raised a hand to run it through my hair and brought it to rest on the nape of my neck. I felt his hand tighten on a handful of curls, stopping just short of pain as he tugged my head back.

'You remember this, Reema?' His fingers were on my mouth, tracing the outline of my lips. But there was nothing sensuous about it. 'I couldn't get enough of these lips.'

He brought his mouth down on mine.

'Amit, stop,' I said, jerking away.

'So beautiful. Even when you were angry. And now there is nothing there? Even the other day when we kissed, you were impassive, cold.'

I raised my arms and shoved against his chest. His grip on my hair tightened.

'You used to love me, Reema.'

'Amit, stop it.'

He ignored me. 'So soon to forget.'

'You are the one who forgot,' I said, trying to keep my voice calm.

'That's a lie. For four years you left me on my own. Did you ever think what you were doing to me?'

'I didn't ask you to cheat on me.'

'But you gave up on us for some fancy foreign university. You explored the world while I endured a mother whose every word was about a dead husband who had left us with nothing. Who looked to me for every emotional need.'

'You never said any of this to me before ... ever.'

'A good woman would have known.'

'A good woman?' Between those words and being pinned to the wall, I felt my anger rise.

'Yes, a good woman.'

'Like Aloka?'

He didn't reply.

'I didn't take you for a man who likes his woman docile and primed to put her husband before herself.'

'Shut up!' he shouted, tightening his grip on my hair.

'Amit, let go.'

Silence.

'Why are you doing this, Amit? I am only trying to help.'

'And I asked you why! Why are you helping me?'

'I am helping you because of what once was. Not what is, or what I hope it to be. I am helping you because I am not willing to taint twenty years of memories with hate. But we are over, Amit. Now get your hands off of me.'

He released his grip and I pushed him away. I went into my room and locked the door. Never again would I let Amit see me cry.

SIXTEEN

The next morning, I arose and found Amit sipping coffee on the sofa.

Once again, my cup was waiting for me on the kitchen counter.

'Good morning,' he said.

'Good morning,' I replied.

No apology. No explanation. No offer to leave. He seemed quite at home in my living room, as though nothing really could faze him – not his wife's abduction, not his behaviour the night before. All traces of the spark I had loved in him seemed gone; Amit had allowed himself to grow into the very worst version of who he could be. The dreams of a poet are bound to be fragile, but I hadn't thought Amit was so ready to be broken.

I retreated to my room with my coffee and sent a text message. I quickly showered and changed before leaving the room again.

There was Amit, still on my damn couch. I was beginning to think that he had become attached to it like resilient mould.

Halfway through breakfast, I heard footsteps. I peered out

the window and, as orchestrated, saw my landlady approaching my door.

'Shit,' I said. 'My landlady is here. You need to go inside.'

'Where?'

'The bathroom. Stay there till I tell you to come out.'

Amit complied and I slipped on my shoes and went outside.

'You wanted to see me, Reema? I just got your message,' said Mrs Banerjee.

'Yes, thank you for coming at such short notice.'

'How have you been?'

'I'm well. What about you? And Mr Banerjee?'

'It hasn't been too good. The doctors are hopeful but the treatment is so harsh.'

Mr Banerjee's cancer had been detected in time for a positive prognosis, but it was still early days yet.

'Your rent for the month,' I said, handing her the envelope. 'I'm sorry it's late.'

'Thank you,' she said. 'Reema, there is actually something I think we should discuss.'

Here it was. The conversation I had been sidestepping for months; and now I had opened the door to it myself perforce.

'You've been staying here for so long now, my husband and I are happy to have a tenant like you. You've taken care of the place, which is why we haven't raised the rent before. But now it is really time for a hike. With Mr Banerjee's health the way it is, we have no choice.'

'I understand. What kind of an increase are you looking at?'

'At least 20 per cent. It has been so long, and Mr Banerjee's treatments are so expensive.'

'I know, Mrs Banerjee. I really appreciate the warning.'

'I can also see that you've had trouble paying the rent of late. I know your contract is till the end of the year but if you'd want to leave before that, I'd understand.'

'Thank you for the offer. I think for now I am okay. I may have to take you up on it soon, though. Are you sure you don't need the extra funds now? If so, I can move out.'

'There is no rush, Reema.' I gave Mrs Banerjee a hug. 'Thank you.'

Mrs Banerjee got into her car and drove away. I watched her turn the corner before walking back into the living room. It looked like my decision regarding full-time employment at *Face* was being taken out of my hands. If I valued the freedom of living on my own, I would have to take the offer. If I valued my professional freedom, I would have to give up my place.

I took a moment to compose myself. 'You can come out now,' I finally called out to Amit.

He emerged, unfazed even at having to hide in the bathroom like a schoolboy playing hooky, and sat back down on the sofa.

'You need to leave.'

'Why?'

'The landlady has heard rumours and has made it clear that she doesn't expect her place to be a co-ed facility.'

'How typical.'

'Maybe, but she is a lovely lady who has been kind to me over the years. I don't want to abuse her trust.' I felt no guilt at the lie.

'Where will I go?'

'Anywhere but home. And not to your mother's place either. You could stay with another friend, perhaps? How about the one you have been visiting?'

I saw a bleak look creep into his eyes. 'Okay,' he said at last. 'I know some place I could go.'

He began to pack the few things he had brought with him. It didn't take long.

'You can stay till the end of the day, I suppose,' I said.

'No,' he said. 'I should go.'

At last, a hint of ego fighting back.

He stood by the door, poised to go. 'You've been,' he began haltingly, 'you've been good to me.'

'Amit—'

'No, Reema, it needs to be said. I'm sorry about last night.'

'What we need now is for you to take care of yourself. I am still on this thing. I just can't have you here, not now.'

'Reema, I don't know what to say.'

'Be safe, Amit, don't do anything stupid.' I leaned forward to kiss his cheek, but he jerked his head so my mouth grazed his. As he reached for my arm, I stepped back. I closed my eyes, shook my head just a fraction and, as I forced myself to look into his face, I could no longer keep the sadness from my eyes — or the pity. Amit didn't miss it and, as he opened the door to leave, in the cleansing light of day I saw the faint edge of desperation that had hung around him since this business began drop away, replaced by a hard glint of anger.

And there was nothing more I could do for him.

A moment later, Uncle Kumar called.

'You, my dear, seem to be onto something.'

'What do you mean?'

'I have in my hand a copy of the register recording the complaint filed in the police station by the girl Prakash Agarwal had assaulted.'

'That was quick.'

'You have the New Market police station to thank for that. The official complainant was Samir Sinha. His daughter, get this — Mallika, aged fifteen — had been molested by a shop owner at a

New Market store. Their residence address was listed as 15/1/13 Chetla Road. That could not be far from Sharma Sweets.'

Mallika Sinha. She would be about forty years right now. In all probability, married, name changed.

'Could this be your Mallika Mitra?' he asked.

'Name aside, the address is also a match. It would be a hell of a coincidence if it wasn't. Do you have anything else?'

'The complaint was dropped soon after it was filed.'

So it was likely that the police had done nothing at the time – the New Market businessmen would have kept their pockets jangling through the year, and an allegation like this would be buried before you could say 'pujor bakshish'.

'Did you find anything else on Mallika or her family?'

'No, do you need me to look?'

'I think this will do for now,' I said. 'Thank you, Uncle Kumar. Things are beginning to make sense.'

'Happy to help.'

'Will you be sharing this with the police?'

'Why should I?'

'I don't know – it is possible motive in a recent murder investigation.'

There was a long silence at the other end. 'So far, all the evidence is purely circumstantial. Why don't you pursue this angle on your own? If you come up with more, you can always go to the police with it yourself.'

'Uncle Kumar, are you telling me that I should interfere with an investigation on the basis of a hunch and a name in a twenty-five-year-old police complaint?'

'No, I think you should substantiate your suspicion with fact, using the skills I know you have and should have respected a long time ago.'

'Uncle Kumar–'

'Don't you dare thank me again!'
'Just don't tell my parents.'

I rang the doorbell and waited. It was finally time for some real answers.

Mrs Agarwal opened the door herself, and didn't seem surprised to see me. 'Come in,' she said, leading the way into the living room where it had all started.

Mrs Agarwal appeared more and more self-possessed every time I saw her and now her poise was softened by something like relief. Her eyes were bright as she looked at me.

'Mrs Agarwal, I have some questions and I need you to answer them honestly.'

She nodded.

'But before that, I have a confession to make, one that I should have made some time ago.'

Confusion flickered across Mrs Agarwal's face but I ploughed on. 'I am a trained private investigator. I am now primarily a journalist, but I still take some cases on the side. I should have mentioned it that first day when we met but at such a time, it didn't seem right. And later, I became somewhat invested in this whole business and I suppose I was afraid that you'd tell me to back off.'

The sparkle in Mrs Agarwal's eye hardened. 'Yes, I probably would have. But at least that explains all the questions.'

A mild reaction compared with what I may have received, which only served to reinforce my theory. 'I have been wondering from the beginning why you chose me to confide in. Yes, as a journalist I might have been privy to some information, but how would that benefit you? Unless it was you who had killed your husband, of course. And from the beginning, I have to admit, I didn't quite buy into that theory.'

Mrs Agarwal sat perfectly still, her eyes never leaving my face.

'But there was another possibility – that you were protecting someone other than yourself. And that person was Mallika Mitra, wasn't it?'

The blood drained from Mrs Agarwal's face. 'How did you know?' she asked, voice icy.

'Dhyan showed me something he found the day after your husband died – an earring recovered from the dustbin in your kitchen.' I held it up for her to see.

Mrs Agarwal's eyes widened. 'He shouldn't have done that.'

'It was the only thing he could do.'

'It was so silly of me,' said Mrs Agarwal, shaking her head slowly 'I panicked and threw it the first place I could find. I realized later that I should have just left it amongst my own jewellery. Who would have even noticed?'

'You knew the earring belonged to Mallika?'

Mrs Agarwal nodded. 'She had come to the office the evening the day before we took my husband to hospital. He had gone briefly to the warehouse close by and I had seated her in his office. It was the first time she had ever been here, or approached us in any way. Given their history, I just assumed she had to be somehow connected with what happened to him. She was the last outsider in his room that night.'

It was finally starting to make sense to me, but Mrs Agarwal's confusion was a long way from being dispelled. 'I thought I was helping her.'

'Because your husband had hurt her all those years ago?'

'Because he continued to hurt her every chance he got till he died!' she said, eyes flashing. 'Every time he bumped into her, I saw the way he looked at her. It was vile. It was as though he were taking revenge on her for making those accusations public. The ultimate power trip for him, watching her suffer whenever they happened to be in the same room, till she started to do her best to avoid him. But he could be charming when he wanted to, and ... But what a fool I've been!'

'No, Mrs Agarwal, you've been anything but. Mallika too believed that suspicion would fall on her if she was connected to the scene. That's why she left town.'

Mrs Agarwal shook her head. 'What exactly happened here?'

'I still have a little way to go before I can say for certain.'

Mrs Agarwal closed her eyes, unable to face the mess her husband had left even after his death. 'I don't know why I didn't leave him!'

'Why didn't you?'

'Oh, you know. Same old sob story,' she said with a harsh laugh. 'My parents wouldn't hear of a divorce and I had no way out without their help. I got married when I was twenty. No college degree. Who would employ me? Where would I go?'

'Your family wanted you to stay with him even after the dowry incident you reported?' I asked.

'Of course. Even after they coughed up the money. Even after I had a miscarriage following a particularly bad encounter. So I did what I could to make him unhappy. I made sure Prakash Agarwal would have no children. But I couldn't stop him from inflicting harm elsewhere.'

'You knew about Mallika when it happened?'

'Oh yes! It was soon after my miscarriage. I managed to piece together what was going on, though the family tried its best to hush it up. I knew what my husband was capable of. I was sure there had been many more like her. But I think that incident scared him, and for a time he kept himself happy with his whores. The high point of my life has been that he didn't touch me for years. No doubt I rapidly became too old for his taste anyhow,' she spat out.

'Why do you think Mallika came here that night?'

'I knew my husband was involved with someone of late, and I thought that it might have been her.'

'Your husband was having an affair?'

'Yes, I'm fairly certain of it. Not one of his usual flings or prostitutes.'

'And what made you think it was Mallika?' That seemed a rather improbable jump to me when she couldn't stand to be in the same room as him.

'I thought she was looking for an opportunity to get her peace. That she had got close to him for a chance at revenge at last.'

Now it was my turn to close my eyes. How could I have been so blind! How could I forget that all crime is essentially the same, that in all crime, it is the details that give away the big picture; that what is missing is often more important than what is staring you in the face?

I began to create a timeline of events. Agarwal is ill for at least twenty-four hours – quite possibly more – before he is taken to hospital. But not so ill that he can't go about his work, even making a trip to the warehouse. Sometime around then, Mallika visits, but leaves without seeing Agarwal. Agarwal doesn't emerge from his office for dinner, and is discovered still at his desk the next morning. By evening, his wife forces him to the emergency room. When Agarwal does not respond to treatment, Dr Mitra is called in, but to no avail. Agarwal dies, and Dr Mitra alerts the police. Mrs Agarwal comes to the conclusion that Mallika must have had something to do with it and rushes the body away for cremation. The doctor too changes his story. The police, with no evidence to go on, drop the case.

What was increasingly clear now was that the action triggering this chain of events – the poisoning of Prakash Agarwal – happened well before Mallika's ill-fated visit. The two people who had feared that Agarwal's death was a murder both suspected Mallika, but they were both wrong – they must be.

※

Once again, my phone had rung out on silent mode while I was at Mrs Agarwal's home. As soon as I stepped out, I saw that it was Mr Ojha and called him back. I was feeling particularly generous towards the CCC right now, thanks to Santosh da's role in my current state of enlightenment.

'Reema ji? I thought you would want to know that tomorrow they are launching a search for your friend Amit.'

I bit my lip. It had only been a matter of time, and I had already set the wheels in motion to prepare for just such an eventuality. 'Thank you for the information.'

'How is your other case going?' he asked. 'What about the old molestation accusation you were looking up?'

If I expected Ojha to continue to give me information, I knew I would have to give some myself – even though I suspected DDG had instructed Ojha to play nice. 'It could be nothing more than a coincidence, but it was the molestation victim's husband who treated Agarwal at the end. I am looking into the angle.'

'Oh my! Reema ji, very good work.'

'Thank you, Mr Ojha. I am not sure what any of it means yet, but at last I am getting somewhere.'

'Do keep me posted on anything else you learn.'

※

I arrived at the gate of the Mohta residence once again, but this time I rang the bell. A guard opened a small window within the door and peered out at me.

'Kisko chahiye?' he said. All I could see were his eyes.

'Mrs Mohta, please.'

'Aap kaun?'

'Reema Ray. Friend of the family.'

'Please wait.'

I stood outside. I was not surprised by the security, given the circumstances. In a few moments, the guard reappeared with a cordless phone and opened the window within the gate again to hand it to me.

'Hello?' I said.

'Yes? Who is this?' replied a woman's voice.

'Mrs Mohta?'

'Yes.'

'This is Reema. I am a friend of Aloka's from school. I wanted to come in and meet you if possible.'

'Reema?' Not surprisingly, it didn't sound as though she remembered me from that solitary Digha holiday. 'I am sorry, but we aren't receiving visitors now. If you can leave your number ...'

I knew it was pointless but I gave her my number and hung up. I had to stretch into the small portal to hand the phone back to the guard; he had stepped back into his booth, giving me enough time to spot a police jeep parked in the driveway, behind which was a fleet of cars that must belong to the family.

I handed over the phone and then stepped away from the gate, walking a little down the pavement and standing behind a tree.

I kept an eye on the gate and fiddled with my phone. Now was the time to multitask. I tried to call Mallika once again. No answer. I called Abhimanyu next.

'Have you heard from Mallika at all?' I asked.

'She did call to say she'd be gone for a couple more days.'

'Did she say where she is?'

'No, just that she had to get away for a while. Can I be of any help?'

'Um, no, I just wanted to check how she was doing.'

'She sounded better, to tell you the truth.'

I saw the gate opening and knew I had to hang up. 'That's great. Chat later?'

I hung up over Abhimanyu's friendly goodbye just as the police car drove out. In the back seat was Ravi Sharma. Seated beside him was Shayak Gupta.

I was grateful for the shelter the tree provided, for exposed, with my mouth hanging open, one of them would have been sure to see me.

Then, for once, my luck held: just when I needed it, there was a cab, and the driver didn't ask where I wanted to go before I stepped in, and when I asked him to follow the police car, he didn't so much as raise an eyebrow.

We drove for a long time. My state of confusion and not knowing where I was going made every moment stretch even longer. Why was Shayak Gupta at the Mohta home? No explanation made itself clear. Twenty-five minutes of open road later we took a turn off the highway and onto a narrow, pot-holed road that led to Green Acres Golf Club.

The car disappeared inside the gate, and I released the cab outside and quickly made my way in. I found myself not far behind Ravi Sharma and Shayak who had parked and were headed for the greens.

And that is when my luck ran out.

'Ma'am, are you a member?' asked a young man in a black suit.

'No, but–'

'Then I am sorry but the clubhouse is out of bounds. You can use the driving range if you like.'

'Driving range?'

'Yes,' he said, pointing to the large netted area to his right. 'Would you like me to show you around?'

I followed him to the counter, where he gave me a rate chart. 'Half an hour – ₹200.'

The upside was that I could get a fairly decent view of the course from where I stood, as well as the exit.

I took a club and a bucket of balls and headed for the bay. I was inappropriately dressed, in black shirt, jeans and wedges, but it would have to do. And though I had never held a golf club in my life, I felt that there was enough angst bubbling just beneath the surface that whacking a few balls into oblivion couldn't but help.

I have always prided myself on being quicker on the uptake than most people you might encounter in the general course of things, so it only took me a couple of minutes to realize that hitting a ball any distance took much more than a golf club and suppressed rage. The only thing I had working in favour of my club making any kind of contact with the devilishly small spheres were the long hours spent watching Nick Faldo, during his day, dominating the greens with regal imperiousness. I summoned the image of his stature and swing in my mind, trying to channel all the information that must have filtered down to my latent golfer psyche through the adolescent adoration. I brought the club down, and completely missed.

No matter, I told myself. The range was relatively empty, and no one was watching. Besides, I had a job to do. Shayak and Sharma were still within sight, though well out of earshot. But I wasn't in the mood to budge. I brought my club down again. The ball didn't make it far, but at least there was contact. Progress!

In about fifteen minutes, I hit as many balls as I could with varying degrees of success, none making it farther than five feet away from me, though one may have gone a considerably greater distance – behind me – had it not been for the net it encountered. I am still not sure how that had occurred; my only consolation was that the presence of the net indicated I was not the only one who was directionally challenged.

That was around the time when Shayak and Sharma moved out of sight. With the guard standing behind me, there was no way I could slink outside to the course. But then I realized that the last hole was beside the first hole and, if I was patient, they would loop around back to where I could see them. I kept at it and soon began to make consistent contact: the ball headed in roughly the right direction. If I couldn't catch a killer/kidnapper, I could at least work on my game.

'You can hire an instructor, you know.'

The words were dangerously close to my right ear, threatening to throw me off balance. I turned to face the speaker, knowing full well who I would see there.

'I am beginning to think that you are following me,' I said with a smile. All the reasons I had to be suspicious of Shayak came back like a montage in the movies. Though now I fancied I knew better, there was surely much to be wary of.

'I could say the same about you,' said Shayak.

'What happened to your golf buddy?' I asked.

'He was called away.'

'How does a venture capitalist know a police officer?'

'He's an old friend. How would a food writer happen to know one?'

'Who said I did?'

'You recognized him, didn't you?'

'He's in the papers all the time.'

'If you saw us, why didn't you say anything? You could have joined us.'

'I'm still a novice.'

Having seen my swing, he couldn't argue with that one.

'I'd better be going,' I said.

'Me too.'

I handed the near-empty bucket over to the attendant and walked quickly down the steps that led to the path to the lobby.

And then I saw a familiar rotund frame, hobbling on dangerously small feet, approaching me.

It was Manoj Chakravarty. 'Reema ji!' he exclaimed.

'Hello, Mr Chakravarty. I didn't know you played golf.'

'I don't, I don't. But my son is learning now. He is on the hole.'

Then he saw Shayak standing beside me.

'Arre wah! You and Shayak ji know each other! How splendid!'

I turned to Shayak. 'Another old friend?'

'Mr Chakravarty and I had some business.'

'Venture capitalists do seem to get around, don't they?'

'Why don't we go to the coffee shop downstairs? It has some lovely snacks,' said Mr Chakravarty, grabbing hold of my arm. Shayak fell into step behind us.

Mr Chakravarty seized the opportunity to wax eloquent about my articles to Shayak. 'Some people didn't like that last one of yours, where you talked about how mediocre most of the Continental restaurants in town are, but what kind of a journalist are you until you have ruffled a few feathers, eh?' he said with a chuckle.

'So how is it you know each other?' I asked Mr Chakravarty.

'Shayak? Oh, we are in talks about–' he began.

'Mr Chakravarty is very well connected. I've been picking his brain about some boring business matters,' said Shayak, interrupting. I was certain he didn't want Mr Chakravarty to finish whatever he was going to say. And nothing like flattery to do the trick.

But there was an upside to the exchange – Mr Chakravarty had called the man by my side 'Shayak'.

A waiter arrived and we ordered tea and spring rolls. I barely listened as Mr Chakravarty rattled on about his son's golf. Soon, he looked at his watch. 'Oh dear, it is quite late, quite late. My son must be finished by now,' he said.

'But your tea!' I said. Somehow I didn't relish the thought of being left alone with Shayak just now.

Mr Chakravarty shook his head. 'My missus will be waiting for me at home! We have a lunch invitation.' Shayak stood up. 'No need for you to come with me, Shayak. You young people finish,' he said, waving him back down in his seat.

'I'll walk you to your car,' he said. He then looked at me and, in a voice so low that only I could hear it, said, 'Don't run away now.'

I have to admit that I did contemplate it. But perhaps I didn't really want to move. Perhaps the spring rolls were too tasty for me to abandon them. Perhaps I was tired – my back did ache a bit – from all that fake golfing. Perhaps hearing Mr Chakravarty refer to the man I knew as Shayak as 'Shayak' had lulled me into a false sense of safety. Whatever it was, by the time I began to seriously consider it, it was too late for me to flee. I saw Shayak returning, crossing the room with long strides. In a moment, he was sitting in his chair, black, black eyes boring into mine.

'Truth time,' he said.

'What? Shouldn't that be my opening line?'

'Perhaps,' he said, not ruffled in the least. 'But I got there first.'

'You are Mayank Gupta's brother?' I asked.

I was happy to note that he looked at least a little unsettled by this. 'Yes,' he said.

'Why didn't you mention it earlier?'

'You didn't ask.'

'But you lied!'

'Did I? No, I am fairly certain I never lied.'

My mind was a mess. I tried to remember at least one thing that this man had actually lied about. 'What about all that venture capitalist stuff?'

'Well, my brother is a venture capitalist and I am representing him. So that is my job for now. I was here on my brother's behalf even before his prickly ex-partner very inconveniently got himself murdered.'

That was a shamefully thin explanation. But I had more important questions at hand. 'Why *ex*-partner?'

'Little known fact. My brother and Prakash Agarwal had parted ways some time ago. It seems Agarwal hadn't bothered to mention it to anyone.'

That explained the silence from Hong Kong. 'Why are you here then?'

Here Shayak paused. 'There were business matters to tie up and I am ... somewhat better equipped to handle the situation than my brother. He is far too soft to have dealt with Agarwal with a firm hand. And once Agarwal was dead there was even less reason for him to be here.'

I tried to think of a reason why this wasn't an acceptable answer. Mayank Gupta was not wanted by the law. And just in case there were any issues, his brother was here to represent him and was clearly in touch with the police.

'Who are you?' I asked.

'I think I just gave you the answer to that. The real question is, Reema Ray, who are you?'

'I am not the one keeping secrets,' I said, acutely aware that he still had not answered me.

'Aren't you? What do you have to do with Mrs Agarwal, exactly? Why did she choose you to confide in?'

My jaw almost dropped. How could he know that? 'As a journalist, she thought I might have information, that's all. She was in the dark about her husband's death, for heaven's sake.'

'And your being a trained detective has nothing to do with it?'

I paused and stared. 'How did you know that?' I coughed out.

'Later.'

'Fine. How is it relevant?'

'Had it ever occurred to you that Mrs Agarwal might have been using you? That she needed certain information not for her peace of mind, but for a more insidious reason?'

I sat there stony-faced. Of course it had.

'What kind of a position would you be in now, Reema, had she been the killer?'

I opened my mouth to protest, but Shayak put his hand out and stopped me. 'I know it isn't her. But it was a very distinct possibility at the time you chose to get involved, and you had no evidence to the contrary.'

I was surprised by the words and the vehemence with which they were delivered. I felt my hackles rise. 'I didn't break any laws and I didn't hurt anybody.'

'What about Mallika? Is she your villain or your hero? And what will she think of you now that you've unearthed her deepest, darkest secrets?'

'How do you know about that?'

'Does it matter?'

'Of course it does,' I yelled. My mind was racing and my face was burning, but Shayak was not finished yet.

'A little knowledge can be a dangerous thing, Reema. Isn't your ex-boyfriend's wife's disappearance enough to teach you that valuable lesson?'

His voice was cold and clinical; mine was now a cracked whisper. 'How much do you know about me, exactly?'

'Enough.'

'Well, how do I know it wasn't you?'

Shayak smirked. 'If it were me, I would have killed you that first night I met you in the bar, after you left Mrs Agarwal's house.'

In a flash it all made sense. He had followed me! In fact, he had been following me all along!

It was as though he could read my mind. 'And you were wrong about another thing: it is extremely unlikely that you'd bump into an acquaintance not once but thrice within days in a city of fourteen million people.

'But it is a funny old world,' he continued. 'Because this meeting – well, it really *was* a coincidence.'

'Sorry, but you are wrong on that front,' I said, standing up and throwing some money down on the table. 'This time it was I who followed you. Perhaps you'd care to explain what you were doing at Aloka Mohta's house?'

'As I said, Sharma is an old friend. What were you doing there? Is it possible you were spying for your former lover? The one that you happened to be harbouring till very recently?'

The fury rose up to choke me as I turned and walked away as fast as I could.

I left the golf course and had to walk for a kilometre or so before finding a cab, but my anger propelled me with speed. By the time I was off my feet, Shayak's message was clear – I had been reckless, endangering myself and, more importantly to Shayak, possibly the investigation with my ill-advised snooping.

Now, more than ever, I wanted to talk to Mallika Mitra. I tried her number again, in vain. Why wasn't she taking my calls? Why didn't her friends seem to know her whereabouts? Had the circumstances been different, I told myself, I would have gone straight to the police with what I had learnt some time ago. But I knew there would be no controlling what happened afterwards.

But Shayak was wrong: I still could help here. And there was only one thing left for me to do: track Mallika down.

It was lunchtime at Khana Khazana. Vineeta was behind the counter, flipping through a book, and she didn't notice me approach over the bustle of mealtime chatter and cutlery striking the plates and doors swinging shut – the rhythmic music of a restaurant.

'Vineeta,' I said, stopping in front of the cash counter behind which she was perched, dressed in a lavender silk sari, silver earrings dangling from her ears, hair pulled tightly back from her face. Luckily, her husband was nowhere to be seen.

She looked up and, for a split second before the smile came, her eyes narrowed.

'Reema,' she said. 'What brings you here? Not lunch, I suppose.'

'No, not today, Vineeta. I need to have a word with you.'

'This isn't a good time, really,' she said.

'I didn't think it would be. But I think you know where Mallika is.'

'Why would you think that?'

'Why did she leave so suddenly?'

'I don't know.' She held her hands very still. I knew she was lying.

'Perhaps you could hazard a guess.'

'I don't see why I should answer any of your questions.'

'Vineeta, she's your friend. All I want to do is help her. And I think you know a lot more about her than you have let on. Like what happened between her and Prakash Agarwal all those years ago.'

Vineeta's kohl-lined eyes widened, and her veneer of civility slipped for just a second to reveal a deep vein of panic. She stood up and looked around quickly. There were far too many people too close at hand, and though I had spoken in barely a whisper, it was undoubtedly wiser not to carry on this conversation in public.

'Come with me,' she hissed, walking towards the wide doors that led to the kitchen. She ushered me in after her, her confused staff watching as we disappeared through another door after that. The room was in darkness, but as soon as Vineeta closed the door behind us the aroma told me where we were. The shelves lining the narrow space in which we stood were laden with the essentials of every Indian kitchen: spices. And when Vineeta flipped on a light, I saw that underneath them were vats of provisions – dals, rice, flour. Despite the ugliness that had brought me here, I couldn't help taking in an extra lungful of their combined perfume.

'How do you know about that?' Vineeta whispered.

'It was a police case. It wasn't so hard to find out. She shared it with you, didn't she? That is why you got so defensive when your husband mentioned him that night at the dinner.'

She nodded slowly. 'The only reason she told me was because we were close to the Agarwal family a few years ago. Mallika warned me that leaving my daughter alone with him would not be a good idea.'

'But you were on good terms with him after that?'

'Yes.'

'Why?'

'Why not? Who Mallika likes and doesn't like isn't the sole determiner of who I associate with.'

'He's a friend.'

'Yes.'

'And that doesn't affect your relationship with Mallika?'

'Whatever happened with Mallika was twenty-five years ago. And it was never proven. In some way, it was her word against his.'

'You believe him?'

'It's not like that!' she said. And then, it was as though she finally remembered who I was. 'Anyway, I don't see how any of this is your business.' Her mouth was a snarl of contempt.

'I told you – I need to know for my article.'

'You write about food, Reema, not murder.'

'Not this time. So you can either tell me what you know or put me in touch with Mallika. Or I will have to print whatever information I have, and it won't look good for your friend.'

'You don't understand,' said Vineeta.

'So explain it to me.'

'When Mallika's marriage hit a rough patch, she blamed Agarwal.'

'Why?'

'She said that she had never been able to trust men after what he had done to her. When she and Siddhartha couldn't have children, he wanted to adopt. She refused. She said it never felt right. I don't think she ever got over it. And Agarwal wouldn't back down, even for a moment. But I never thought she would go this far.'

'You believe Mallika killed Agarwal?'

I saw a flash of hesitation in her eyes. 'I don't know what I believe.'

I would get nothing more from Vineeta. She was already moving away from me, towards the narrow door of the pantry. As I turned to leave, I saw through the corner of my eye a shelf of spices, the new labels on their green-and-orange jars peering out at me. It looked as though there were enough saffron in there to cover a small field. Beauty blooms in the unlikeliest of places.

As we stepped out of the pantry, I cringed. There before me was Manish Solanki. He looked from my face to his wife's with surprise. 'Did I interrupt something?'

I shot Vineeta a look, and she hardly seemed capable, in that moment, of coming up with a plausible reason for the two of us hanging out in the pantry. 'No, Vineeta was just showing me the lovely batch of saffron you have in stock.'

'It's very expensive, you know.'

'Yes, I am aware of that.'

'And it's real. From Kashmir. None of that fake stuff that most people use.'

I smiled, too exhausted to care.

'You better write that down. Don't you go printing lies about our restaurant.'

'Manish, she isn't here to write about us.'

He gave a snort. 'No, of course not. We don't sell pig dumplings, do we?'

'Perhaps you should try castor bean halwa instead. That would make it into the news, no?' I said with a smile.

'Very funny, Reema,' said Manish, finally cracking a grudging smile. 'Why make the lifestyle pages when I can make headlines by killing my wife's customers?' Like every bully, he backed off when pushed back.

I turned to his wife. 'Goodbye Vineeta,' I said.

Vineeta looked disgusted with both of us, and gave me only a cursory nod of dismissal.

SEVENTEEN

I felt like I wasn't thinking straight. Between Aloka and Agarwal, the magazine and the mystery, my overloaded head was simply unable to sort and file and analyse in the manner it was used to.

I could think of only one activity that would help me recalibrate: baking. And lightweight muffins or brownies, the kind that I could handle in my kitchenette, simply would not cut it. I needed to pull out the heavy-duty baked goods.

I called my mother. 'Ma, can I use your kitchen tonight?'

'Only if we can eat what you are cooking.'

'It will be dessert. And it might be a little bit late. Is that okay?'

'If you have to ask about that, you don't know your mother at all.'

She promised to organize dinner. I headed to the grocery store to get my supplies. And then I rushed to my mother's house as quickly as I could. I let myself in and was almost taken down by Batul's enthusiasm and girth. The next fifteen minutes were spent scratching the retriever's demanding belly, then I headed to the kitchen. For the next few hours, Batul aside, I would have the house to myself. Exactly what I needed.

It wasn't often that I worked up the courage to attempt puff pastry. But I knew the theory well enough, and I was in the mood to be patient. I began by bringing the dough together as delicately as possible, before stashing it in the fridge. Then, with Batul passed out at my feet, I pulled my notebook out of my bag and started to jot down my thoughts.

Unlike my pastry, there were no clear steps to solving a murder. And I had too many suspects with too many motives and decidedly too little evidence.

A man was dead. Poisoned.

The wife had once accused her husband of attempting to extort dowry. She admittedly disliked him, if not hated him.

And then there was this ancient accusation of molestation. Where did that leave Mallika and her husband?

What about the Solankis? Hateful Manish. Cold Vineeta. Undercurrents with every word spoken.

I had at least ruled out business partner Mayank Gupta and Shayak. Dhyan I had never considered as a suspect. He had brought me a piece of evidence, which he had had no need to do. It was a different matter that I was convinced that the evidence had nothing to do with the murder of Prakash Agarwal.

I left my notepad and returned to my pastry. The dough was cool enough to work with. I took it out and shaped an obscene amount of butter into a square. I rolled out the dough into a rectangle and wrapped it in the dough and then began to slowly, painstakingly roll again.

I rolled and folded, folded and rolled. As my pastry began to take shape, ideas came together in my head. About both Aloka and Agarwal. And then I put the dough in the freezer to rest once again before heading back to my notes. Then another round of rolling, as I ignored the ache in my arms. The amount of discomfort I could endure now was directly proportionate to how good the end product would be; an unfathomably complex result of skill, patience and a good deal of chemistry. Every mouthful should be light and rich all at once, and the eater would never know the effort that had gone into it.

The skilled chef knows never to take simplicity for granted.

Just like the skilled detective. Every crime is as flawed as the people who commit them, and it is usually the most predictable people who are the perpetrators, acting for the most predictable reasons. But when it all came together, sometimes the mechanics were difficult to recognize; hidden under layer after layer of light-as-air deceit.

I heard the main door open. The ladies were home.

'I smell pizza,' I yelled out. Not the gourmet precursor I had expected for my dessert.

'Yes, but it's the good stuff. We stopped by Fire & Ice.'

'Great. It's going to be a rich dinner.'

'Which is why we have some very light white wine to give it company,' shouted my mom from the living room.

Hema Masi walking into the kitchen. 'Ooh, Reema, puff pastry? That's very impressive.'

'Try it first before you decide that.'

'I am sure it will be lovely. What are you making?'

'It's a surprise.'

'How long will it be?' asked my mother.

'Not long now. I'll put it together at the end, after dinner.'

'So come and sit with us.'

'Soon.'

I had begun to lose my pleasant concentration when luckily my mother cracked open the wine and she and Hema Masi retreated to the living room, leaving me alone, once again, with my thoughts.

It was back to the fridge one last time. As I stashed the pastry in the fridge, I turned my attention to the cream. After all that trouble over the pastry, I was going to keep the filling simple. I added sugar and a few drops of vanilla extract to the cream and turned on the electric beater. Once it had turned into a pillow of goodness, I stashed it in the fridge and took the pastry out. More rolling and folding followed before it was finally ready for the oven.

I briefly joined the ladies for my slices.

'What did I miss?' I asked, grabbing my Fire of Bengal and taking a sip of wine.

'Another shopping spree,' said my mother.

'This time, it was only gifts from New Market.'

After dinner, they showed me the day's loot before I retreated to the kitchen to finish up dessert. I cut the pastry and popped it into the oven. Then I chopped up the strawberries, which were too tart to do without some sugar. Soon, I was assembling my mille-feuilles. I chose pristine white plates and layered the beautifully browned pastry with strawberries and dollops of cream. Three individually plated tiers, covered by a final snowy dusting of icing sugar.

I carried out the plates to a chorus of oohs and aahs. Taking her first bite, my mother looked at me with awe. 'Reema, this is fabulous.'

'Really?' I said.

'You've come a long way, sweetheart,' said Hema Masi with a smile. And she would know. Many of my holidays during my four years of college involved staying with Hema Masi for weeks. We'd spent so much time in the kitchen – I'd be at the oven while she cooked for the family. Muffins, brownies, cakes, many of which had set off the smoke alarms and ended up in the trash can. 'This is restaurant quality.'

I took a bite. I had to agree with her. Silently, of course.

'Reema, wake up! Wake up!'

I opened a bleary eye and saw my mother's anxious face inches from mine, her hands raised, poised for another shove.

'What? What's happened?'

'Aloka Mohta is on TV!'

I sped to the living room where Hema Masi was seated on the couch.

Aloka's distressed face filled the flat-screen. It looked like she was reading from a script.

'We have kept her safe for this long,' she said, voice trembling ever so slightly. 'If you don't pay the ransom within twenty-four hours, that will no longer be the case.' Aloka looked into the camera, eyes filled with distress.

And then there was darkness.

'How horrible!' my mother said. 'I had read about the kidnapping, of course, but this – this is just awful! No matter what she has done to you!'

'What *has* she done to you?' asked Hema Masi with alarm.

'Nothing at all,' I said.

'What do you mean? She stole your boyfriend – your fiancé!' my mother objected.

'That is the woman Amit married? She's been kidnapped?'

'He married her only for her money,' said Ma.

'Even if that were true, this is hardly the time to discuss it.'

'Poor girl,' said Hema Masi.

We continued to watch the news broadcast. The words 'Breaking News' filled half the screen; the newscaster was doing a recap of the events that had led to the dramatic airing of the tape. Aloka Mohta is kidnapped from one of the main thoroughfares of Calcutta a little after 11.30 pm by a masked man. The following day, a phone call is made to Aloka's father, a steel baron, for a ransom of ₹2 crore. Then, an e-mail, followed by more silence, ended by the arrival of a video at News Now, hand delivered to the lobby by an unknown person. It is left on the stairs of the building in an oversized box in the early hours in a package guaranteed to arouse

The Masala Murder

suspicion. A security guard opens it to find a note saying that the CD contained in the box is of the utmost importance. The guard alerts the chief of security, the chief of security alerts the chief of news and the video is on air almost continuously ever since.

And now, it was back on. This time I saw it from the beginning. There was Aloka on a cheap plastic chair, with a blank white wall behind her. She looked straight into the camera, and apart from her weary look and a few dirt smudges on her face and arms, she looked unharmed. She wore a pink T-shirt and jeans. It had a handheld-camera, reality-TV kind of feel.

She cleared her throat and began to read. 'It has been ten days and we have been very patient with you. Just because we have chosen not to make threats of violence, you seem to think you will get your daughter back somehow, without making the payment. What we ask for is not much, and is surely nothing considering it is in exchange for the life of your daughter. And yet you seem unwilling to pay. So if it is threats that you want, it is threats that you'll get. As you can see, we have kept her safe for so long. If we don't get the ransom within twenty-four hours, that will no longer be the case.'

Cut to the studio. There sat Barsha Das, Calcutta's hottest news anchor.

'What will the Mohta family's response be to this latest video? Keep watching News Now to find out.'

Ad break. I ignored my mother's searching look as I walked out of the room to the bedroom. I shut the door and called Amit. 'Are you watching the news?'

'Yes,' he said.

'Have you heard anything apart from this?'

'No. But I have to do something.'

'What can you do? And now, with the police officially looking for you.'

'I don't know, but I have to think of something. I can't let this charade go on any longer.'

I hung up and called Ojha. Perhaps he could tell me what the police intended to do after this latest threat. The phone rang and rang and, just as I was about to disconnect, he answered.

First there was silence.

'Hello?' I said.

'I'll call you back,' he whispered, hanging up.

I paced my old bedroom as I waited, considering what I had just seen. Something, I wasn't sure what, was bothering me about the video. Finally, in about five minutes, Ojha called back.

'How are Sharma and crew reacting to this ransom video?'

'We are at the house now; that is why I couldn't talk. The family are panicking. For the first time, I think they feel it may actually be another gang that is behind the kidnapping, not the husband.'

'Finally.'

'Yes, Sharma is not very happy.'

'Are they getting ready to pay?'

'I think so.'

'When?'

'I am not sure. A text message has also come with instructions on how to pay, where to pay. There is a drop point somewhere. I think the time is noon tomorrow. I don't have those details. They are keeping that information very secret for now.'

I returned to the living room, and found that the news channel was playing the ransom video almost on loop. I kept watching, trying to figure out what it was that was bothering me about it.

The anchor was interviewing everyone the station could find – distant relatives and friends of the family, none of whom knew anything but pretended to – and then finally, about an hour into the non-stop coverage, they seemed to find time for something else.

'While the city waits with bated breath for the safe return

The Masala Murder

of Aloka Mohta, there have been sudden developments in the investigation into the death of Prakash Agarwal, a prominent city businessmen,' Barsha Das began. 'Agarwal died eight days ago after a brief illness. The police had looked into the events surrounding his death but soon dropped the case, citing insufficient evidence of foul play. But new information has surfaced, casting a shadow over the very doctor who had treated Agarwal on the day of his death. In a dramatic turn of events, a twenty-five-year-old case has been unearthed in which the doctor's wife accused the deceased of sexual molestation, though the charge was eventually dropped. The connection, say the police, is enough for them to reopen the investigation. Though with no dead body for autopsy and enough time for any physical evidence to have been possibly destroyed by now, one police insider confessed, on condition of anonymity, that it may be too late for justice.'

I felt a shock through my system. How had this happened? Had the police made the connection between Prakash Agarwal and Mallika Mitra independently? It seemed highly unlikely, especially coming so soon after my own discovery.

Who else knew what I had learnt? Uncle Kumar and possibly the underling he had sent to physically search for the case files. I first had to rule out his office as the source of the leak. I called Uncle Kumar.

'Did you hear what they said about the Agarwal case?'

'Yes. How did that information get out?'

'That is what I wanted to ask you.'

'I assumed you had decided to take it to Sharma.'

'No. I needed some more time before I did anything with it. I am not even sure what it means yet.'

'Well, I can assure you the information didn't leak out at our end. I have no time for these Barsha Das types.'

'What about the officer you sent to dig out the files?'

'I doubt he would even connect the information he found with the Agarwal case.'

'Are you sure?'

'Quite. But I will still ask. I'll let you know if I hear anything noteworthy.'

'Thank you, and sorry for hurling these accusations at you.'

'Not at all. You need to know how your lead ended up on the morning news.'

I hung up and thought fast. Shayak had seemed to have some inkling of what I had learnt when I met him yesterday afternoon, only hours after I had found out myself. And he had been hanging out with Sharma. That would explain his irritation with me if he thought I was the source of the leak, especially as he seemed annoyed that I had discovered that link at all.

If Sharma himself was behind the news flash, that left me with one question – how did he get wind of it? And there was only one possible answer.

I dialled again. 'Mr Ojha, did you tell Ravi Sharma about my break in the Agarwal case?'

Silence.

'Mr Ojha?'

'No, actually, you see ... actually I mentioned it to DDG sir, and he mentioned that it was a good lead, police would look like fools when it came out.'

'And then what did you do?'

'Then I met sir, and I told him that there was something he might want to look into.'

'Mr Ojha, that was my lead! Why didn't you at least check with me first?'

'But Reema ji, I didn't see the harm. Our group, you know, we always aim to help the police, isn't it? So now police can find Mallika Mitra, who is absconding, and they can arrest her, no?'

'Mallika Mitra is not the murderer!'

'She isn't? But I thought ... Then it is the husband?'

'No, it isn't him either! It has almost nothing to do with either of them!'

'Then what—'

'I am not sure yet. But what I do know is that I have to figure it out fast, before Mallika Mitra is arrested and put through hell because of our meddling!'

I tossed the phone onto the bed and shook my head. While I knew I was on the verge of a breakthrough, there was still some distance to go before I came to a definitive conclusion. On top of that, everything had escalated all at once. But the living always came before the dead, so the kidnapping case would have to come before the murder.

I had to get my hands on Aloka's ransom video.

*

When I finally came into the living room, my mother and Hema Masi were still watching the drama unfold on TV.

My mother looked up at me. 'Reema, tell me what is going on.'

'What do you mean?' I asked, sitting down.

My mother pursed her lips. A powerful action, in an instant able to remind me of her constant dissatisfaction, a memory I had carried with me for as long as I could remember. And now those lips in a still almost painfully pretty face moved to renew their censure. 'You are worried about something. I can tell.'

'It's just work, Ma,' I said, looking at Hema Masi for support. But this time, she seemed to be on my mother's side.

'Don't look at your biggest cheerleader. You can't hide from me,' said Ma.

'It is nothing to do with you ... It's just ...'

'Nothing to do with me? What is that supposed to mean?'

I quickly interjected. 'I don't mean it like that. What I am trying to say is—'

'You have a case, don't you?' Hema Masi had spoken. Always saw too much, did Hema Masi.

I found my mother staring at me with round eyes, aghast. 'Oh Reema! Is that true? Are you involved in Aloka's case? Are you having an affair with Amit?'

'Ma! Of course not! What's wrong with you?'

'Then what?'

There was no point in denying it any longer. 'Amit came to me for help.'

'You are in touch with him? How can you let him near you after what he did?'

'We met again a few months ago. He wants to be friends.'

'Why? Why would you let him back into your life?'

'We've known each other since we were babies.'

'And then he treated you like you meant nothing.'

'We were young.'

'You were in love!'

'Without really knowing what any of that meant.'

'So you are helping him?' 'Yes. What kind of person would I be if I didn't?' How many times would I repeat those words before this thing was through?

'I don't understand you.'

'Why not?'

'You've been doing so well in your new job!'

'It's not new any longer. I've been doing it for two years now and—'

'And what?' she interrupted. 'You are bored of writing about food, too?'

'Too? I don't remember ever saying that I was bored of being an investigator,' I scowled.

'So then why did you stop?'

I had never gone into the details of my failed business with my parents. 'I didn't stop. Not really. I work on whatever cases I can find.'

'And this is the only case you could find!'

'Why can't you ever be happy about anything I do?'

My mother turned to face me at last, and even through my anger I could see I had hurt her.

'What makes you say that?'

'What was the last decision I made that you were actually happy with?'

My mother's expression turned to dismay. 'I am not unhappy with you! I am just worried – I want you to be happy in your career, in your life, that's all! If this is what makes you happy, then do it. I am only wondering why you left it in the first place.'

I said nothing. I had assumed they would be so happy that my PI chapter had ended that they wouldn't care what had brought it about. 'But you hated my being a detective!'

'At first, maybe. But once I realized that you weren't putting yourself in danger, I came to terms with the fact that you were just following your heart. Just as I had when I decided to become an actress. In my day, it was just as unacceptable a choice. But it was my dream. So how could I hold your dreams against you?'

'Oh, Ma.'

'Why else do you think I stopped badgering you! Not only did I approve, I was so very proud! And I still am.'

My mother gave my hand a tight squeeze and I could stop the tears no longer. She reached over to wipe them away. 'Why should that make you cry?'

'You've never said that to me before.' Now it was my turn to watch a tear roll down her face.

'Well, that was very, very stupid of me,' she said, handing me a tissue. 'I am so proud that my beautiful daughter can do anything she sets her mind to. What mother wouldn't be?'

But then all conversation came to a halt, for on the news was Amit.

'What!' I cried.

'What is the matter?' asked Ma.

'The police are looking for him! What is he doing there?'

Barsha Das blabbered on, but I had eyes only for Amit. Since I had seen him last he had shaved his beard, had a haircut and found a nice kurta. He'd also lost the air of anxiety somewhere. He looked angry, alone, vulnerable and determined.

'BREAKING NEWS', the screen screamed.

'A News Now exclusive. The prime suspect in the kidnapping of Aloka Mohta – her husband Amit Majumdar – is now in our studio.'

'That swine,' my mother said.

'Shh.'

'Amit, why did you choose to come to the News Now studio despite the fact the police have launched a city-wide manhunt for you?'

'Because my priority right now is finding my wife.'

'But the police have been treating you as the prime suspect in her kidnapping. You were believed to be in hiding.'

'I was not in hiding, and if they want me, then they should come and get me right now. But before that, I want Kishan Mohta to know that his daughter is at risk. He has stuck to the belief that I am the man behind Aloka's disappearance. I am here to say that I am not, that I want my wife back as badly as he wants his daughter back. If I had the money I would pay the ransom myself, but I do not. If he wants the police to arrest me, I am here, in the studio; they can come here and I will make no effort to escape or resist. But please, please, do whatever it takes to bring Aloka back to safety.'

'Oh dear,' said Hema Masi.

Even my mother, despite herself, seemed moved by this dramatic appeal.

'What are you going to do?' my mother asked me.

I shrugged. 'I have to wait for some information. I hope to get it by the end of the day, but till then there is nothing much I can do.'

'That will be cutting it close. They have given the family till tomorrow to pay up. Final deadline, apparently,' said Hema Masi.

'Poor boy,' Ma said. 'Up against the crass Mohta family with all the money in the world.'

Despite my anger at Amit, I had to try hard to suppress a smile. If he could move my mother with that little performance, he could move mountains. Yes, a public appeal had been quite the PR masterstroke.

'I understand now, Reema. What kind of a person could resist trying to help him through this?'

Not Amit's ex-girlfriend, for sure, the one with the superhero complex.

Amit was right about one thing: I hadn't changed at all. How well he knew me.

EIGHTEEN

As I waited, I found it impossible to sit at home and watch the endless drama unfold on TV. I knew that once the kidnapping case was resolved, Sharma would waste no time in shifting his attention to Prakash Agarwal's murder now that the spotlight was back on. That didn't leave me very long to right the wrong I had done to Mallika Mitra.

I walked into Middle Kingdom through the front door. No disguise; the all-black outfit was usual enough for me. It was late for lunch – there were just two other tables occupied. It was also late enough that I knew that Abhimanyu would have most likely left – in fact, I was counting on it. But there was another unexpected problem: the waiters, who still recognized me from my meetings with Mallika and the chef, were very attentive, so attentive, in fact, that I couldn't help a moment's hesitation. But I reminded myself that if I was patient, an opportunity was bound to present itself.

The restroom was upstairs. Just across the narrow hall was Mallika's office. I hoped to find what I was looking for there – some indication of where she was now. I could then track her down and

The Masala Murder

tell her what had happened, and warn her to lie low till I was able to sort out the mess I had created.

I finished my meal, paid my bill and waited for the servers to leave the area in which I was seated, which I had chosen specifically because it was far enough from the kitchen and sufficiently obscured to be inconspicuous. As soon as the dining room was empty of staff, I slipped up the stairs, treading as gently as possible on the hard ceramic tile, soft-soled shoes making barely a sound.

I entered the restroom and flipped on the light. After an appropriate pause I left, closing the door behind me. If I managed to return quickly, my reappearance downstairs wouldn't arouse suspicion. But if I couldn't find what I needed, I would have to slip inside Mallika's flat. I knew that the level with the office and restroom were connected to the rest of the house. I hoped that her staff would simply assume that I had left or, if they had heard me going up to the restroom, they would think I had finished my business and exited when no one was around.

The lock was of good quality but luckily I had spent my idle time during my detective agency days well, mastering the kind of tricks they hadn't taught in college. In under twenty seconds, I found myself inside Mallika's dark office. The only light was streaming in from between blinds on the solitary window. As my eyes slowly regained focus, I was able to distinguish the outline of the desk. I walked around and found the switch to the table lamp. I turned it on and quickly scanned the surface for anything out of place. There was nothing except a pen stand, a ledger and a diary with a few scribbled recipes. If Mallika had left in a rush, there was no sign of it here. I went through the three drawers and found little of interest – a draft for a food-festival menu, some loose change, a well-thumbed copy of the Gitanjali.

I looked around and saw that in the corner of the small room was an armchair beside which stood a small, beautifully crafted antique Chinese table. The woman undeniably had taste. There were a few books on top of it and, as I approached it in the dim light, I saw what looked like an appointment book.

I picked it up and began to leaf through the pages. I flipped to the day before Agarwal's death; there was no mention of a trip to his house. I moved forward to the day after the dinner – the day that she had stopped taking my calls. She had penned in some sort of engagement or task to carry out everyday. So leaving town had definitely not been on the cards.

Then I heard a noise. I moved towards the door but before I could make my exit, I heard footsteps. I stood perfectly still, listening. No need to panic; it was probably just the waiters checking the bathroom. They'd see the light on, think someone was in there and go back downstairs.

But no, something was terribly wrong. The steps were getting louder, and closer, and coming not from outside the door I had entered but from the other corner of the room, from Mallika's flat.

I desperately looked for a place to conceal myself, but I was too late. The door swung open. I had nowhere to go, nowhere to hide.

I was too afraid to look up so I gazed at the floor. I knew at once that the shoes were familiar. And the white of those pants left me in no doubt.

Sharma. The man who had made it clear that if he'd see me anywhere near anything to do with his cases, he would teach me the lesson I seemed to have missed in biology class: that my nose belonged firmly on my face and not in his murder investigation.

There was nothing to do but stand my ground – and lie, lie, lie.

Eye to eye, Sharma saw no need to mask his reaction. 'You!' he said.

'Nice to see you, Uncle Sharma,' I said, smiling my warmest smile.

'You! What are you doing here?'

It seemed Sharma was content to let me hog all the good lines in this latest act of our ongoing drama. 'Quite a coincidence, isn't it?'

'What are you doing here?' he repeated.

'Mallika sent me.'

'Mallika?'

'Yes. The owner of this office.'

'I am aware of that! But what has she sent you for?'

'This,' I said, holding out the diary for him.

He narrowed his eyes at me, deeply suspicious – as usual. 'Why?'

'I suppose she needs it.'

'Why you?'

'It seems that not everyone thinks I am as irresponsible as you do.'

'How did you get in?'

'Through the door.'

He glared. I pointed.

'Check it for forced entry. I can guarantee that you won't find any.'

'What does she want the diary for?'

'I don't know, she didn't tell me that.'

'Where is she?'

'I don't know that at the moment.'

'Then how will you get it to her?'

'She said she would call later tonight to let me know.'

Sharma glared at me. He walked up to me, an inch or two closer than necessary, and took the diary from me. He quickly glanced through it.

Thankfully, Sharma seemed indisposed for further conversation. He looked around the small room, rifled through some drawers and picked up a ledger. His eyes then rested on the small antique table in the corner, and he crossed the room as I had done minutes earlier. Finding nothing more of interest, he continued to glare at me and I could only guess what was going on behind those contemptuous eyes.

'Come with me,' he said at last.

'Where?'

'You'll see.'

Sharma, hot on my heels, led me through Mallika's flat and to the ground floor; a squad car was parked just outside the building. I was going to see the inside of a jail after all.

My shoulders threatened to slump as I was led away. But then I remembered my mother's words of advice to me, when I was auditioning for a high school play. 'Never let them see your discomfort. Head back, chin up. Even if you are dying inside, it's the illusion of confidence that matters.'

What was this if not a stage? What was I doing if not play-acting? For it was becoming increasingly clear that a real detective I was not.

But I would rather spear myself with my lock pick than let the inspector see my doubt.

※

If Sharma's strategy was to bore me into a confession, it was working. After we got to the police station, he had me sit in a back room and sternly instructed me to not move an inch. I wouldn't have dared, of course. I may not lack for courage, but suicide wasn't on the day's agenda.

I had a feeling I was being watched, but I could not for the life of me figure out how. There was no telltale mirror – which decades of police shows had taught me were one-way glass – and there was no camera in sight. But I knew Sharma had his eye on me.

I reached into my pocket and felt for it: the pearl earring. It was such a pretty little thing, girly in the way that Mallika Mitra was and I was not.

Who knows what other evidence she had left behind the night she was there?

It didn't take me long to grow restless. I may have been quite content under different circumstances to play Sharma's game of patience, but I knew the longer I was here, the harder it would be to get to Aloka in time. Sharma had even taken away my phone so I had no idea whether Shweta had managed to get a copy of the ransom video I had asked her to. That was the key to this whole thing: I needed a better look at that video.

It must have been a good two hours later when the door finally opened. I didn't have the energy in me to look up, to take on Sharma again.

So much suspicion. That is what my days of work amounted to.

So many dreams. That is what my whole life could be reduced to.

Once again, I started with the shoes. But those didn't belong to Sharma, who wore round-toed, black, chunky schoolboy regulation issue. These were brown, beautifully crafted and tapering. I looked up.

Shayak.

I groaned. Out loud. I couldn't help it. If there was one man who trusted me less than Sharma it was Shayak Gupta.

'What are you doing here?' I asked. 'Dropped by to rub it in?'

Shayak glared at me without saying a word. After a brief, blank second, a flash of – what was it, could that actually be approval? – he took a step forward and Sharma followed on his tail.

'Yes, Inspector. I sent Reema to try to find out Mallika Mitra's whereabouts.'

'Why?'

'Because I don't believe Mallika is guilty. In fact, I am sure she is not.'

'But till yesterday, you hadn't mentioned Reema was working for you!'

'Sir,' Shayak interrupted, 'I assure you, I would have had it come up. But right now, the need is to locate a woman who may hold the key to this case. Reema is a detective by training and quite a good one at that.'

'A detective!' exclaimed Sharma, looking at me with a mix of disbelief and surprise.

I didn't respond.

'But she is a journalist.'

'That is merely one of her many talents.'

Sharma seemed far from satisfied, and my own confusion mounted with every word Shayak spoke. But I maintained my stony silence, looking with what I hoped was some degree of assurance from one man to the other.

*

'And how exactly did you plan to get out of there?'

Shayak was livid. No sooner had we stepped out of the police station did he flung those words at me with barely concealed fury.

I didn't answer.

'Are you incapable of paying heed to advice?' he said.

'Advice? What advice? And whose?'

'I am referring to our chat at the driving range.'

'Advice!' I laughed. 'More like condescending officiousness.'

Shayak's lips formed a thin line. I realized too late that my words could be interpreted as lacking gratitude for his saving my hide.

Too bad – I hadn't asked to be saved.

'Get in the car,' he said coldly.

He pointed at a black sedan by the curb.

He stood with the driver's side door open, looking at me with clear impatience. 'Get in the car.'

'Why should I?'

'Are you aware, Reema Ray, of how close you just came to becoming a serious suspect in the murder of Prakash Agarwal?'

'Me?' I let out a dismissive laugh, feigning amusement when I felt nothing of the sort.

'Hardly a laughing matter, I would think.'

'It's a ludicrous suggestion. Give me one reason why.'

'Why not? You were seen coming and going from the victim's house, lurking around on other occasions, asking questions of the police and anyone else who would listen, at complete odds with your professed profession of food writer. Add to that a break-in and you have been displaying pretty suspicious behaviour in anyone's books.'

I was guilty as charged, but I would not dream of letting him hear me say that. 'And what about you? You obviously have more to do with this business than you have let on. You are working with the cops!'

'For which you should be grateful! This was not the first conversation I have had to have with Sharma about you – who is a hardly at fault here, by the way – and I have had increasing trouble convincing him that you are a well-intentioned, if overly inquisitive, young journalist. Thus his surprise at suddenly finding us suddenly "working together".'

By this time I needed a seat, so I finally sat in the car as ordered, trying to process what I had just heard.

'But–' I began.

Shayak sat in the driver's seat and pulled away from the curb.

'Why didn't you tell me?'

'I tried. Without revealing my own position. You weren't very receptive, were you?'

I let that sink in.

'Only incidentally, of course, but how were you planning on getting out of that spot, exactly?'

'Just like I got in – through the front door. He hadn't charged me with anything.'

'He could have.'

'I would have liked to see him make it stick.'

'Believe me, you wouldn't. Why were you in Mallika's office anyway?'

'Why were you at the police station?'

'I happened to stop by to speak to Sharma. Lucky for you, I would say.'

Silence.

'Coming back to you,' he said pointedly. 'What possessed you to break in?'

'I didn't – the door was unlocked. I merely turned the handle,' I lied.

He took his eyes off the road to glare at me.

I glared back. 'Why have you been following me?'

Shayak exhaled a long, pent-up breath. 'When I first arrived here–'

'Which was when?' I interrupted.

'Three days before I met you.'

'Before Agarwal died?'

'Yes. I was at the house when you showed up, presumably to pay your respects. The door was open – some guests were leaving – and I let myself in. I was speaking to Mrs Agarwal's brother – I didn't know if I would be welcome in their house, as my brother and Agarwal had parted ways under rather bitter circumstances. Still,

I thought I would visit to make my position clear, as there was a lot of unfinished business that needed to be concluded, including a large amount in dues. And then I overheard what Mrs Agarwal said to you about hating her husband and wanting information about his death.'

'But I was as shocked by that as you were!'

'I didn't know that at the time. I wanted to know why Mrs Agarwal chose you to confide in.'

Shayak stopped talking. We had reached the gate to my home and he parked just ahead of it before turning in his seat to face me.

I looked at him expectantly. 'You know you can trust me, right?' Now I need to know I can trust you. Who are you?'

Shayak handed me his business card.

It was a simple white rectangle with only the words:

Shayak Gupta
CEO
Titanium Securities

'You are a detective?' I asked.

'Something of the sort.'

'You are the private security expert consulting in the kidnapping of Aloka Mohta?'

'How do you know about that?'

'You aren't the only one who has sources. And I followed you and Sharma from the Mohta residence to the golf course, remember?'

Shayak nodded. 'I happened to be in town to help out my brother and it is a rather high-profile case, so my friend called me in to consult on the matter.'

'Friend meaning Sharma?'

'No. Higher than him.'

'Like the commissioner?'

Shayak merely shrugged.

I moved on. 'How do you know that I am trained as a private investigator?'

'There aren't that many detectives in India, and fewer who write film reviews.'

I gaped. 'You have read my crappy reviews? You've known all along?'

'They aren't crappy, by the way. And the introduction to your first piece was quite memorable: "Reema Ray, a real-life gumshoe on the reel-time dicks".'

Ooh, I could kill Shweta about now. 'That was not my doing, I can assure you.'

'The first night I met you, I hadn't made the connection. But it came to me fairly soon after that.'

And here I was thinking that I was being mysterious.

'To answer your question, yes, I know I can trust you,' said Shayak.

'Well, that's progress.'

'Though I really can't understand what possessed you to get so deeply involved in either of these cases.'

'I guess it had been a while. I needed my fix,' I said flippantly.

'Why did you quit in the first place?'

'I haven't given it up entirely, at least not yet. But the whole private practice thing hasn't worked out as well as I may have liked.' I glared out the window in silence, a lump in my throat. I felt his fingers brushing a strand of hair away from my flushed cheek.

And then he dropped them, as though the world had not just skipped a revolution. He reached behind me to the back seat, from where he retrieved a brown manila folder.

'I think it's time to talk.'

'Talk,' I said somewhat blankly.

'About both these cases. Can we go to your place?'

My place? I nodded.

Walking towards the gate, I tried to concentrate on what might be inside the folder in his hands to avoid thinking about his fingers on my face.

But before we made it inside, my phone rang. It was Shweta. 'Reema, I have your tape.'

Finally, things were beginning to move! 'Thank you, thank you, thank you! When and where can I pick it up?'

'We're working late today. Swing by the office any time.'

I looked at Shayak. 'There is something I need to take care of. It's important.'

'More important than murder?'

Shayak Gupta had, somehow, become entwined in both my cases. There was no need to hide the truth any longer. 'Aloka Mohta. Come with me,' I said. 'I need a lift.'

We returned to the car. I gave Shayak directions.

'Do I get to know what is going on?'

'It's a hunch right now. I'll find out soon.'

'Where are we going?'

'To pick up a copy of the ransom tape that has been on air all day.'

'Why do you need that?'

'To enhance the background. You are an investigator. You don't by any chance have image enhancement software, do you?'

'No, but I could send it to Mumbai.'

'No time,' I said, taking my phone out of my bag.

I had already started walking back towards the car. Shayak and I got in and I gave him directions before pulling out my phone to call Terrence. He had always claimed to have access to high-end surveillance equipment. Now was the time to see whether or not he was all talk.

'Terrence, I need your help.'

'Do you, now? After the way you spoke with Ojha, I don't know if you are welcome in the group.'

'Did he tell you what he did to deserve it?'

'Well–'

'Then stop acting like an outraged mother hen. People could be in danger.'

I heard him sigh. 'What do you need?'

'I have some video footage. I need to enhance it.'

'When?'

'Now.'

'God, Reema, you don't ask for much. The office is closed.'

'Look, I know it's late. I wouldn't have asked you if it wasn't important to do this right away.'

'Geez. Okay. You know where my office is?'

'Yes.'

'Meet me there in half an hour.'

꽃

After a detour to the *Face* office to collect the tape, we met Terrence outside the offices of World Wide Eye, the detective agency for which he worked, under a slightly surreal winking logo of the Earth, half of which was covered by a rather stoned-looking eye. It was one of the biggest detective agencies in the city.

Terrence gave me a smug smile before he spotted Shayak.

'Who is this?'

'A friend. He's helping me on the case.'

'A PI?'

I looked at Shayak for the answer. 'Not quite,' he said.

Terrence tried staring some more information out of the

unexpected guest. He got nothing but a stonier stare in return and, bravado sufficiently withered, he turned around to open the copious numbers of locks protecting the door.

'From an agency of this calibre, I had expected something a little more hi-tech than – what is it, ten? – locks.'

'There's nothing wrong with a lock,' replied Terrence. 'Imagine what happens to those fancy electronic alarm systems when the power goes out.'

'Power back-up,' I heard Shayak mumble under his breath.

Terrence finally had the door unlocked and we followed him into the dark hall, at the end of which was a room. Terrence flipped on the light to reveal three computers with large screens, scanners, audio equipment and other paraphernalia.

I handed him the DVD and paced the small room as the system started up.

'What will we be looking at here?'

'Aloka Mohta's ransom video.'

'Why bother, just turn on the TV. It's been playing all day.'

'I need an enhanced view of what's going on in the background.'

'Okay,' said Terrence, opening the file.

'It has been ten days and we have been very patient with you,' I heard Aloka say again, for the nth time. 'Just because we have chosen not to make threats of violence, you seem to think you will get your daughter back somehow, without making the payment.'

And the unsaid message: anything happens to Aloka and the whole world knows that it is because Kishan Mohta was too greedy and selfish to pay up the ransom.

As the video approached the end, the handheld camera shifted an inch or two.

'Here it is, freeze this frame,' I said.

The shaking hand holding the camera had inadvertently provided the briefest glimpse of the window behind Aloka.

'Blow up the part of the frame with the window.'

It only took a few seconds to bring it into view, but I still could not be sure what I was seeing. 'Can you enhance this green area?'

Terrence got to work and in a couple of minutes, he had cleared things up as best as he could.

When he finished, my hands were shaking.

'This isn't as easy as they make it look on TV, you know,' he said, defensive in the face of my silence.

'No, it's not, but you've given me exactly what I need,' I said softly.

'A palm tree is what you need?'

'A palm tree, and this grey protrusion,' I said, pointing at the screen.

'It looks like a dirty rock.'

'And I know exactly where it is.'

'You can tell from this picture where this rock is?'

'Yes.'

'This rock is enough to tell you where this woman is being held?' asked Terrence with surprise.

But I was already on the move, 'Thanks Terrence, I owe you one.'

'A big one!' he shouted after me.

Shayak followed me out.

'Thanks for your help tonight,' I said.

'I'm coming with you.'

'Where?'

'To get Aloka.'

'No, you're not.'

'It could be dangerous.'

'I'm not going alone.'

I pulled out my phone.

'Who are you calling?'

'The police.'

'Sharma?' Shayak asked with a raised eyebrow.

'Hardly.'

'Sharad Kumar?'

'Is there anything you don't know about me?'

'Plenty, I'm sure. Tell him I am here. And that I am coming with you.'

I was shaking my head in a loud 'no' when Uncle Kumar picked up.

'I need your help,' I said. 'I know where she is.'

'Who, my dear?'

'Aloka.'

'And here I was in the middle of a dinner party.'

'Sorry, but this can't wait.'

'Of course not.'

I gave him an outline of what I believed had occurred.

'Sweetheart, it pains me to say this but it's not me you should be calling, it's Ravi Sharma. This is his case.'

'But—'

'He's not a bad cop, Reema.'

'I thought you hated each other.'

'I wouldn't put it that way. Our politics don't match, but that is about it.'

'That's not what I've heard from Baba.'

'People make more out of professional disputes than there is. That case, the one we fell out about. You remember it?'

'A woman was killed. They believed it was the lover. Sharma asked for a CBI enquiry.'

'Exactly. And it was that simple. Except that since the boy was Muslim and the girl Hindu, it became a huge issue. Local politicians jumped into the fray and Ravi Sharma, always on the alert when a TV camera is in the vicinity, tried to squeeze every inch of mileage out of it.'

'But that's so unethical.'

'Unethical, yes. Crooked, debatable. I was angry, of course. We had it all wrapped up – confession and all – and the media whipped it into a storm.'

'But Sharma won't listen to me. He hates me.'

'Why would you say that?'

'He arrested me today.'

'What! Why am I hearing about this now?'

'I couldn't call. He took my phone away.'

'Why?'

'He found me where I shouldn't have been.'

'Reema,' he said. 'Breaking in, were you?'

'Yes,' I admitted.

'I'm afraid you've lost my sympathy, seeing as how you are not in the slammer any longer. I'll call him and alert him to your news. If he doesn't respond, I'll go over his head and come in myself. Give me five minutes.'

'Okay. And one more thing,' I said, moving to the side. 'I am with Shayak Gupta. He says he knows you.'

'Shayak is there? Take him with you.'

'Why?'

'He'll keep you safe.'

'But–'

'No buts. That's an order, young lady. Get moving – you've already wasted enough time yapping with me. In fact, get Gupta to call Sharma on the way. He knows him better than I do.'

'Really?' I asked.

Uncle Kumar had hung up. I stared at the receiver before turning around and glaring at Shayak.

'I told you he knows me.'

'Oh, stop.'

'Just stating a fact.'

'What the hell is Titanium Securities anyway?'
Shayak smiled.
'Uncle Kumar said you should call Sharma.'
'Good idea. But we should get going.'

We got into the car and Shayak plugged in his handsfree before pulling out of his spot. I listened to him telling Sharma what we knew.

'He's on board, he'll meet us there. He's asked us to wait before we go in.'

'But—'

'Reema, when all this is over I will give you a long lecture about the merits of working within the system. But for now, please stop asking questions and tell me where the hell I need to go.'

*

We started our drive in silence; Shayak seemed to realize that I didn't want to speak about the case just yet. He played music, extracted as much back story he could about me. He had guessed that food was the best way to soothe me, so he rolled out story after story about his world travels and the crazy things he had eaten. Antarctica to Antigua, he seemed to have been everywhere and tried everything. But he still had told me as little about himself as possible.

Finally, after about three hours on the road, we arrived outside a narrow lane that was overgrown with trees and shrubbery. It had been years since I had been here last – over a decade – but I still recognized it. 'This is it,' I said.

'Are you sure?' asked Shayak. 'There doesn't seem to be anything here.'

'The house is at the end of the lane. Right by the beach.'

'Okay, let's wait.'

'Shayak, I really need to do this myself.'

'That's out of the question. It could be very dangerous.'

'I think it would be safer. They wouldn't harm me,' I said.

'Why?'

My silence, more than anything I may have said, seemed to convince Shayak how much I needed to see this through on my own.

'Are you sure?' he asked.

'Yes. But just in case, back me up.'

Shayak nodded reluctantly. He didn't give me grief about what Sharma might say; I knew he would handle it. 'You'll be unarmed,' he said, pulling his own gun from a compartment under his seat. 'But I'm right behind you.'

I got out of the car. It was an all but uninhabited stretch of coastline. In the darkness, Shayak and I walked along the narrow pathway. Soon we came into view of the house, which was just as I had remembered it.

The rusty gate was locked, but we had no trouble scaling the boundary wall. The small garden had been abandoned to the elements. The grass was overgrown in places and dead in others, the rows of bushes crowded with weeds, palm trees heavy with unwanted coconuts. Underneath one tree was an old water feature, a rock which had been forced onto the sandy landscape. When I had come here as a teenager, the iron-laden water had already discoloured the stone, streaking it with red rivulets. Now, it stood there dry and barren. It was so out of place and so grotesque, it was a dead giveaway, poking its rusty presence into the ransom video.

I pushed the main door; it was unlocked and I let myself in. It was a shoddy job all around: kidnapping wasn't for amateurs.

The house was musty and there was no sign of life as I entered. But I followed my ears and they led me to a room at the rear of the building.

Raised voices. A woman. 'You said it wouldn't go this far!'

'How would I know they would guess so soon!' replied a man, voice hoarse with anger. 'I thought it would be over long before this! But anyhow, what does it matter now? The money is coming, isn't it?'

'So now what?'

'We wait!'

The woman was silent.

'You aren't thinking about giving up, are you? We'll go to jail!'

'He wouldn't–'

'Your blessed father wouldn't have to do anything. The police would–'

I pushed open the old wooden door and it announced my entry with a creak. The room was lit by a flickering hurricane lamp and there stood Amit and Aloka, aghast and exhausted but otherwise none the worse for wear.

'Amit is right. The police can take action, even if your father doesn't, Aloka,' I said.

Aloka let out a cry and covered her mouth, the flickering light accentuating her horror.

Amit closed his eyes. When he opened them, they were drained of every emotion, as though somehow he had been waiting for this moment. 'How did you know?'

'She gave it away, not you,' I said.

'What do you mean?' Aloka asked.

'You once had a birthday party here, remember? We must have been about fourteen years old, you brought us all to your fab beachhouse near Digha. Then I saw that picture of the two of you, here, on your bedside table. The ransom video you took, Amit, was fine till the end, but your shaky smoker's hands eventually gave you away. You provided just a glimpse of a window that revealed a palm tree and that hunk of rock that I recognized as being part of the travesty of a waterfall in the garden. But you really should blame it on the TV channels; they played your little sketch so many times that I couldn't help but notice at some point.'

Husband and wife stared at me without motion, without words. 'It was a good plan,' I continued, 'except that Aloka's father guessed what was going on from the get-go. You've got to give him credit for that, Amit. He could see right through you. And then you had another brilliant idea – you could turn the story around by going to an ex-girlfriend with convenient connections and allege persecution. Who wouldn't lap it up?'

They still said nothing, not even looking at each other.

'In fact, you had prepared for trouble, months in advance. When you started planning this operation, the two of you realized that help might be needed, at some point. Amit, you called to test the waters, to revive our friendship, so you could come to me as a route to Uncle Kumar and the influence and information he could provide, if and when required. When things started off so wrong, you landed up on my doorstep.'

He hadn't counted on getting found out so quickly, however, or on me asking him to move in. No, that had been even beyond his imagination. He couldn't refuse for fear of arousing suspicion.

'When I foolishly allowed you into my home, you thought you'd unnerve me, throw me off balance with your sudden intensity every time I asked uncomfortable questions. Did you really think I'd fall for that?' I said with a coldness I did not feel.

'There must have been someone guarding this place. A caretaker. What did you do to them?' I asked. 'Pay them to leave or will we find them locked up somewhere? Or dead?'

'We didn't hurt anyone,' said Amit.

'So you paid them. At any rate, I can think of a few people you did hurt – Aloka's mother, for one.'

'And you,' said Amit, still clinging to his badge of defiance.

'You needn't worry about that. I had too little faith in you left for hurt.'

The rest would remain unsaid: though my emotions were unscathed, I would never admit to him that he had me shaken to the core. How could I have been deceived of the very fibre of which Amit was made? How could I have trusted him now, loved him then?

'You staged the break-in at your house for my benefit alone?'

'Just a little insurance in case you had doubts.'

'You chose a bad way to do it. It only served to make me suspicious. Why would a kidnapper break into his victim's house? It's too risky. And then when I went back, I found a pair of jeans missing, the hairbrush gone.'

Aloka slouched back on the bed, face in her hands.

'You wanted your wife to be comfortable. You love her, though you have strange ways of showing it. My only question now is why.'

When Amit spoke, his veil of languorous irony was back in place. 'I always knew money couldn't buy me happiness, but desperation – something my father-in-law taught me – was not something I had ever known. He ensured that every path I could have honestly taken was closed to me. Believe it or not, this was almost the only alternative we had.'

'What about starting afresh in another city where he couldn't get to you? Like you'd said?'

He let out a brief, derisive laugh. 'We couldn't even put together enough money for a security deposit to rent a house.'

'And I guess it would have been far too bourgeois of you to have asked someone for financial assistance rather than stage-managing your own wife's kidnapping.'

'It was my idea,' Aloka said, finally finding her voice and injecting far more spirit into the statement than I had imagined her capable of.

'Why?'

'I'm pregnant.'

I saw shame come over Amit's face like a baby's blush.

'We need the money. I can't let my child suffer because my father is too stubborn.'

'Does he know?'

'No. No one knows.'

'You don't think if you told him he might have softened his position?'

'Who gives him the right to decide when to accept me? His opposition to our marriage was always about controlling me and my choices, no matter how personally Amit takes the rejection. Why should he have that kind of power over me again?'

'This is your way of getting back at him?'

'Not of getting back,' said Aloka. 'Of breaking free. Of taking what's mine; what I am entitled too.'

'It's your father's money and he has every right to dispense with it as he chooses.'

She shook her head impatiently. 'I would have agreed with you at one time, till he left us without any means to support ourselves. Even your own father doesn't have the right to doom you to a life of penury. I wasn't looking for a paid holiday for life. ₹2 crore isn't so very much for him, but it is enough to set us up somewhere so we could start afresh, make our own way in the world and keep something aside for our child.'

'But what will happen to the baby now?'

Aloka shrugged. 'It's no worse than when we started out.'

'What if you both end up in jail?'

'On what charges?'

'Fraud, extortion, who knows what else.'

A look of contempt came over Aloka's face, and she shrugged. 'We'll see about that. Maybe Daddy darling, who didn't want to cough up the ransom, will pay to keep his daughter out of jail and scandal away from the family.'

'I think it is a little late for that.'

I had heard what I needed to. I turned to the door behind me; it was the signal Shayak had been waiting for to enter the room. There was not a word of protest as husband and wife were led away.

I think it was the intensity of my gaze that forced Amit to look at me. All I saw staring back at me from those bleak eyes was confusion and perhaps a little fear.

NINETEEN

As Shayak led Amit and Aloka away, I fell in behind them. Before stepping out of the shadows of the house, Shayak turned to me.

'Are you okay?'

'I will be.'

'You did well in there.'

I attempted some sort of smile. I was thankful for the darkness.

'And now you know.'

Shayak gave a brief nod. 'It looks like the police are here.'

Two uniformed men came in and Shayak handed over his charges. We followed them out of the dark hallway. I stepped out from behind Shayak and into what used to be the front lawn. What I saw next left me fuming.

'Camera crew?'

'Bastard,' mumbled Shayak.

'But how did they get here so fast?'

'Let's get out of here.'

The cameras got as much footage of Amit and Aloka as possible before the two were stashed safely in the back of a police van. Then they turned their attention back to Sharma who was holding court at the centre of the decrepit lawn.

As we walked towards the gate, one of the policemen stopped me. 'Sa'ab wants a word with you.'

'Why?'

Before I could make my objections known, I had a camera in my face and Sharma by my side.

'Reema Ray, how does it feel to have solved a case of this magnitude?' asked a reporter.

'Uh–'

'And the perpetrator, Amit, is your friend? Your ex-boyfriend? You were all in school together?'

'No comment,' I snapped, stepping away.

The reporter backed off, but Ravi Sharma's hand was on my arm.

'Reema, what is wrong with telling the truth? All they want is a story.'

'How did they get here so quick?'

'I don't know about that. They have their sources.'

'And that wouldn't by any chance be you?' I said before walking away.

Reema–' he called after me.

Shayak led me back to the car and I collapsed into the passenger seat. It was 3 am; it had been a long, wretched day. In the car, I let out a long lungful of expletives.

Shayak listened.

'Why the hell would he do that?'

'Because Ravi Sharma's biggest turn on is seeing his face on the news.'

'He could have had that without me. He could have hogged all the credit and no one would have been the wiser.'

'Then you don't understand the media.'

'Huh?'

'With Amit going on air like he did this morning, Sharma feared he had made a major blunder in his advice to the Mohtas. Which is why he went public with the news about reopening the Agarwal case when he did. He had hoped for a distraction. But now that he knows he was right all along, though he failed to act, he wants to gloat in the spotlight. And since no one wants to see an old mug like Ravi Sharma's on TV, his best bet at maximizing air time is to have a woman like you by his side.'

'A woman like me?'

Shayak smiled. 'Having got to know you over the past ten days, it doesn't surprise me one bit that you can be decidedly obtuse when you choose to be.'

'What is that supposed to mean?'

'Only that TV channels prefer pretty faces over ugly, moustachioed ones. And even a self-obsessed prick like Ravi Sharma is observant enough to see that you are downright beautiful.'

I turned to the window to hide my smile. I couldn't help but think he was handling me like he might an angry child. But in the moment, it worked.

Once my anger at Ravi Sharma had come down a notch, I put my head back on the plush seat.

'It was you who figured out the kidnapping was a hoax, wasn't it?'

Shayak was silent.

'From the beginning, you saw it all,' I said, watching the ghosts of trees zip by.

'I've had an unfortunate amount of experience in kidnap and ransom,' he said softly.

'I knew it was all wrong from the beginning. I simply chose the wrong person to trust. He had me convinced that it was Mohta's doing.'

'In your position, I may have believed that too. It was only natural.'

'A bit too natural, I would say. A bit too naïve.'

'You found them, Reema. I didn't.'

I closed my eyes and, at first, only pretended to doze. But soon, once the adrenalin had worn off, the past few hours caught up with me and I slipped into a deep sleep.

I awoke with a jolt to find us parked in front of my house and Shayak watching me with a smile. 'Sorry,' I said, fruitlessly running my hands through wild hair.

'No need for apologies.'

'What time is it?'

'Around 6.30 am.'

'What a day.'

'Yes, and it hasn't ended yet. We have one more matter to conclude: the Agarwal murder.'

My head snapped to the left.

Shayak looked at me; there was nothing in his expression to indicate that he was anything but serious. 'Now that we are on the same side, there is no reason to work separately. Take this,' he said, handing me the file from last night which I never got the chance to see. 'Go through it. Give me a call when you are done.'

'Want to come in for breakfast?'

'Maybe later. I'll be back in about an hour.'

'Where are you going?'

'There is something that can't wait.'

I entered my house and paused to put on the coffee maker before frantically grabbing the file. And there was that business card again.

Titanium Securities. First things first: I hit Google, and found absolutely nothing.

How could that be? Every company had a website nowadays, even if it was a page that read 'Under Construction'.

I tried calling Uncle Kumar but unsurprisingly, given the hour, he didn't answer.

And then, I dialled the only bona fide person I knew in the security industry: Terrence.

'What time is it?' came his groggy voice.

'I'm sorry, it's early, I know. But this is urgent.'

'If you like me, Reema, come out and say it. Calling me late at night and first thing in the morning is a funny way of showing it.'

'Terrence, please.'

'What happened last night?'

He'd probably turn on the TV and see my enraged face outside the house in Digha soon enough anyway. I saved myself the trouble of an explanation.

'What do you know about Titanium Securities?'

'Titanium? What business do you have with them?' Terrence suddenly seemed wide awake.

'Nothing really, as of now. But I might.'

'Wow, Ray. They are only the best security agency in the country.'

'Then why haven't I heard of them?'

'Because that is how they operate. Titanium is an elite security company, possibly the most elite in India. Based out of Mumbai. Over the past decade or so, they have revolutionized the way private security is run. They are famously discreet about their operations – who and what they guard, and how. The head of Titanium is a mystery. I did my fair share of digging around when I had toyed with the idea of applying for a job with them. It was rumoured that the chief had been an army man who had quit the game to set up his own shop. But that was about all I could unearth, since he does no press. Ever. Not to promote himself or his company. And he has never breathed a word about a client, though around half of Bollywood, the entire cricket team and a number of parliamentarians have been spotted with guards who may or may not belong to the Titanium clan.'

I felt relief clouded by a surge of dismay. How could I have missed it? First Amit, and then Shayak – how could I have been so wrong about them both? Though I had been drawn to Shayak from the moment we had met, I had let my imagination run so far away from me as to have severed all ties with reality.

'Hey, how about it, Ray,' said Terrence, interrupting my thoughts. 'They just mentioned you on TV!'

'What are you talking about?'

'On News Now – they are showing Amit and Aloka being led away in handcuffs. The newscaster just mentioned you, that you had helped the cops crack the case! Woohoo!'

'Did they show any footage of me?' I said, bracing for the worst.

'No. Too bad. But why don't we celebrate this over a drink tonight?'

'Thanks for the offer, Terrence, but I think I'll pass.'

He was still trying to convince me when I hung up.

Name mentioned, but no video. It could be worse. But I knew the damage, for the time being, had been done. Anyone associated with the Agarwal business who had watched that news story would know that all the questions I had been asking had nothing to do with my story – and that suddenly made me a significant threat.

It was with a sense of urgency that I turned my attention back to the contents of the file. There was a document compiling the data that had been gleaned, I assumed, by Shayak through his sources.

The police found nothing at the Agarwal home. No signs of poison in the food or other household sources.

And then, crucially, there was the doctor's preliminary report. Agarwal had been brought in with diarrhoea and resulting dehydration, respiratory distress and a host of other problems. He didn't respond to any medication and finally suffered multi-organ failure. He had been ill, according to these documents, for seventy-two hours.

A poison that took days to act? That did not show up in the blood work in any way?

And then there were the photographs. Mrs Agarwal's spotless home. Agarwal's bedroom. His office. The desk. The computer. That strange snuff bullet.

Finally, the list of visitors Agarwal had received in the days before his death. One name stood out, prompting a forgotten memory to the surface.

I closed my eyes as it finally all came together.

TWENTY

It was 10 am and Khana Khazana was already bustling with activity. I walked in to find the dining area empty, but I could hear the shouts of the kitchen staff, the clatter of pots and pans, the sizzle of tarka, the smell of spices.

Spices. I had known at once that something had been wrong with what I had seen in the Khana Khazana pantry. The stockpile of saffron in those small jars: it was way too much saffron for any restaurant to stock. And from a distance, how had I recognized it as saffron in the first place? It hadn't been a brand I had seen before on a store shelf somewhere; I had seen it last in Agarwal's office. They were the samples for his gourmet store. The saffron wasn't real – it was orange thread used for mock-ups for Agarwal's investors, the ones he had shown me during our interview. They shouldn't have been in the Khana Khazana pantry but they were, stolen from a man dead or alive.

I needed those samples.

I decided the best way was to brazen through it. I walked straight into the kitchen and turned the handle to the pantry. It was locked.

'Can I help you?'

I turned around and found Manish standing there.

'What are you doing here?' I asked.

'This is my wife's restaurant. What are you doing here?'

'The other day when I visited,' I said, falling back on what was becoming an old trick, 'I think I dropped an earring in the pantry.'

'So why didn't you call or something?'

'It was a gift from my grandmother; I'm very attached to it. Can you please open the door so I can check?'

'I'm sorry but I don't have the key.'

Just then the kitchen door swung open and there stood Vineeta, panting for breath.

I took a step forward. 'Vineeta.'

She let out a little cry and looked about in panic. The kitchen stopped in its tracks, everyone watching Vineeta as she scrambled towards the counter and grabbed a knife.

Arm raised, she turned to face me, her features twisted into an ugly grimace.

'What are you doing?' cried Manish.

'Vineeta,' I said, 'put down the knife. It's over.'

The weapon trembled in her hand.

'The police will be here any minute. You can only make it worse for yourself now.'

She looked from me to her dumbfounded husband, her face contorting with despair. 'How did you know?' she asked.

'It doesn't matter now. But there are a lot of people in this room and you don't want to hurt any of them. Give me the knife, Vineeta.'

I took my eyes off Vineeta only long enough to register that Shayak had entered the kitchen through the back entrance. He crept down the passage filled with open-mouthed cooks to about five feet behind Vineeta. He pulled his hand out of a pocket in which I assumed was his gun. But firepower would not be required. On seeing Vineeta's listlessness, he simply closed the distance and reached out and grabbed her knife-wielding right arm with his left from behind. She let out a small cry, but Shayak kept his grip tight around her wrist while he quickly removed the knife with his other hand.

And it happened in a second. Shayak let go to hand the knife safely back to one of the cooks behind him and Vineeta dashed past him towards the back door. I didn't even bother to chase her – I knew see she wouldn't get far. Since Shayak entering from that way, a rotund lady in a chef's hat had placed a big round vat right in the doorway before stepping forward to ogle at the action.

Vineeta ran straight into it and fell down in a heap.

'Oh, my rasgullas!' cried the chef, watching the round white sweets fly through the air and land all around her grimacing boss. Vineeta was sprawled in an awkward heap on the floor in the centre of a galaxy of confectionary.

*

'I wish I could say I was sorry. But I don't think I am.' Vineeta sat at a table in the restaurant mopping sticky syrup off her arms.

There would be no lunch service today. I had hung the 'Closed' sign outside the restaurant and Shayak had asked the bewildered staff to leave. Manish sat sulking in a corner.

Vineeta was in a daze, passion spent, anger diffused. Far from being sinister, she seemed more than a little ridiculous, hair clinging to her skull, the smashed remains of rasgulla stuck to her kurta. She sat there in syrup-drenched clothes, vaguely smelling of cane sugar and staring through the window onto rain-lashed streets, the suddenly grey sky mirroring the mood. 'So you have really called the police?'

'Yes, we have,' Shayak said gently.

'What will happen to me now?'

'I really don't know.'

There was a pause, and I watched Vineeta's expression turn from fear to cold composure. It was the look I had come to associate with her, the mask summoned to hold her demons at bay.

I roughly knew the chain of events, but I still couldn't understand what triggered it. 'What happened, Vineeta?' I asked.

She shook her head, sadness returning to those elegant features. She looked from me to Shayak and back again. 'You know where they are?'

'Yes,' I said.

'Bring them,' she said, handing me a key.

I walked over to the pantry, where she had brought me in haste for the hushed, hurried chat the other day. I unlocked the door and quickly found the crate of jars exactly where I had last seen it, on the shelf – the green-and-orange labels with the words 'Spice Route' in a Devanagri-inspired font. The dal starter kits were behind them. Cheesy in execution but a good idea nonetheless. An idea that could never have come from Agarwal. I had instinctively realized this even as he was sharing the concept with me. But I had no idea that it would become a motive for murder.

I carried the crate back to the dining area and placed it on the table.

'This was my idea,' said Vineeta. 'A chain of gourmet stores that would change the way Indian food is perceived and prepared. I made the mistake of sharing it with that bastard Prakash Agarwal.'

Vineeta dipped her towel in a glass of water, and continued to rub the syrup off her hands.

'He stole my plan. He went to Mayank but by then your brother,' she glanced at Shayak, 'had had enough of his slipperiness. So he found another investor for whom these mock-ups were made and was getting ready to open his first store in London. I assumed I would be involved, of course, but he just laughed in my face when I suggested it. That is what I get for pillow talk.'

Try as I might, I couldn't imagine this woman letting Prakash Agarwal touch her.

She shook her head slowly. 'That was my biggest mistake, of course. Letting him get under my skin. I was in debt, and he bailed me out. Big time. I hadn't paid him back for the past year; I couldn't with my husband cutting the restaurant loose. Through it all, Agarwal supported me. He enjoyed it, having power over me, to use that leverage to squeeze everything he could.'

'You knew what he had done to Mallika?'

'Yes, she told me, though not for years after we became friends, after I was already in debt. By that time, I have to say I wasn't inclined to believe her, though I was careful not to leave my daughter around him alone. Mallika was always so different with the men. Always looking to be rescued. Siddhartha, Abhimanyu, it was the same with all of them, and I wasn't so sure – or perhaps I didn't want to believe what she said about Prakash.'

I thought of Vineeta's husband's brazen appreciation of Mallika at the dinner. I had wondered then that their friendship had survived such strains. It apparently hadn't.

'But I wouldn't have done anything this drastic till I realized that if I didn't act, my daughter would have to drop out of college thanks to my debt and I would have to lose the restaurant. And then I saw these.'

She picked up a jar of faux saffron and unscrewed the top. 'I asked him why he couldn't include me in this business; I didn't mind being his partner if he was willing to invest in it. He just laughed and said he had already made enough of an investment in me, that he expected something in return apart from sex.'

'And then you learnt you had access to a powerful poison,' I said. 'Ricin. A waste product of the castor oil manufacturing process, which your husband was just beginning to extract.'

Vineeta nodded slowly. 'Yes. My husband's latest business venture. A pharmaceutical company doing research into cancer treatment approached him for a small supply of the stuff, which they believe may help kill tumours. It wasn't hard to go to the factory and take a little.'

'Swallowing ricin doesn't always result in death, and an injection is difficult to orchestrate. So you came up with the idea of putting it in a snuff bullet.'

'He couldn't live without that vile snuff. I loaded the dispenser with care, so the first dose was already measured out with the poison to ensure it was inhaled at one go.'

'And then he got sick.'

'I went to visit him when he was ill, the afternoon of the day before he was taken to hospital. I still wasn't sure if he'd die. I took the samples when he went to the bathroom.'

'Even if he had gone to the hospital earlier, there is no antidote. And no hospital in Calcutta would run a test for ricin as a matter of course, even if poisoning had been suspected.'

She nodded.

'Did you know Mallika was intending to confront Agarwal that night?' I asked.

Vineeta looked confused for the first time that morning. 'No. I never meant for her to take the blame.'

'But it didn't hurt when she came under suspicion.'

'It wasn't like that. I didn't want it to happen that way. But what was I to say without confessing the truth?'

Vineeta sat increasingly listlessly in her seat. 'What was it that made you suspect me?' she asked.

'Those saffron jars had no business being in your pantry. Agarwal had shown them to me only weeks before he died, and made no mention of your involvement in the project. But it was also a series of other things. Mrs Agarwal had told me her husband was having an affair. By all accounts you both were friendly – perhaps a little too much so. And then I had been told that your husband worked with castor beans, so when I saw Agarwal's symptoms in the doctor's report, it seemed like a strong contender for the mystery poison. And then I think it was the way you told me what happened between Mallika and Agarwal. It was decidedly without sympathy, and your apparent willingness to pin the blame on your friend was surprising.'

Her expression had turned stony. It seemed I had yet been able to fathom the extent of her resentment for Mallika.

Vineeta said nothing more.

The police arrived at last, led by Sharma. He did not look pleased to see Shayak or me there, but he saved it till after Vineeta was taken away.

'I'm sure the two of you are feeling very pleased with yourselves,' he said.

'I think I can say we are,' said Shayak with a smile.

'Care to enlighten me about this evidence that you claim to have against Vineeta Solanki?'

I showed him the crate of fake saffron.

'What is this?'

I explained about the stolen idea for the business venture.

'She could have taken them at any time.'

'But this is part of the motive. She confessed the rest.'

'So now I have two cases in which our leading evidence is confession to Reema Ray.'

'Only fitting since the two cases were solved by her,' said Shayak.

'As if the police needed her help. We knew all along that Amit was guilty.'

I didn't point out afresh that so was Aloka – that the kidnapping wasn't a kidnapping at all and they hadn't been able to find her on their own. None of that really mattered anymore. Except to an angry Sharma.

'Lucky for you your *friend* here came along otherwise you would have been in jail as well after I found you snooping around in Middle Kingdom. Don't forget that private detectives aren't above the law.'

'Coming back to the case,' Shayak said, 'you don't have to rely on Vineeta's confession alone. If you look at her financials, you will find that she was deep in debt and was receiving large amounts of money till quite recently. I think you will also find evidence that a quantity of ricin was stolen from Vineeta's husband's factory.'

'And you will find traces of it in a snuff bullet that is currently sitting on Mr Agarwal's desk. It was a present from Vineeta Solanki, to which Mrs Agarwal can testify,' I added.

Sharma, apparently out of other accusations to hurl at us, gave a brusque nod. 'Then I'll need to see you in my office for a full debrief,' he said before he strode away.

'Why is he so angry all of a sudden?' I asked Shayak.

'Probably something to do with the fact that he got less face time on TV than he expected.'

'I understand his irritation with me, but why is he upset with you?'

'Because I may have had something to do with his sound bite being shortened even further.'

'What do you mean?'

'After I dropped you home, I paid Sharma a visit to try and

get him to tell the channel to axe the footage where he ambushed you. I tried to be nice but when he refused to hear reason, I threatened to tell his boss that he had leaked information to the media about an ongoing case, putting a number of people at risk. He made the call.'

'You did that? Why?'

'Because I understand your need to remain low profile. Just see – your name being mentioned on TV gave Vineeta the heads up and a chance to get away.'

'Thank you,' I said softly.

'You'll soon discover that almost everything I do is entirely selfish. Anyhow, how did you recognize the symptoms of ricin? It is hardly a commonly seen poison,' asked Shayak.

'College sometimes does pay. I was an espionage enthusiast.'

He nodded. 'Georgi Markov.'

'Assassinated by the KGB using an umbrella rigged as a gun with a tiny pellet containing a minuscule amount of ricin. London, 1978. Similar symptoms. Notoriously difficult to detect. But you seem to know all about it without my help.'

'I was missing the critical piece of the puzzle – how the poison was administered. And also why.'

'How did you figure it all out?'

'There is a lot you can piece together from boring things like financials and security-camera footage. Didn't I say working within the system has its upside?'

TWENTY-ONE

It was dusk by the time we emerged from Sharma's office. He had seen me first – a gruelling session in which he wanted me to reveal every detail of how I had got involved in the case, what had led me to the discovery of the link between Mallika and Agarwal, how I had focused on Vineeta as the suspect.

'I still don't know how you ruled out Mallika. She had the strongest motive,' said Sharma.

'Did she? A molestation that occurred twenty-five years ago? If that was it, why now? Why not when she had just returned to Calcutta from China? It just didn't make sense.'

'She went to his house to confront him.'

Which had confused me, and I still couldn't understand what had pushed her to it. 'And yet, when Agarwal went to the hospital, he had already been ill for a few days. That means the poison had to be administered well before Mallika's unexpected visit. She was merely in the wrong place at the wrong time.'

Sharma grudgingly let me go, and then called in Shayak. While I waited for him to finish, I saw Mallika herself walking in.

'Mallika!' I cried.

She gave me a tight, sad little smile. 'Hello Reema. I was told I would find you here.'

'I've been so worried about you.'

'I know. I have to tell you how sorry I am for all the trouble I've caused by disappearing.'

'No apology required, Mallika. If anyone should apologize it should be me, for raking up the past.'

'You were just trying to figure this all out. I should have stayed and explained what I was doing there that night. But it all felt like it was terribly, terribly out of control.' Mallika took the seat beside me. 'I was so afraid, and then I felt so relieved that he was dead,' she said, voice cracking.

'But why did you go to Agarwal's house in the first place?'

'For years I have wanted to confront him. To have my say. I could never forget his breath on my face, in that tiny dressing room in the New Market shop. He had come in to take my measurement for a pair of trousers that needed alteration. My mother had just stepped into another section of the store to take a look at something. He stopped an inch short of raping me, and then left the dressing room and thoroughly charmed my mother. 'Such a nice man,' she said as we left. If it were not for those words, I may have found a way to put it behind me. But I remember that moment, that feeling of complete and utter humiliation. That no one, not even my mother, could be trusted to protect me. So I spoke out.'

'Why did you withdraw your complaint?'

'The police did their best to be difficult at every stage. There was no evidence, they said. My word against his. That he'd at best receive a slap on the wrist for eve teasing.' She shook her head.

'Eve teasing,' she repeated. 'What a cruel joke. So we gave up. I regret that decision even now. But when I learned that Vineeta's daughter may be at risk, I had to say something. I never thought Vineeta would use that information against me.'

'I don't think she did either. Though I can't understand how Vineeta could have been so blinded by Agarwal.'

'I think she wanted an escape. You've seen how her husband treats her. Attention, even from someone so beastly, was better than Manish's contempt.'

'She's a completely different woman when he's not around.'

'Yes, and I think she just wanted to be loved. But of course Agarwal didn't know the meaning of the word. He was doing his best to ruin Vineeta. And she was too enamoured of him and too resentful of me to see that. I thought I could give him a little push in the right direction, to get him to spare her some self-respect.'

'You brought yourself to face him for her?'

'Well, finally I couldn't see it through. I waited at the house but when he didn't show up I lost my nerve.'

'But that was the plan.'

She nodded. 'I thought he might respond to a threat of fresh exposure. If nothing else, maybe he would have agreed to write off some of her debt, and she could have kept the restaurant. But then I ran.'

'And on the way you dropped an earring.'

Round-eyed, she raised her hand to her breast, still horrified at the memory. 'I was sure that would be the death of me. After everything, I couldn't imagine going to jail for that man! I still don't know how it escaped the notice of the police.'

'Because Mrs Agarwal moved it before they got there.'

'Oh my. That poor woman.'

'Is that why you went into hiding?'

'That, and because you started asking so many questions, my dear! You scared both my husband and me with your interview.'

Mallika stopped me before I could apologize. 'When Agarwal was taken in for treatment,' she continued, 'Siddhartha realized he had been poisoned, which is what he reported. But when I told him that the Prakash Agarwal in question was the same man who had assaulted me, he told the police he had been mistaken. He knew that I had been to visit Agarwal, and I'm not entirely sure he believed I was innocent!'

'Why did you come back?'

'I suppose some part of me wanted the story to be out — at last. And when I heard the police were looking for me, I thought it best to come forward. I hadn't intended to run from the police.'

'Only from me?'

Mallika laughed. 'Perhaps. But that just means you were doing your job right.'

'Her PI job, not her food-writer job,' Shayak interjected, stepping out of Sharma's room. 'An important distinction that has caused me much grief.'

'Mr Gupta, you look like you can handle it.'

'So you know each other too?' I asked.

'Not really,' she said. 'We've spoken, though.' 'When?'

'Yesterday morning. Mr Gupta called to encourage me to come back and clear my name.'

'How did you find her?' I asked.

Shayak answered my question with a dark smile. 'I'm famished,' he said. 'I haven't eaten since last night.'

'I won't keep you,' said Mallika.

We walked out into the parking lot and I saw Shayak's car as well as a silver sedan with a familiar man in the driver's seat. And there to the side stood Abhimanyu.

'There you are!' said Abhimanyu, coming forward to wrap his arms around Mallika.

'I told you not to come!'

'The restaurant won't collapse without me there. Dinner isn't for another couple of hours.'

'Oh, you silly man,' she said, holding his arm.

'You had me worried there for a while.'

'Did you honestly think I was capable of murder?'

'Don't even joke about it,' he said.

'I'll see you tomorrow, Abhi.'

We walked toward the cars. 'There's Siddhartha,' Mallika said softly. 'Maybe you two can come to our place for dinner tomorrow?'

We accepted the invitation and Mallika slid into the passenger seat beside her husband, who reached out to squeeze her hand before driving away.

I felt drained of my last stores of energy, but Shayak, incredibly, seemed ready for more. 'Hungry?' he asked.

'Never been hungrier,' I said. 'But can you give me a minute?'

Shayak got into the car as I walked over to where Abhimanyu still stood. He gave me a wan smile.

'The morning news said you are a detective. Unless I've got the wrong Reema Ray?'

'I'm afraid not.'

'I wish you had mentioned that while I was spilling my guts to you.'

'I'm sorry I had to keep the truth from all of you.'

'I guess it doesn't matter. Mallika is safe,' he said softly. 'For now.'

I saw the pain simmering under the surface. 'How long have you felt this way?' I asked.

Abhimanyu leaned against the filthy, paan-stained wall of the police station. 'For almost as long as I have known her. A dozen years now, maybe more.'

'And you've never told her how you feel?'

'No, but I didn't really need to. It's plain enough, isn't it?'

'And?'

'And what? She was married when I met her and whatever cracks appeared in the marriage weren't deep enough to cause a split. And Mallika is hardly one for a tawdry affair. So now it is up to me to move on. I had myself fooled for a while in Shanghai that I had. But no relationship ever lasted and now I just sort of live with it. It doesn't hurt much anymore, for the most part. It's more like a bruise that never quite fades.'

'If you ever need to talk, you have my number.'

'Thanks, I will. I've liked talking to you a little too much, I would say. Particularly since it seems that the man waiting there for you in the car wouldn't mind wringing my neck for keeping you here for so long.'

'Who? Shayak? He's just a–'

'Yes, yes, I know the drill. Just remember, you're not the only one who can see things that are meant to be secret.'

'No, really, he's just hungry.'

'I'd say,' Abhimanyu said with a naughty grin.

I felt my face flush as I turned and walked towards the car.

TWENTY-TWO

I needed comfort food but Shayak was headed in the direction of Strand Road where, apart from a tired old sundae shop, there was nothing to feed us famished souls. 'I don't think you'll find much here,' I said.

'Patience isn't one of your many virtues, is it?'

'Dead on, detective!'

He gave me a quick look, his smile lighting up the car. My stomach revolted again, this time not from hunger.

He entered the underground parking of a complex I had never noticed before. He parked and I followed him out onto a road that lined the river. My confusion mounted as he led me through a garden and onto a wooden gangway. Lining it was a row of yachts gently swaying to the rhythm of the Hooghly.

'You're joking, right?'

Shayak had stopped before a small, beautiful boat. There was just enough light for me to see the name: Titania.

'Don't I strike you as a seaman?' he grinned.

'This is yours?'

'I surely don't intend to break into someone else's.'

'You have perfected the art of taking me by surprise.'

Shayak climbed in, but I wasn't ready to abandon land just yet.

'That is a brave name,' I said. 'You aren't afraid of history repeating itself?'

He held a hand out to me. 'I stay away from icebergs and Oscar-winning film directors.'

I stared at him with some hesitation.

'You aren't afraid, are you?'

'I might be. Never really been on one of these before.'

'You aren't daunted by a murderous restaurant owner, but a boat throws you off?'

'Not the boat; the water underneath it.'

'You can't swim, can you? Well, don't worry. I can. And we aren't going anywhere tonight.'

'I can swim.'

'So what are you afraid of?'

I took his hand at last and climbed in. It must have been the strain of the day or the lack of sleep, for I felt myself tense almost immediately. I gave Shayak a nervous little smile.

'If you are free tomorrow, we can take her out for a spin, perhaps before dinner at Mallika's place. Something tells me you will enjoy it.'

We went inside the small cabin and I sat down. The gentle rocking must have soothed my anxiety, because by the time Shayak pulled out a bottle of red wine and uncorked it, I was at ease.

'Pizza, pasta or curry?' he asked, handing me a glass.

'Are you going to start cooking now?' I asked incredulously.

'Hell, no. Maybe on land, but not in this little thing.' He opened the freezer that showed off an impressive array of frozen foods. There were labels from across the world. Not quite gourmet fare, but not too shabby either.

'When you said you had been in the neighbourhood of Calcutta when your brother asked you to drop in, what did you mean exactly?' I asked.

He smiled into the freezer. 'Pizza it is then.' He grabbed a box and headed for the microwave. He popped the frozen pie into the oven and turned to face me. 'I had sailed from India to Hong Kong on my annual boating holiday, making a number of stops on the way – Sri Lanka, the Andamans, Thailand, Malaysia. I was on my way back when my brother alerted me to the situation with Agarwal.'

'It's a good way to live.'

Shayak nodded. 'When I disconnect, I need to do so completely. This boat is the best thing I ever bought.'

How rich are you exactly, is the question that came to mind. But I pushed it aside – for the time being. 'Disconnect?' I asked instead.

'We need to run away sometimes, with the kind of work we do,' he said softly. There were at least two feet between us as we leaned against the railing, but suddenly he seemed too close. I squirmed and moved away.

'Sorry, but you are alone on this one. I don't do your kind of work, not anymore at least.'

'Giving up on your practice?'

'I need to close it down.'

'Why? I didn't think you were one to run away.'

I frowned into my glass. 'I wouldn't say I am running. I need to keep a roof over my head.'

He looked at me, his head cocked slightly to the right. I knew he would wait for my real answer.

'Don't you ever feel like it is all a little too much?'

'Tell me about Amit.'

'Does it matter?'

'Reema, the case is making national headlines. Someone will drag it all up. I'd rather hear it from you.'

'First tell me how you know so much about me.'

'As I said earlier, there aren't too many private investigators in India. And it is my job to keep tabs on the ones who matter.'

'Me? Matter? At best, I am the city's leading expert in cheating spouses.'

'All experience is good experience – at the end of the day, even the Agarwal murder case hinged on infidelity, didn't it?'

I couldn't tell whether Shayak was being kind or honest, but his words softened my stance. 'Amit was the first man I ever loved. And the reason I can't do this anymore,' I said.

'Ah.'

'I didn't love him when this happened,' I added quickly.

'Then what is the problem?'

'He was capable of kidnapping his own wife. A character flaw that escaped my notice entirely for years. And even now he managed to manipulate me.'

'Which you figured out for yourself.'

'Just soon enough.'

'You blame yourself for not being able to look into the future?'

'No, for not being able to look into a man's heart.'

'Almost as impossible, if you ask me.'

'Not always. Look at Prakash Agarwal. One interview and I knew he was a creep.'

'But my brother – a very intelligent, successful man, by the way – trusted him enough to do business with him.'

'True. Why was that again?'

'Because people will ignore instinct enough when they wish to. Agarwal had something to offer and he seemed valuable at the time, and easier to control than he turned out to be. The world is full of unpleasant people, Reema, and sometimes it is unavoidable having to deal with them.'

I shrugged. 'I guess I'd have preferred not to have dated one.'

Once again, Shayak's face softened. 'You must have been young – a little too young to take it all so seriously.'

I shook my head. 'I was foolish. And blind. Not good qualities for a detective to have.'

'I have an alternative explanation. Could it possibly be that you are afraid of your own success? That you aren't prepared for what solving two high-profile cases could bring?'

I started shaking my head even before he had finished. 'But it's what I wanted all along!'

'Was it?' Again, those eyes.

'Of course!' I said. My voice didn't sound like my own.

Shayak was unrelenting. 'You don't find yourself just a little frightened of your own abilities?'

I let out a short, nervous laugh, Amit's old taunts coming back to me. 'I hate to disappoint you, but they are not exactly superpowers.'

'No, definitely not superpowers. But the ability to look into darkness and make sense of it where others cannot is not insignificant.'

We stood in silence for a few moments, listening to the sound of the water as it kissed the sides of the boat. At last, unable to stop my voice from cracking, I asked, 'How do you deal with it?'

Shayak took a step closer, reaching over and putting his hand under my chin, forcing me to look at him. His eyes smiled into mine, soothing me with their heat. Despite myself, despite the fact that I found myself unable to breathe, I smiled back. He dropped his hand and leaned on the railing once again.

'I didn't go into the security side of the business for nothing,' he said. 'I would prefer to prevent crime rather than solve it, when I can. I am an investigator when called upon to be one but I choose my cases carefully. And off the job, I make it a point to spend as much time with people who make sense to me, who are willing to stand for the truth and what they believe in.'

'And that helps?'

'To the degree possible. You don't need to be a detective to be confronted by evil in this world. Our beautiful species will drive you mad if you let it. We too easily forget the goodness, and the fun. Which is why I am asking you to come on board.'

I looked around his beautiful boat. 'I thought I already was!'

'I mean professionally.'

'Work for you?' Tumult took control of my brain. What was happening?

'For me, with me.'

'But I–'

'But what? You'd rather be a food critic?' Shayak said the words lightly, but I detected a note of disdain beneath the surface. 'Given a choice, I would have thought you'd decide to stick to what you do best.'

'Eating?'

'Solving crime. And since you need a roof over your head, a salary might help. I can promise a generous one.'

I gave in to the confusion. 'But just the other day you shouted at me for putting my nose where it didn't belong!'

'Yes, and there was a reason for that.'

I looked at him with a questioning brow.

'The information you unearthed about Mallika was, out of context, dangerous. It could have easily led to her arrest. If you had been working with the police to begin with, that kind of fallout would have been easier to control.'

'And that is what you do.'

'When I can,' he said with a shrug. 'So, as I said, you should really think about making a return to full-time detective work, with a proper agency.'

'Like yours?'

'Like mine.'

'But I was wrong about almost every assumption I made!'

'That is because you had little choice but to make assumptions. You were on the outside looking in. Once you had the facts, you put it together. Which is the other point I want to make about working within the system. You need access to official evidence. You seek information according to what you already know. Real data is, in a situation like this, vital. When time is short and there is much at risk, you don't have the luxury to hunt down the unknowns like you were forced to here.'

'But the molestation angle proved to be a red herring.'

'In isolation, yes. But in a roundabout way it led you to Vineeta and the truth.'

'So what convinced you it wasn't Mallika? My theory was just that – a theory.'

'I had seen the security camera footage so I knew she had been in the building. I couldn't explain it at first but either way, it didn't fit in with the timeline of the poisoning, which took place a couple of days before his death.'

I nodded. Had Agarwal's symptoms not appeared as early as they did, Mallika may have been in very real danger.

'So you see, Reema,' Shayak continued, 'had you known what I had known, or if I had known what you had known, we could have figured this out some days ago. Lucky for us this still ended well.'

Shayak was right, I thought, in essence, but I couldn't think of this as a satisfactory conclusion to the week. 'You don't always do good in this profession, do you?'

'What do you mean?'

'Well, a truly unpleasant man was killed. He got, some would say, what was coming to him. And a woman – not blameless, but a good deal less morally bankrupt, murder notwithstanding – will pay for it because of our meddling.'

I could see a dark smile on Shayak's lips. 'Would you have wanted any other outcome?'

I thought about whether I would have let my judgement come between a criminal and the law. 'No, this ended as it had to.'

'And you are glad to have been the one responsible for that?'

I ignored, for now, Shayak's transfer of full credit to me. 'Yes,' I said, sounding more convinced than I felt.

He gave a sharp nod. 'Good, then you accept the job?'

I watched him through narrowed eyes. I wasn't sure why I continued to resist. 'But I am ...'

'What? What are you afraid of?'

'I don't know!'

'Leaving this comfort zone of yours?'

'Well, is that so wrong?' All of a sudden, I missed the simplicity of food, the clarity of choosing between the best cheesecake in the city and the rest. Even there, there was a need for objectivity and fair play and no room for emotion. Who you are eating with, how hungry you are, the loudness of your neighbouring diners, your mood, the memories attached with each individual flavour impact your eating experience.

But though the answers of the food world may not be easy as pie, the outcomes were still a lot less weighty than life and death.

'I didn't expect you to run away from who you are.'

I heard the disappointment in his words. 'I feel like I have been spending my life doing nothing else.'

'You know the solution to that.'

'Give it all up and go with you, to Mumbai? Live the dream – till it turns into a nightmare again.'

'I am not so idealistic, nor so pessimistic. I'll simply say that you have a head and it is your responsibility to use it as best you can.'

Once again I was torn between yearning and fear. And his voice, deep and low and resonant, wasn't helping much either.

I knew which universe I would rather be a part of. Given the choice, I would take the path my heart had led me down all those years ago when I found myself in criminal psych class. It was the same path I had always taken, except for once, but even that detour had somehow curved back here, to where I began.

Of course, I knew one reason why I was slow to reach full excitement about Shayak's proposition – because it was not the proposition I had hoped he'd make. But, I told myself, there were many possible men for me out there but only one possible job, and only one person on the horizon capable of turning it into a reality.

I stared out onto the water. And just as I seemed a little closer to a decision, he put an arm on my shoulder, turning me to face him. The harshness of a few minutes ago had been replaced with a smile touched by a trace of irony. He bent down, his face in my hair, hands cupping my face. I couldn't breathe yet never felt as alive as in the moment that his lips touched mine.

Hungry, warm, soul-stirring, I wanted that kiss to go on forever. I leaned into his arms as his hands swept up my curls.

I was lost, and I don't know where I found the strength to break away. But I knew I had to, and I did. 'If we work together, that can't happen again,' I gasped.

'Why? It's my company. Last time I checked, I made the rules,' he growled.

I shook my head slowly, not quite knowing why, but knowing I was right. 'Sorry, but I can't jump into another mess.'

'You are so sure it will be a mess?' he asked, eyes still stormy.

Every cell in my body wanted to be back in his arms, and to push him overboard, all at the same time. 'Yes.'

'Don't test my patience; I haven't slept in thirty-six hours.'
'Sorry, but that's how I feel.'
'Okay,' he said all too soon.

I searched his face, unable to mask my disbelief. Why did I know I hadn't heard the last of it?

'Really,' he nodded, in an attempt at sincerity, 'any way you want to play it.' And then he ruined it by running his thumb across my lower lip.

I moved away, putting a few feet between us. 'Shayak, I'm serious.'

'So am I,' he said, eyes still smouldering. 'And to prove it, I am withdrawing my invitation.'

'What invitation?' To work with him?

'Well, I hadn't made it yet but I was planning to offer you a lift to Mumbai in my boat, but under the circumstances I think it's best that I didn't. I'd rather see you in office.'

My jaw had dropped as he spoke but I quickly shut my mouth and nodded my agreement. No way could I share this tiny space with this man and hang on to any distance, decorum or decency. And painful as it was, I knew the sacrifice was worth it. The old buzz was back, and it had to do with so much more than this man alone.

I looked back into those eyes and returned the smile that had started there even before I finished what I had to say. It was short.

'When do I start?'

ACKNOWLEDGEMENTS

To want to be a writer is one of those ambitions it is almost embarrassing to nurture. But at some point, the seed of this dangerous idea was planted in the brain and took root, and I am ever grateful to the following people for not laughing it out of me.

Not a word of this novel would have been written if it wasn't for Bappa, my most constant cheerleader, whose unflagging enthusiasm kept me going through the very dark times I traversed to get here. Thank you for refusing to let me give up. And thank you for two magical years in Shanghai, where this book was written, much of it sipping coffee by the riverside like a woman of leisure.

Thank you, Sujata Sen, for that shining star that sits on my bookshelf, and to the BC competition with a very embarrassing title that gave me a glimmer of hope that my writing was not, in fact, rubbish. Thank you, Nonda Chatterjee, for introducing the idea that words could be mine. Thank you, Sumit Das Gupta, for making me a better writer and for giving me a name and a foot in the door.

Thank you, Didi, for revitalizing my interest in Agatha Christie after I thought I was done with her. I was very wrong.

Thank you to the team at Pan Macmillan, for making this possible, and enjoyable.

Thanks to my friends whom I have bored to tears with the travails of writing and the hopelessness of it all. You know who you are.

And to my parents, missed every day.